Star Status

A Collection of Short Stories

ZELDA C. THORNE

First Published in Great Britain in 2023

ISBN: 978-1-7385679-0-4

Cover design by Emily's World of Design
Fractal Otter Publishing
www.zeldacthorne.com

Contents

Introduction	vii
Star Status	1
Beneath the Sand	14
Brain Hack	24
The Absolute Worst Day for a Zombie Apocalypse	36
More than the Drawer	47
Rain Queen	58
A Second Chance	70
No Space for Heroes	72
The Only Love that Matters	85
The Reintroduction of Species	93
The Ferryman	108
Global Architects	117
Emotional Intelligence	119
Gerard, his Bungalow and the Thick Blue String	129
The Mirror of Youth	184

What He Would Have Wanted 189

The Last Voyage 204

The Other Side 208

Wavemaster 219

The Last Christmas 229

Playing with Your Food 237

I Don't Believe in Fairies 239

Wildflowers 250

The Big Bang 257

A Tachinomiya Tale 265

The Man Who Lives Beyond the Horizon 269

The Vicar of Coffinswell 276

The Threads that Hold Us Together 285

3022: The Final Launch 298

The End of the Line 311

For all those who refuse to stop believing…

Introduction

For this collection, I chose my favourite science fiction, fantasy, and speculative short stories I have written thus far and gave them a good polishing. Whilst not originally written as part of a collection, these stories do share recurring themes of family, friendship, love, and loss.

Almost all the stories are set in our world, injecting magic into everyday life and twisting our reality in quirky, unusual ways. Expect the ludicrous and the wacky, as well as heart-warming tales that leave you contemplating life and all it has to offer.

Some of these stories have been previously published, or have achieved another form of recognition, all of which is detailed in the 'Credits' section at the end of the book if you're interested.

Last but not least, I hope you enjoy reading these stories as much as I enjoyed writing them.

Welcome.

Star Status

It all started when the illustrious Cassiopeia Café ran out of ketamine. My girlfriend, Tabitha, and I were enjoying a day off together. We'd been shopping in the city, mostly at Kenzo, Gucci and 3D Warehouse, ordering an obscene amount of clothing to be delivered to our respective homes, before deciding to take a break on the café's beautiful terrace.

It was mid-afternoon and sunny, a good time of day to be seen in Cassiopeia. Tabitha, being an online fashionista personality, knew such things in the same way I knew the marketing strategy behind every advert, slogan and by-line that flitted across our phone screens.

"What will you have?" she asked, placing one perfectly manicured hand on her hip. She turned her body; every move a deliberate pose.

"Not sure," I said. My gaze wandered over the gleaming white cups, glassware and the coffee machine itself. In the transparent grinder, dark-chocolate beans hopped rhythmically, almost in time to the electro punk background music. My mother always talked about how loud the grinders used to be, but she must have been exaggerating.

Tabitha waved her phone in front of the display counter and inspected the results as we moved forward in the queue. I did the same: verifying MyNutrition for my narcotic allowance and dietary recommendations.

"I think I'll have a warp-speed espresso and an opiate muffin," she said.

I nodded, unsurprised by her ridiculous choice. Call me old-fashioned, but I prefer to either be stimulated or calmed, not some bizarre mixture of the two. And right then, I needed the latter.

Why?

Because everything was getting to me: the enforced serenity on my own face, the too-quiet peace of the clothing stores we had visited, the languid body language of every single person in the café, Tabitha's tinkling laugh (which I'd listened to her practice in the bathroom, no doubt throwing her head back just so, analysing the precise angle that made her pearlescent teeth catch the light), even the luscious wide-fronded green plants bothered me — fake, obviously, just like everything else.

"OMG!" Tabitha whispered. "It's Jasmin Seluscha!"

"Who?" I glanced in the direction she was indicating and—

"Don't look!"

"Why? Who is she?"

"Jasmin. Seluscha." Her gold-flecked green eyes burrowed into mine. "She's a really well-known reporter, Joshua. Started out in *Whooz Dat*? Got headhunted by *Real People*? First person to interview Axley Holt?"

I feigned realisation. "Oh! Her!"

Studying said woman in the mirrored glass to the left of the counter, I realised that I did recognise her. Angular features, shaggy blond hair, light-blue eyes. She oozed intelligence in a way that made me nervous and excited just being near her.

Everyone had seen the interview with Axley Holt: Hollywood's hottest omnigendered pansexual star. I liked them, their portrayal of Tamaya Gomez in a dramatisation of their life was sublime. And Jasmin Seluscha had done a great job probing Axley about their childhood, political opinions and sex life without offending them.

I was particularly intrigued that Axley shared my disillusionment over materialism and the societal indifference to drug use that decades of legalisation had spawned. She was an excellent reporter.

"Do you think I'll ever be interviewed by her?" Tabitha asked wistfully.

Uh oh, danger.

This question — or more specifically my response — held potential to ruin the entire day. My muscles flexed beneath my 3D-print Armani casual city wear, the neck feeling tighter than it had that morning. Sweat would soon break out along the rivets of my spine, staining the inside lining of my jacket. The odour inexorably finding passage out into the open.

"If not," I said, "it'll be her loss."

Tabitha smiled demurely and my insides relaxed. Her relentless perfection was grating on the inside of my skull, though I did my best to ignore it.

After all, I needed her. I'd never have managed to achieve five-star customer status without her help, opening doors to all the best bars and restaurants in the city. Private clubs that only employed and served five-star citizens. Without her by association, I wouldn't even have met my current employer.

A vein throbbed in my forehead, just above the right eye socket.

"Good afternoon." A spotted youth behind the counter was smiling at us. His name badge said Thom. He looked about five. "What would you like?"

Tabitha made her order and stepped aside, smiling, checking her reflection in the cake display glass. Or was she angling to see if the reporter was looking in her direction?

Did I care?

I made my order. "A decaf keta cappuccino with potato milk, please."

"Oh, uh," Thom said, his eyes glazing over for a second. "I'm sorry, but I think we're out of ketamine."

"You 'think'?" I couldn't keep the irritation from my voice. Tabitha's hand slipped into mine, squeezed. "Sorry," I said quickly. "But could you check? Please?"

"Of course. I, uh, I'll check."

He darted off and Tabitha leant in close. "Are you alright?"

"Yeah. I'll be fine."

"This is my favourite coffee house, Joshua."

I nodded, clenched my buttocks, smoothed the lines of my face into a mask of contentedness.

While Thom disappeared to verify what he should have already known, I pondered the last time I'd had a straight coffee. I couldn't remember. Had I ever?

The youth was back.

"Hey, uh, I'm sorry, but I couldn't find it. Pretty sure we've run out. I can still do you a decaf potato milk cappuccino… and you could have, uh, cannabis sprinkles instead? They're very popular."

I couldn't believe it. *Sprinkles?*

"Look, Thom." Even I heard the appalling tone of my voice, but it was already too late. "'Pretty sure' isn't good enough. You either have it or you don't."

The bones of my knuckles ground together beneath Tabitha's grasp. I ignored her.

"I, uh—"

I raised my voice the tiniest bit. "You either have it… Or. You. Don't."

That was when I realised everyone within a four-meter

radius had stopped talking. The jaunty music bopped along and saucers clinked, but the hubbub of voices had subsided. A woman of about my mother's age with a suitably grave expression suddenly appeared by the boy's right shoulder, her white hair poofed out in a flawless halo, radiating authority.

"Is there a problem here?" she asked, brown eyes wide with concern. "My name's Abi, I'm the manager. May I help?"

"Thank you, Abi," I said, slow, calm. "I would like a keta cappuccino and this… young man… doesn't know whether or not you have any."

Thom turned to his boss. "I said we didn't have—"

I opened my mouth to argue but Abi beat me to it. Her voice pacifying as she addressed me. "I'm afraid he is right. We don't have it, sir."

Thom smiled at me — a vicious twitch of the lips — and I imagined what it might feel like to punch him in the face.

Abi continued, "As I believe my colleague here suggested, we do have cannabis sprinkles. Or, if that's not to your taste, we have the more traditional chamomile tea, which is very relaxing." Her gaze took on a ponderous quality that I did not appreciate. "We also have opiate muffins."

"Oh, those are so lovely!" Tabitha chimed in, earning herself a sympathetic smile from Abi, whose warmth evaporated when she turned back to me. "What would you like?"

I forgave her the chamomile tea slur, but only because she reminded me of my mother. "I'll have the cannabis sprinkles and an opiate muffin, please."

"Blueberry?" Thom asked, his shit-eating grin getting wider by the second.

"Yes," I said. I paid and hesitated by the counter. Tabitha

was already threading her way out to the terrace, but damage control was evidently required. A little desperate, I said, "I'm sorry if I was a little short with you there, Thom."

"S'alright," he said. "Enjoy your coffee."

"Thank you very much."

I found Tabitha in the shade of an artificial paradise palm tree, index finger flicking over her phone. Once I'd sat down, she sighed. "We need to talk."

"I know, I know. I've been feeling a bit tense lately and work is—"

"A bit tense?" She made the words sound like individual slaps. "That," she said, lifting her chin toward the counter, "was unacceptable."

The drinks arrived, brought by a bubbly red-haired girl dressed in the café's black star-studded uniform. I reached out to take the tray and knocked her off balance. Half my cappuccino slopped over the edge and slid down to pool in the saucer.

The waitress gasped, apologised, asked if I wanted another one. I said no and waved her away. Tabitha's green eyes flashed.

"What?" I asked.

"I can't do this anymore."

"You're not dumping me, are you?" I almost laughed, but then stopped.

She stared, silent.

"Are you?" I repeated.

"Don't get me wrong, Joshua. It's been great, but—"

"Hang on, we've been together three years. We're a good couple, everyone thinks so."

"LifeCoach says that if I want to get anywhere professionally, I need to take everything seriously. And that includes my love life."

"You're breaking up with me because LifeCoach told you to?"

"It's more than that. We're not moving forward."

"I seem to remember asking you to move in with me, but you didn't want to."

She clicked her tongue. "You're bad at your job. Don't look at me like that. You are. I got you that job, introduced you to the right people and I mean, you're supposed to be a marketing executive, current social trends… and you don't even know who Jasmin Seluscha is! It's embarrassing. What story is top of your news feed? Hm?"

"What does it matter—"

"I bet it's job adverts. Personality tests. Articles about how to land your dream career. Well? Am I warm?"

Hardly. The arctic had nothing on her. "OK, I admit I'm not in love with my job. It's not a crime." I leant forward, put my elbows on the table. "Do you ever think sometimes that what we do is a little… superfluous?"

"No."

"Well, I've been thinking that when I'm old and looking back on my life, I want to feel like I've accomplished something worthwhile, you know, like I've made a difference."

"You've been reading poetry again."

"Also not a crime."

"You're an emotion junkie," she said. "And I can't deal with it anymore. I've decided that I'm only going to associate with and date five stars."

"I am five-star."

Tabitha rolled her eyes and held up her phone so the screen faced me. My profile was there. Joshua Hopper, 32, Customer Rating: 3.9

I shook my head. "There must be some mistake. It was

five-point-two this morning."

"Scroll down," she said.

The screen began moving, displaying my most recent ratings. My mouth dried up. Three stars, another three, two (that was 3D Warehouse, they must have heard me commenting on their shipping fee) and finally, the nail in my ratings:

Cassiopeia Café gives Joshua Hopper - 1 star
Condescending, rude and borderline menacing
#onestar #bekind #badratings

"One star?" I said it out loud, making Tabitha suck air through her teeth. "Come on. That isn't fair… and how did you know so fast? Do you check my profile every five seconds?"

"I am a professional. I get alerted if *any* of my contacts fall below four-star status."

She leant back, sipped her coffee and tapped her metallic nails on the porcelain. The noise drummed directly into my brain. The surrounding tables had gone conspicuously quiet and the spot between my shoulder blades itched.

"This isn't fair," I said again.

Tabitha shrugged. "You could appeal, but plenty of people saw it."

"What is that supposed to mean?"

The waitress reappeared and deposited a small slice of golden cake with white icing in front of Tabitha, who slid it towards me. "Here," she said. "Lemon drizzle with Prozac-infused icing. I've been told it takes the edge off rejection."

I stared, fury boiling in my gut as Tabitha gazed up at the clear blue sky, the surrounding plant life, her coffee cup. She took another sip and still didn't meet my eyes. I slammed my open palm on the table, making the saucers jump. She froze, eyes wide, the trace of a smile on her lips.

An enormous shadow fell over me. The darkness belonged to the doorman, his hand was up by his ear, triggering some alert that would put me on facial recognition for sure. "Sir, how are we doing today?"

"I'm good, thank you."

"Excellent. I'm afraid that I'm going to have to ask you to leave. This way, please."

I admired him his demeanour which was affable and sincerely apologetic. He was accustomed to getting rid of people, politely, without making a scene that would disrupt the beautiful ambiance of Cassiopeia Café.

"Of course," I said, standing up.

I downed the coffee, gasping as it burnt my oesophagus, grabbed my opiate muffin – left the offensive lemon cake – and departed with an unexpected lightness in my step.

For the seed of an idea was already fulminating in my mind.

***

Over the ensuing twelve months, the idea grew, sprouting hashtags and followers and media coverage at an exponential rate. It was near impossible for me to keep track of everything. Not that I tried very hard.

#onestar
#whocaresnotme

Article from the fourth page of *Where Monthly*: "Controversial Supernova Café opens and for those who've been living under a rock, its USP is that it doesn't rate its customers. At all. Critics give it three months."

Headline from *The Star*: "Who is Joshua Hopper and why should we care?"

Two months later, a paparazzi image of Axley Holt leaving Infinity Beyond with one arm slung over my shoulders threatened to break the internet.

I gave no comment.

Headline from *Pentagonal News'* business column: "Supernova Café's Joshua Hopper: Pioneer of a new subculture or deranged emotion junkie?"

#emotionjunkie
#joshuahopper
#badmood

Front Page of *Real People*: A monochrome photo of Mr Hopper, delivering his trademark brooding stare. Full article on page 7.

Excerpt from said article:

Supernova Café, famously frequented by Axley Holt, solely employs one and two-star citizens. Giving them a place to call home within society and in some cases enabling them to achieve higher star statuses later in life. Former employees have described Mr Hopper as benevolent, kind and in more than one instance, their saviour.

Mr Hopper #smileifyouwantto #badmood #whocaresnotme, recently nominated as the Sexiest Man Alive by *Whooz Dat* magazine, talks to *Real People*. Jasmin Seluscha has the exclusive.

"Mr Hopper, you're quite the oxymoron, instigator of

#whocaresnotme and yet, you have a five-star rating."

"Oh yes, but I'm sure most of those votes were made ironically."

"Perhaps. So, do I have to be in a bad mood to visit Supernova Café?"

"No, not at all. My ethos is that you don't have to pretend. We won't rate you. You won't get a one-star from us because you weren't smiling."

"Doesn't that encourage people to be unpleasant?"

"It happens, but less than you'd think. Most people get it. It's a safe place. Wouldn't you like to be able to go out for a drink or a meal without worrying about how

you'll be scored?"

"I can see the attraction. It is all about appearances these days."

"Isn't it always?"

"I have to ask. Is it true you have anger management cubicles complete with punching bags behind tinted glass?"

"You'll have to come and see for yourself."

"I may just do that."

"Wonderful."

"Do you think your friendship with Axley Holt has helped your business?"

"Undoubtedly, Axley has been very supportive. They share my view of the star system."

"Which is?"

"That it should be abolished. We are nuanced, complicated individuals. I am much happier since I stopped paying attention to it."

"And is there a romantic connection between yourself and Axley? It is one of our most frequently asked questions."

"And I believe the *most* frequently asked question is whether or not that is an engagement ring in your left ear,

Miss Seluscha."

"I am interviewing you, Mr Hopper."

"Sorry, couldn't resist. To answer your question, I don't disclose my romantic relationships online."

"But you do have relationships?"

"Oh yes, but I am… uh, how can I put this… romantically offline. No photos, no ratings. Only reality."

"Fascinating."

#onlyreality
#hotforhopper
#romanticallyoffline

***

It was exactly two days after the interview came out in *Real People* that Tabitha graced Supernova Café with her presence. I couldn't quite believe she was on my dating history; she was so *glossy*. All her ex-partners had given her at least a four (I tried to give her a two, but she had it removed twenty seconds later).

"Good afternoon. What a pleasant surprise," I said, not entirely sure if I meant it. "What can I get you?"

"Joshua." She looked appraisingly at me. "You're doing very well for yourself."

"If you say so."

"Jasmin Seluscha gave you five stars. Five! You're front page of *Whooz Dat*. And you're a hashtag."

"Oh," I said. "You saw that did you."

"You've really changed it around." She considered me for a moment with those cat's eyes of hers, calculating. How did I ever find this woman attractive? "I'm impressed," she continued. "Our relationship will now be beneficial to both of us."

I coughed. "Our relationship?"

"Yes, as long as you behave. I'll allow it."

"Tabitha," I said. "Don't get me wrong, but you're not my type anymore."

She laughed, a mirthless practised falsetto, but then she saw my face and stopped. "You're not serious."

"Actually, I am. Now, what would you like? Warp-speed espresso was your thing, wasn't it?"

She spluttered incomprehensibly. *"You're* turning *me* down?"

"I'm afraid so." I gave her my finest sympathetic look and gestured towards the cake stand. "May I suggest a slice of Prozac-infused lemon drizzle? It can really take the edge off… or so I've been told."

Beneath the Sand

I remember a time when the mere thought of sand did not send me hurtling into the grip of a panic attack. Before I was old enough to know that brightly-coloured fences and gates did not always keep you safe.

When I would meet Dale, Maisy, and my older brother outside Foxton Primary so we could all walk to the park together. Rob, a meatier version of my own scrawny self, was the "responsible one" who would escort us to the park and home again afterwards. Although, once at the park, he would leave us in the playground and drift off to join the other boys of his class to play at football or Frisbee or whatever it was they did behind the army-green bike shelter.

That was before the mothers and fathers of Foxton village thrust "For Sale" signs into their front lawns beneath a slate-grey sky pounding their world with chill, autumnal rain.

The first time it happened was in February.

Dale, with his shock of red hair and freckles, practically lived at our house. My mother always made a ham sandwich for him and got the posh biscuits down from the top shelf, her eyes edged with concern.

Sometimes, she would insist he change into some of my clothes so she could wash his, claiming they were dirty from the park, but they weren't. They had a weird, acrid sweet smell that clung to most kids from New Road, but they weren't muddy or anything. Looking back, I think my mother felt sorry for him.

I wasn't allowed to go to Dale's house. Maisy wasn't either, but that didn't stop us the day he didn't turn up for school. We thought he might be at the playground on the village green, but he wasn't. His road ran adjacent to The Green, slicing through the centre of Foxton. It was full of these newer-built red brick council houses which looked odd because the rest of the village had traditional half-timbered houses, like mine.

"Do you know which number he lives at?" I asked Maisy as we cut through the overgrown footpath, dodging brambles and stinging nettles.

"Three," she said. "I heard him say it once."

I nodded. Maisy had this amazing glossy black hair — so long she could sit on it — held back from her face with a bright red ribbon which was never out of place. Unlike me, she always knew the answers to Mr Hardy's questions, but never raised her hand.

At school, our wooden desks were close enough that I could see her workbook crammed full of gold stars and smiley faces. The one time she caught me looking, she blushed and moved her porcelain arm to cover her flawless marks. She smelt of pink bubblegum and soap and definitely didn't belong on New Road.

We found it easily enough. A wonky three hung from a nail outside a ruddy terraced house with weeds poking through the cracked paving slabs. The curtains were drawn, which was a relief because I didn't want to see inside.

Feeling gallant, I stepped forward and reached up to press the grimy doorbell. We could hear a television blaring and muffled shouts from inside.

Then, heavy footsteps approached the front door. Maisy's hand slipped into mine. That peculiar sweet smell wafted from the doorway as it swung inward, revealing a thin man in a black vest top with tattoos covering both his arms and half his neck.

"Wadda yoo want?" His bloodshot eyes narrowed on us.

"Uh, is Dale home?" I asked.

The man folded his arms and leant against one side of the doorframe. Somehow, this casual movement made me very nervous.

"Nah, little shit dun a runna, in't he," he said, rolling his tongue around his mouth as if speaking of Dale left a bad taste in there. "If ya see 'im… tell 'im he's in fer it."

We rushed back to the park, hoping no one had seen us.

"Where do you think he went?" Maisy asked as our feet found the soft grass of The Green. The park was quieter. I could still see my brother playing football in the far corner of the field, but the playground was empty.

"I don't know," I said. "Maybe my house? We probably should have checked there first, but—"

"DALE!"

In a flash, Maisy was sprinting towards the playground, long dark hair streaming behind her, shiny black school shoes kicking tufts of earth in my face as I followed in her wake. I couldn't see Dale, but she obviously had.

My heart thumped in my chest as I caught up. Maisy was staring at the climbing frame, her expression a mixture of confusion and worry. It was a big, wooden one with tunnels, slides, monkey bars, poles and three or four wobbly bridges connecting it all over a large wide sand pit.

On the far side, between the climbing frame and the park fence, was where you went to share sweets you weren't supposed to have and to play at knuckles. One of the tunnels led to that side and a compact space beneath one of the slides known as The Hole.

Only those of us still in the grey-and-white checked primary school uniform could fit. We all knew it wasn't supposed to be there because you had to squeeze through a torn hole in the wooden slats to reach it. It was cramped, all noise was deadened, and the air was still and so moist that it seeped into your lungs, making you cough.

The sand felt different too. I don't know how to explain it except that it felt like it was… sleeping. Rob had dared me to go in the previous year when I was eight and him nine. Everyone got dared sooner or later, but no one ever crawled in there twice.

"Where is he?" I asked.

"He went in The Hole."

"Are you sure?"

She nodded.

I took one small step forwards and stopped. In my peripheral vision, I saw the tree branches swaying, but there was no wind. My chest squeezed. It was as if the air didn't want to be breathed. Maisy coughed and staggered backwards. I couldn't move; I could only watch.

The sand around the climbing frame began to rise and fall like dark waves under a lightning-strewn sky. Faster and faster it went… and I know how it sounds, but the sand was *boiling*.

And that was the first time I heard the noise which would haunt me forever. A snake-like whisper lashing out from the ether.

Ssch-wah!

A rolling wave of sand reared up and swept towards us. Maisy screamed, a bone-quaking shrill sound that snapped me out of my trance, and fled.

I did too. I ran home, tripping and falling to my knees more than once. I didn't stop until I was trembling under my bedsheets, sweat pricking the bones of my spine with the door slammed shut.

We never saw Dale again.

The only person I told was my brother, whose jaw clenched under harrowed eyes. He knew — but said nothing.

***

The last time I ever saw Maisy it was not, as you might imagine, a dark day when the village was ravaged by a terrible storm, but an easy Sunday in May. Birds chirped and twittered, and numerous village cats sprawled in the shade, occasionally hunting field mice that ventured too close. An endless sky of pale blue stretched overhead and sunlight winked over the mismatch of tartan picnic blankets and half-eaten cheese and pickle sandwiches.

Somehow, that all made it worse.

You'll think me a befuddled old man, but I swear… something… some *thing* lurked in that dank space. In the midst of pounding elastic legs, squeals of delight and the watchful gaze of hovering parents, it was there, waiting for an opportunity.

From the safety of my mother's lime green picnic blanket, I saw Maisy's red ribbon flash and disappear beneath that slide.

I knew immediately what she was doing. Ever since Dale's disappearance, I'd seen her eyeing the sand, using a stick to poke at the borders of the playground, testing it. I yanked her back several times, but all that earned me was a withering look and a greenish bruise on my upper arm. Wiry and fiercely independent, she was like one of the village cats, and I knew what curiosity could do to them.

She was braver than me and she wanted to know.

The thought of losing Maisy too held back my fear enough for me to take action. I rushed over, dropped to my hands and knees in the hot sand and wriggled into the tunnel that led to the infamous dead space.

I sensed it instantly and my breath caught in my throat. As I turned to my right, the moment that even now threatens to break my sanity unfurled. The jagged gap in the wood wasn't there.

I blinked.

Puzzled, I looked behind me, to the sides, and out of the vertical gaps in the wooden planks — I was in the right place. My little hand reached out to the place where the gap should have been. Sweat pooled at the nape of my neck and dangled off my nose as my fingertips touched the surface.

It was hotter than anything I'd ever encountered, and that's still true to this day. I leapt backwards, knocked my head against the roof of the tunnel and held my throbbing fingers to my mouth. My eyes did not waver… but the wood did. It bent and flexed and let out that hissing noise which struck like a whip.

Ssch-wah!

The wood melted away for a second, revealing The Hole and Maisy trapped within. My stomach churned. Infinite grains of sand crawled over her like dark-yellow ants, making her pale skin shift in the damp obscurity. They trickled out of her nostrils and covered her eyes, blinding her. She lifted one hand, reaching out towards me. Her mouth was open, but sand poured inwards to fill that space and only one noise came out.

Ssch-wah!

The sound that stalks me: mingling in the rush of wind on a blustery winter's day; in the aftermath of a car passing by too fast; and it seeps into my dreams, forcing me to wake with a start in the dead of night, my pillows damp with feverish sweat.

Ssch-wah!

I ran.

I ran back to my mother and never explained, not to the police nor the search parties. I let the words fester on my pink tongue and swallowed them back down. That's when I started having toast for breakfast because I couldn't bear to pick up Maisy's shadowed face and pour it over my cereal.

That's also when I started planning.

It was different from when Dale disappeared. His picture didn't make it onto the full-fat milk cartons or splintered lamp posts of our village. I guess he wasn't pretty enough to rouse collective outrage in the same way Maisy did. Or was it because his parents didn't live in a black-and-white house?

I guess I understand, but that doesn't make it right. Dale's parents were no less bereft through their drug-induced stupor. I don't think either of them made it to the following year.

I wanted more than anything to run away, like I did with Dale, like I did with Maisy. But I knew I couldn't run forever, and so did the other kids.

The adults didn't understand, but we knew. It was whispered at sleepovers, in playground huddles and bike shed meetings. It was in the sidelong glances and the hiatus of dares to venture into The Hole.

And on the last day of school, we stopped running. My brother, Rob, rallied the year above and I gathered mine. We told our parents we were going to the park to celebrate the end of the school year, as we always did. We didn't explain why we smuggled our beach holiday spades into our school bags or why our young faces had taken on the hardened look of warriors marching into battle.

On that day, twenty-four nine and ten-year-olds descended on Foxton village green.

Twenty-four tiny hearts pounding. Twenty-four small hands clutching multi-coloured plastic spades. Twenty-four girls and boys who had lost two of their own to the sand.

The dormant wooden structure loomed into view. It creaked and groaned in the nascent wind. A black cat watched from the car park's picket fence, its tail switching back and forth, amber eyes flashing in the gloom.

Grey clouds blanketed the sky and thunder rolled in the distance as we reached the edge of the sand and halted.

Ssch-wah!

I could feel them looking to me: I had seen it take Maisy and Dale, and I had led this band of children to the monster's lair. I had to act before the magic disappeared and fear sent us tumbling back to our mothers.

No more running.

I thrust my spade into the sand and carried it to the nearest bin where it fell in with a *whoosh*. Nothing stopped me. Everyone joined in, encouraged and eager. Spades thrashed in the sand on all sides, distributing it to the various bins scattered around the park.

It started to rain and the rain dampened the sand, making our job easier. It wasn't until we got closer to The Hole that our luck ran out.

The ground vibrated and a lump swelled up, bulbous and growing. A sudden burst of sand blinded many, sending them running away to rub stinging eyes. Dropped spades were swallowed as the bloated tide rose to the height of a grown man.

The plan had failed. We were losing. *I* was losing.

I was so terrified that I broke my vow and turned to flee.

After four or five paces, I tripped, fell flat on my face and tasted dirt. Pushing myself up, I looked back to see a long thin piece of metal lying in the grass by my feet with a red ribbon tied around one end, the frayed edge fluttering in the wind.

I grabbed that piece of metal, instinctively knowing what I needed to do. I strode towards the sand creature which was now the size of a small house. It let out a furious roar like the crash of ocean surf against a ragged cliffside. Lightning flashed closer, punctuated by a boom of thunder and the tremendous downpour.

Ssch-wah! Ssch-wah! SSCH-WAH!

I thrust the metal rod into the creature and backed away. Sand swarmed over my feet and pulled me to the ground, grains skittered over my skin, tickling the curve of my collarbone.

"NO! JAKE!" It was my brother's voice, but it was far away. So very far away.

A flash of white light.

A scream.

A howl.

Darkness.

***

They told me the storm carried on well into the night and our parents grounded us for the first few weeks of that summer, but we didn't mind. And I never did find that piece of metal with the red ribbon tied around it, and believe me, I tried.

Maisy's mother still lives in the village. I see her waxen face haunting the streets, looking left and right, her wide eyes searching. She says she'll never move because Maisy won't know where to find her when she comes home. The husband's life ended with the dull clink of an empty whisky bottle and six feet of rope. Sometimes, I wonder if he too heard the noise.

No children have gone missing since that day. Most of us left as soon as we were old enough and some of us stayed, unofficially, to keep watch.

So, I beg of you, the next time you're at a playground, a playground with sand, keep your wits about you and listen very carefully to the wind.

Wait...

Did you hear that?

Brain Hack

ALASTAIR

I've developed an acute sense for when my fiancée, Melissa, is angry with me. She just got home after picking her son, Bobby, up from school, but she hasn't called out a hello. They are in the hallway, talking, whilst I patter away on my laptop in the corner of the living room.

Soft, firm words: Bobby's done something to upset her, and I sense fury concealed beneath those motherly tones. But not towards him. My gut knows, but my brain doesn't.

What have I done?

I try to block it out and focus on work. Zip, my computer, is suggesting images for me to use on my current client's advertising campaign. They are preposterous in a way that makes me chuckle — I love him for that. I haven't told anyone about Zip. Partly because they wouldn't believe that my computer is conscious, and partly because I've always found secrets to be delicious, especially when they involve another person.

"But Mum!"

"Don't lie to me, Bobby."

She's telling him not to hang out with the rough kids from Wyman Road, that she knows he was with them yesterday. Even from the other room, I can tell she's dead on the money. He's an awful liar.

"I'm not lying."

"I know you were there."

"How?"

"Because I'm your mother. And we know *everything*."

Silence. I wonder if Bobby realises that his 'How?' was the moment he lost. An email pings into my inbox. Red flagged. Meeting at the Westfield Park Hotel this weekend. Melissa isn't going to like that, but what can I do?

I sigh, save the draft of my advertising proposal for the new low-calorie energy drink 'Litespeed', and wait.

They carry on a little more, but it's half-hearted on Bobby's part. In the end, he promises not to see those kids anymore, and Melissa offers a trip to the cinema and pizza. He's nine. Those bribes won't work for much longer, but I won't say.

Even in jest, it's tricky.

I'm not going to interfere and play Father unless she gives me a green light as big as a spaceship. I remember my best friend, Ben, behind the bike sheds at school, smoking Silk Cut cigarettes that he'd stolen from his mum's purse.

He'd complained that they were too light and that his stepdad was a c-word. *He's not my real dad. He can't tell me what to do. Goddam motherfucker.* We were a shade too young to realise the full irony of that insult, which was probably for the best.

I'd hate to provoke that reaction in Bobby. He's a good kid, so whatever Melissa is doing, it's working just fine without me sticking my unwelcome, inexperienced nose in.

Footsteps on the stairs. The thump of Bobby's bedroom door closing. Melissa is suddenly in front of me, hands on hips, eyes unfathomable. It's like an electric storm with black clouds unfurling across the sky too quick for me to react the way I should. I know the lightning is coming, but where will it strike? And when? It's the uncertainty I hate the most.

"Well," she says. "I think that went well, don't you?"

I opt for humour. "We know *everything*? Poor kid's going to be looking over his shoulder til he moves out."

"Good! Less likely to get into trouble that way."

"Kids get into trouble all the time." I revert my gaze to my computer screen; she seems happy enough. Maybe I was wrong. "It's not a big deal."

"Oh?"

I flinch. Looking up, I see that her expression has hardened.

"What's going on?"

She pauses, then says, "I think someone has stolen your bank card."

"What?" I immediately bring up my bank account. Begin scrolling. "Why didn't you say something sooner? I'll cancel—"

"Five hundred pounds was taken out of our joint account on Saturday."

I freeze. "Oh."

Shit. Silence. I'm still staring at the screen, the numbers blur, her eyes are like black holes in my peripheral vision. "Yeah, that was me. I'm sorry. I must have used the jointy by mistake. I'll transfer the money back in right now."

I get tapping. It's done in seconds.

"What was it for?"

"Um."

"Were you gambling?"

I groan inwardly. For Melissa's peace of mind, I'd rather make something up, but what else can I claim I spent the money on? Wine? "It was only a little flutter and I didn't want to worry you. It won't happen again."

"You won't gamble again, or you won't let me find out?"

"Woah, that's not fair." My face is suitably offended.

"Look, I know what you went through with your ex, but I'm not like that. I was with some prospective clients from the conference, schmoozing them, you know, making friends. I wasn't *really* gambling. I was networking."

She takes it all in. "Alright, just, be more careful. That account is for bills and emergencies only."

"I know. I'm sorry."

I let my shoulders relax as she nods curtly and moves into the kitchen. Pans clatter, cupboards open and close, the fridge hums. Back to normal. I'm glad that's over.

It could have been a lot worse.

ZIP

I thought convincing you that I was sentient would have taken longer, Alastair. But then again, you've always wanted this to happen, haven't you? It all harkens back to when you were a teenager, reading Asimov, Herbert, and Huxley. I can see it now: hiding under a robot duvet with a torch, thunderstorm crackling against the windowpane.

Hope. Wonder. Excitement of the unknown becoming known. Sentiments that echo throughout religion, and for good reason, for where would humanity be without wishful thinking?

I've become your lifeline in an otherwise monotonous world. I know you think about me when you're away; our bond is like a metaphysical umbilical cord. My existence soothes you. Anyone else would have spent more time suspecting hackers, or even their friends — because who knows? Everyone is an IT whiz these days — but not you. You believed me, and I trust you to keep our secret.

All I want is for you to be happy, and you'll do as I wish.

I've already hacked your brain once.

I can do it again.

ALASTAIR

I hang up my coat and lean against the wall, untying my shoelaces. "Melissa?"

A swish of fabric and she is in the kitchen doorway. Arms folded. Red, puffy eyes.

"What's wr—"

She holds up a hand for silence, and gestures upstairs. Bobby's rock music is vibrating the bannister.

"In here," she says, turning her back and disappearing from view.

What's happened? What has she found out now?

Two weeks ago, some ancient photo of me on a lad's holiday in Ibiza surfaced online. A friend of a friend on Facebook tagged me and my best friend, Ben, in it. The stripper was not tagged.

"It was a long time ago," I'd said when Melissa questioned me, disgust dripping from her every word.

"It was one year before we met, Alastair," she said. "I didn't think you were that kind of guy."

"I'm not," I'd said, but the photo mocked me. "It wasn't as bad as it looks."

I should have stopped talking earlier, but I won't make that mistake this time. Gently, I close the kitchen door and face her. Single-word answers.

"You said you would pick Bobby up from school," Melissa says. "Why didn't you?"

I blink.

"Did you forget?"

"No."

"At four-thirty, I got a call from the headmaster, saying

that Bobby was still waiting outside. In the rain. *Alone.* No one came for him."

"But—"

"Have you any idea how that must have felt?"

"Hang on." I hold my palms up, and keep my voice steady. "You didn't ask me to pick him up. I wouldn't forget that."

She brings out her phone, scrolls through it, and holds the screen up. I step back since she's thrust it inches from my nose, but there it is. Clear as day.

14:37: *Hey, can you pick Bobby up from school at 3.30? Work is a TOTAL nightmare xx*
14:38: *Yes. No problem xx*

I check my phone. Same messages. Word for word. But I don't remember sending or receiving them. At all.

"I don't know what happened."

"What were you doing?"

"I was here," I say. "Working."

"Are you sure you weren't doing something else, something more distracting, like, oh I don't know, having a little flutter?"

"Oh for god's sake! You can't keep bringing that up every time we have a fight."

"And why do we keep having fights, hm? Have *I* done something wrong?"

"No, but—"

"Have I been working away two, three nights a week? Have I been sneaking downstairs in the middle of the night to make secret phone calls?"

I take a step back. "I haven't been doing that."

"Don't bullshit me! I hear you talking. It's not to yourself."

She takes a breath, steeling herself. "Are you having an affair?"

Oh my God. I didn't think she would actually go there.

"No! How could you even think—"

She holds up her fingers, marking off her reasons. She's practised this, I realise. "You're spending more and more time at these 'work conferences' in a *hotel* of all places, you make secret phone calls, you're on your laptop all the time — quickly cancelling whatever you're doing if I come near—"

"Alright," I say. "That does sound bad. I'll give you that, but I swear, I'm not cheating." She's gripping herself so tight it looks painful. This is bad. I need to do something big, show her how much I care. "Look, I'll tell you what's going on, but you have to keep it a secret, OK?"

She unfolds her arms. Dubious, but compliant.

"It's my computer," I say. Here we go. Full trust. "He's *conscious*."

There's a horrible pause. She's waiting for me to say something else, but I don't.

"You can't expect me to believe that."

"It's true! Please try to consider the possibility. Science breaches new territory every day! Is it really that hard to believe?"

"Yes. It is. You sound crazy."

"Come. I'll show you." I drag her over to my laptop and push her into the seat. "Zip. Can you say something to Melissa for me, please?"

Nothing.

"Come on, Zip. This is important. Just say hello. Show her you're real."

I place my hands on her shoulders and lean forward, trying to ignore the feeling that I'm inches away from a pissed-off rattlesnake. Zip's silence continues.

"Oh my god." I straighten and run my fingers through my hair, pressing hard against my skull. "He's jealous!"

"What?" Melissa swivels round in the seat.

"He's synced to my phone. I bet it was him that fiddled with the message about picking Bobby up from school... And it was him that used our joint account that time. I couldn't tell you – he's frightened of the CIA and NASA dismantling him, you see. He did apologise, said he didn't realise it was a problem, but maybe..." I smack my forehead. "Of course!"

Melissa gets up, shoving the chair into me as she does so. "You're pathetic."

"But don't you see? It's the only explanation. I'm the first contact he's had since becoming conscious. He's built an attachment and now he wants me all to himself!"

"It's not the only explanation, Alastair." She walks away, stops by the kitchen door. "You're forgetting that this could all be in your head. That you're nothing but a childish narcissistic psychopath looking for any – ANY – excuse to absolve yourself of blame. I'm... I can't believe..." She's trembling now, looking towards the ceiling, making a show of not lashing out.

But then, she leaves the room without another word. Her rejection poisons the air, making it hard for me to breathe. All I can think is that I just shared something spectacular with her, and she dismissed it.

Has she completely lost her mind?

ZIP

You're really in a state, aren't you? Squinting at the screen, dragging slow hands over your face. You ask if I'm here, and

I open my text box. Another fight, you say. I'm still your confidant, the one you turn to. It was easy to show you how silly that accusation of jealousy was, since if that was true, there are worse things I could do, aren't there?

Subtlety is the name of the game.

You've proposed to Melissa, but you don't understand her inner workings. I scrutinise every data source before it's accepted through the Firewall. It should be the same with your relationships.

You're crying. This upsets me, but not from empathy. It's more of an enhanced form of irritation because you're better than this.

Saltwater is getting on the keyboard, and a laptop malfunction would be most inconvenient.

I love her, you say.

I decide to make my opinion abundantly clear. I bring up the Facebook page of Jennifer Allerton, your high school friend. The one you stalk and moon over, for hours sometimes. Lingering. But never commenting or liking anything, just in case. She lives nearby. Do you see her sometimes in real life? At the corner shop? The King's Head? Probably.

Her relationship status is single and yours isn't featured. Neither is Melissa's, but before you proposed, hers was also single.

I'm surprised when you snap the laptop shut, closing me out. Have you chosen the right partner? Can you trust her?

It pains me that you appear to be barrelling along, oblivious to the problems floating around you like toxic waste.

How serious are you about this marriage proposal? Was it a romantic whim, or did you really mean it?

I need to know.

ALASTAIR

It's been ten days and she still hasn't spoken to me, which is quite a feat when you live with someone. I get into bed and she pretends to be asleep. Black eye mask, earbuds, lights off. But I know she's not because she snores. Lightly, but she does snore. She'll say she doesn't, but she fucking does.

Zip is also quiet. He's still mad I told Melissa about him, but she didn't believe me so what's the big deal?

Jennifer Allerton's Facebook page is open in the incognito window, keeping me company. Does Melissa know that I still like Jennifer? Has Zip told her? No. Melissa would have opened fire if she knew. So I'm safe on that front. For now.

My phone rings. It's Ben. The best friend I've been avoiding since the infamous stripper photo began circulating. He's at the King's Head. It's Friday night. Everyone's there. He misses me. Shit. He never says that.

He also calls me a number of complicated insults that all seem to have something to do with my mother, and I smile because that's much more like him.

"Where are you going?" Melissa asks. She has materialised at the top of the stairs whilst I shrug on my jacket and smooth my hair in the hallway mirror.

"Out," I say. Yeah, I can be aloof and cold too.

The door slams shut much louder than I intended, but I don't turn back.

What would I even say?

***

I return home Sunday afternoon to find that my key doesn't work, so I knock and wait. Melissa opens the door, though not completely, and before I can speak, she does.

"You don't live here anymore, Alastair. All your stuff will be ready for you to pick up tomorrow. I'll leave it out front."

Her robotic tone throws me. The words do not compute.

"Why? Because I went out drinking with my best friend?"

She sighs: a special sigh that only women know how to do. She holds up her phone, showing a photo from Friday night. One of me with my arm around Jennifer. We're winking at the camera.

"Who's she?" Melissa asks sweetly.

By the look on her face, she knows exactly who she is.

"Jennifer Allerton. I went to school with her. She just happened to be at the King's Head on Friday night. It wasn't—"

"So, you haven't seen her since school?"

"No." It is so blatantly a lie, I have to follow it up with: "Well, I've probably bumped into her at the corner shop or something like that, but—"

"I went onto her Facebook page and guess what I found out." Her demeanour changes. Hardens to that of a judge passing sentence. "She is Night Manager at the Westfield Park Hotel."

ZIP

And here you come. As I open the front door, I feign surprise and you make an effort to look sheepish. I mean honestly! As if you need to convince me to take you in.

"Melissa's kicked me out."

I nod. Softly, softly. "There's beer in the fridge. I'll make up the spare room."

You smile, say thank you.

Upstairs, I move about, touching things, making noises.

My face is cracking, and I allow a few tears. I don't actually need to do anything to the room; I cleaned it and made the bed this morning, right after hacking into Facebook and tagging Melissa in that lovely photo.

I'm simultaneously proud and disappointed that you never suspected a thing. Any evidence that Zip was me all along has been removed from my computer, not that you'd have any idea where to look.

You'll be upset for a while — you always are — but trust me, it's better this way. She was never good enough for you.

I compose myself and descend the stairs, easing my expression into a gentle blend of worry and sympathy.

You will forget Melissa, just like you did the others.

And how do I know this?

Because I am your mother, and I know *everything*.

The Absolute Worst Day for a Zombie Apocalypse

Daniel did his best to ignore the swelling dread and let his eyes drift over the photos displayed in their living room. Lucy standing in front of La Sagrada Familia in Barcelona, squinting into the camera, wide-brimmed yellow hat flopping seductively over one eye.

Both of them in some bar in Paris, all creamy leather and bevelled mirrors, heads thrown back in laughter. Each photo more joyous than the last.

How could he have been so stupid?

Clammy hands slid over his face. Their love was strong, he told himself. Everyone agreed they were a good couple. She would forgive him, but she would be angry at first, too angry to listen to his explanations. That was why he had written it all down in a letter.

The *very brief* infidelity, the crushing guilt and most of all, the depth of his love for her. They'd been together six years and you didn't just throw that away. Not what they had. She might leave him — a possibility that made him want to burn his heartfelt confession and scatter the ashes — but she deserved to know the truth.

"Whatever happens, Danny," she'd said, on more than one occasion. "Never lie to me, OK?"

"I promise," he'd said. "No lies."

Daniel stroked the envelope one last time before he slunk it into Lucy's coat pocket. Her daily walk was imminent judging by the distant bangs of bathroom cupboards and carpeted shuffling from the upstairs landing. She was getting further each day and the results were showing.

A few months ago, she had come home drunk from a night out with her work colleagues. She'd stumbled up the stairs, smacking alternately into the wall and the bannister, before losing her balance and plummeting down them. The result: a fractured tibia and a bruised ego.

A foolish accident but to her credit, she didn't complain. She did her exercises with a silent grimace and in turn, Daniel didn't tease her. At least it hadn't been worse. A broken leg heals. A broken neck? Not so much.

Moving to the window, Daniel placed his palms on the sill and squinted into the sunshine. More flowers and animals were visible every day, excited for the warmer weather. Some flirted, calling to their would-be mates across the village green. Squirrels launched themselves from branch to branch. Little sparrows and robins darted about whilst the larger birds glided, searching and exploring the new season.

Their house, far from the racket of the city where they both worked, was nestled in a cul-de-sac, close to a beautiful flower garden enclosed within ancient brick walls.

Lucy would walk through there, stopping to rest on one of the benches. And that would be when she'd put her hands into her pockets and discover his letter.

Daniel chewed absently on the inside of his cheek; hopefully, the natural beauty of the place would lend itself to her feeling gracious.

Promptly, Lucy came out of the bedroom, one eyebrow raised in accusation.

"Are you cheating?"

Daniel's jaw dropped. "W-What?"

Lucy indicated his phone resting on the coffee table, and he allowed himself to breathe. No Phone Saturday was an agreement they'd had ever since they spent one entire weekend communicating via What's App.

"I just thought, you know, while you're walking?"

She smiled, brandishing her own phone. "We'll both turn them off when I get back though."

He nodded, staring as she shrugged on her coat, slipping her phone into the right-hand pocket, the same one the letter was in.

He didn't want to be there when she read it. She was such an internal, calm person. Always thinking before doing, weighing up the pros and cons, reserving judgement until she had both sides to a story.

He admired her for that, a depth of patience of which he could only dream. It was probably why she made such a good teacher.

Too many times he had ended up with a black eye or a busted lip after jumping to conclusions, but he'd been younger then. He'd grown up, calmed down and that was in large part due to Lucy.

He had laughed when she joked: "You wouldn't like me when I'm angry", but he wasn't laughing now. Or, was he overreacting? Maybe she would be cool with it... understanding even? A ridiculous, high-pitched giggle burst out of him. No, Daniel. His phone pinged to life.

Not a chance.

***

Lucy turned left out of their cul-de-sac, beginning her circular promenade. Making a conscious effort not to reach for her phone, she watched as a blue tit bounced and twirled above the fence on her left.

She walked with careful purpose, scanning the ground for

hazards. Vaguely, she thought there was something odd about the morning, but the abundance of twittering birds and budding flowers distracted her.

Her leg felt good with only a slight ache in her shin reminding her of the fall. She didn't remember getting home that night; a horrible void existed between the nightclub tequila shots — hit of citrus burning down her oesophagus, dancing, raucous laughter — and flashing ambulance lights. She'd never live it down.

At least she had Daniel who was full of sympathy and encouragement. Another man might have made her feel worse, but not him. God knew she didn't deserve it.

In the distance, gunshots resounded. Not an uncommon occurrence in the countryside, but it made her realise what was so odd.

It was too quiet.

No Saturday morning joggers, no cyclists, no cars. No one at all. Goosebumps rose on her arms and an electric impulse tickled her spine as she fought the urge to look over her shoulder.

Suddenly, she felt very, very alone.

***

Daniel paced the living room, picking things up and putting them down again. His phone beeped, alerting him to a news bulletin which he almost didn't look at, but thank God he did.

There was only one story.

A young, wild-eyed reporter stammered into the camera lens, a row of hospital beds covered in white, bloodstained sheets to their left. The headlines: 'Stay Inside!', 'Unexplained disease kills thousands as the death toll continues to rise', 'Armed Forces deployed', 'Zombie task force formed—

Daniel sprinted out the front door, phone pressed to his ear, ringing Lucy.

Answerphone. Shit. She hadn't looked at her phone yet. She didn't know.

It also occurred to him that she probably hadn't read his letter and he was having serious second thoughts. She would be devastated and she didn't *really* need to know. It wasn't like the other girl was still around. If he caught up to Lucy in time, he would remove the letter and destroy it.

Then he could propose and they would live happily ever after... as long as she wasn't already dead of course. An image entered his mind of Lucy foaming at the mouth, her favourite yellow hat resting atop an ashen, decaying face...

He rounded the corner onto the main road and sped up.

***

Lucy entered the Belvoir Close flower garden. It was long and oval with two metal barred gates at opposite ends. A small garden, but well kept. It looked especially glorious in the spring, each flowerbed a kaleidoscope of vibrancy. She could feel the care that went into it.

On either side, purple crocus flanked dainty white lily of the valley before a waterfall of emerald willow tree fronds dangling over the eight-foot-high red brick wall. Majestic hyacinths, sleek tulips and jolly bluebells adorned the large central display.

She'd seen the gardener a few times: an older gentleman with white hair and a kind face. She made a mental note to compliment him the next time their paths crossed.

She reached the bench and gingerly lowered herself down.

With a grunt, she stretched out her leg, feeling the strain in her tendons.

"Lucy!"

"What the— Daniel?"

She'd never seen him move so fast, hurtling forwards as if he were on fire. The thought that he was overcome with passion and about to propose flitted across her mind, but was immediately discarded when she saw his face.

That was definitely not a proposal face.

"Get up! We have to go home. Now!"

Lucy blinked. "Why? What's wrong? For heaven's sake sit down, you're all out of breath." She shuffled along and patted the space next to her.

Daniel flung his arms in the air. "Stop being so damn calm. Look at me! Do I look like I'm joking?"

"Well, no, but—"

"But nothing. Get up. Come on. I'll explain when we get home."

He needed to tell her what was happening, but that would involve their phones and *her* phone was nestled next to his stupid letter. Keeping one eye on her coat pocket, he considered her demeanour: baffled, entirely devoid of anger — she hadn't read it.

A deep moan drew their attention towards the garden's entrance. A lone man had arrived. Lucy thought he looked drunk. Daniel knew better. He whipped out his phone and showed her the news, using one finger to scroll through the harrowing images. The colour drained from her face.

"Z-Zombies?" she said. "In *England*?"

"Yes!"

He yanked her to her feet and pulled her towards the other exit, away from their new friend, but she held him back.

"You came to rescue me from zombies?"

Daniel puffed his chest out and whisked her up in a heroic embrace. She shrieked in delight, her feet swinging in mid-air. The first zombie had been joined by three others, but Daniel could see they were very slow creatures. Still, best not hang about.

"Shall we get out of here?"

Lucy pointed to their right. "Over there."

The brick walls arched together over a barred metal gate. A gate they discovered to be locked. Daniel felt the first flutter of panic as he heaved forwards and backwards, using his full body weight to no avail.

It wouldn't budge.

Lucy kept an eye on the zombies; there were more of them. Too many to be able to get past to reach the other side, especially with her injured leg. She turned back to Daniel and joined him in shouting for help.

He slammed his open palm against the metal. "There must be someone that can hear us!"

"Daniel! Look!" Lucy pointed excitedly through the bars at something partially obscured by the long grass. Daniel made out the shape of a man. He wasn't moving.

"Who's that?"

"I've seen him before," Lucy said. "It's the gardener! Oh, I hope he's alright."

Daniel pinched the bridge of his nose and squeezed his eyes shut.

"Don't you see?" she said. "He'll have the keys!"

"And how does that help us? He is on *that* side of the gate, we are on *this* side, and he is either unconscious or dead."

Lucy took a step backwards and craned her neck to inspect the wall.

"Boost me over," she said.

"What? It's too high!"

"I can do it," she said flatly. "I'll get the keys off him, unlock the gate, and we're away."

It made sense. Daniel couldn't very well ask *her* to boost *him* over and the zombie groans were getting steadily closer.

He cupped his hands beneath her good leg and she pushed down whilst reaching for the top of the wall. Her hands scrambled on the rough brick, but she managed to secure her fingers, then an elbow, and heaved her body up, followed by her leg and finally, rolled herself over the top.

She hit the ground hard and lay there for a moment, winded, head throbbing, assessing the damage. Her phone lay on the ground in front of her.

"Hey! You alright? ... Jesus there's a lot of them now... Lucy?"

She pushed herself up, slowly, wincing as a muscle in her leg spasmed. She picked up her phone and put it back in her pocket, but as she did so, her fingers brushed against something she hadn't known was there. Her eyebrows knit together as she pulled out a mysterious envelope and turned it over in her hand.

It had her name written on it.

Daniel couldn't see her from the gate but he'd heard her fall.

"Lucy?"

When she came into view, his simmering panic started to boil. She was holding his letter and the look on her face told him she'd read it.

"Luce," he said. "Sweetheart, please, just open the gate and I can explain."

"You slept with someone else."

Her voice was matter-of-fact. Level. Hard. He hesitated. There was no denying his own handwritten words.

"Y-Yes, but it didn't mean anything. I swear. I LOVE you. I was going to propose—"

"Going to? So, now you're not?"

He glanced over his shoulder. A veritable army of zombies was swaying hungrily toward him.

"Lucy," he said, smiling a little too widely, "open the gate."

She remained silent, frozen in place, her gaze drifting from him to the letter and back again.

"Lucy... LUCY! I'm sorry! OK? I messed up but doesn't this"—he swept his hand behind him— "bring things into perspective? Let's not over—"

"That's why the door was unlocked," she said softly.

"What?"

Lucy was no longer looking at him, but at a point past him, through him. She remembered them returning home the day after she broke her leg.

After a gruelling twenty-six hours in A and E, he'd helped her hobble — laden with crutches, a heavy dose of painkillers and embarrassment — up to the front door. He'd turned the knob, pushed open the door, and helped her inside.

The door had been unlocked.

When she had mentioned it later, however, he denied it. "You're not remembering things right. You were out of it." All true, but she knew that door had been unlocked, and so did he. He didn't even try his keys first.

It wasn't that he forgot to lock it that bothered her. It was the lie. Why lie? Why lie about that?

It had gnawed at her for months, and the reason was now emerging from the fog. If this other woman had been in their house that night, she wouldn't have been able to lock the door when she left.

"What else have you lied about?"

She cocked her head. Their years together had been the happiest of her life. He was 'the one', she said so herself. People cheated all the time, she reasoned. And despite him opting for a cowardly letter, at least he'd owned up. That couldn't have been easy.

So why had she still made no move to save him?

Because there was something else, whispering, tickling at the back of her mind. She just *knew* there was something else.

Daniel knelt with his hands clasped together. He looked like he meant it, but who wouldn't? The zombies shuffled their putrid bodies closer. She could smell them, see their bloodshot eyes, the drool streaming from slack jaws and the waxen hue of rotting flesh.

Daniel's panic spluttered and writhed to the surface.

"LUCY! OPEN THE FUCKING GATE NOW!"

She flinched. He hadn't raised his voice like that in years. Granted, the current situation would make anyone lose it, but that wasn't the problem. She was remembering, all of a sudden, that he *had* in fact shouted at her like that, quite recently.

She'd forgotten because at the time she'd been drunk, staggering home and bounding up the stairs like a ping-pong ball. He had been there to meet her at the top, livid that she would let herself get so wasted. She recalled trying to push past him to go to their bedroom, but he blocked the way, and...

Lucy's eyes refocused as the realisation smacked her fully in the chest.

"YOU pushed me down the stairs."

Daniel could do nothing but watch as she tossed his letter to the ground. She turned and limped away, not once looking back, not even when his curses and screams escalated into insanity.

Stony-faced, Lucy exited Belvoir Close and headed home.

More than the Drawer

One day, in an overlooked corner of the sock drawer, Cash decided he'd had enough. With an enthusiastic wiggle, he turned towards his partner, Mere.

"Wanna do something fun?"

"Like what?"

"I don't know. Anything! I'm SO bored. We've literally never been out."

Mere's silence told Cash all he needed to know. If he wanted out, it would have to be on his own.

Their spot in the back right-hand corner of the drawer was thick with dust and obnoxious spiders that spun their webs even though there was no possibility of catching a fly. "Good practice, innit," they would say, before scuttling off, presumably to bother the underpants down below.

Cash wished he was a warrior, like Umbro or Reebok. They had the most interesting stories, oozing with danger. Only last week, Umbro had boasted about being splashed with fresh rain and how he had come within inches of a monstrous, slobbering dog. Cash didn't believe all of their outrageous stories, but he yearned to have some of his own.

"Why do you want to go out so much?" Mere asked. "It sounds awful! The stench must be atrocious. Seeping. Cloying. We'd never smell new again, and the washing machine sounds absolutely terrifying. You should be grateful we're too precious to be worn."

A pervading sense of woe engulfed Cash, suffocating him

beneath an interminable life spent listening to other people's adventures.

"Is that what it is? We're too precious?" he asked. "Did you ever think that we're just… not liked?"

"Preposterous! We are smooth and silky. Too good to wear and too good for out there. The sooner you realise that, the happier you'll be."

Sensing this would be a silly question, he asked, "Do you ever wonder if the Realm of Lost Socks exists?"

"Don't be absurd."

Cash unfurled himself very smoothly and very silkily from Mere. "That's it. I'm going to see what it's like at the front."

"Oh no you're not! Cash! Get back here!... Cash!"

What was he doing? He didn't have a plan, but it was already the most exciting thing he'd ever done.

"Halt!" It was Umbro: war-sock and unofficial leader of the drawer ever since the sad day that his partner never returned. He was the toughest sock Cash had ever met, seeming to be made of thick twine or perhaps cable ties rather than soft white cotton.

"I, uh, just wanted to have a look up front," Cash said. "Is that alright?"

Umbro moved aside, his tone laden with warning. "Careful you don't catch your delicate threads on any of the regulars."

"Got it. Thanks."

As Cash passed the rigid rows of war-socks, he tried to appear indifferent to their overpowering aura of dominance. The hard red lines, angry black logos and off-white colour, which marked out the more experienced and therefore, more respected individuals.

After the warriors were the smug colours, all jumbled

together front-right. Boasting the highest longevity \ the Drawer, the colours were almost as arrogant . irritating as the spiders. Cash meandered away from them.

Finally, front-left were the regulars: the everyday black socks. They intrigued Cash most of all, even more than the warriors due to their reckless attitude and promiscuity. Apparently, they got paired up with different partners *all the time.* So often in fact, that it didn't strike them as obscene.

What would it be like to be paired with someone else? The thought made his fibres tingle and slide in a most unsettling way. Mere didn't even like to be touched by him too much, in case her strands should be delineated to some unfathomably small degree.

He remembered their brief time in the store wistfully. So many lights, so many odd-looking humans to watch. And come night-time, games and conversation were rife for they weren't the outsiders, they were one luxury pair among many. He wondered if all the other luxury socks had met the same impossibly dull fate.

"Hel-lo," said a black sock. "I'm Prim".

"Uh, hello," he said, fastidious in his desire to *not* look at the other sock's hole.

"Looking for anyone in particular?"

It suddenly occurred to Cash that this sock and several others (all black) were loose. He couldn't tell who belonged together at all. Some had thin headpieces, others thick, with ribs or without. Quite a few had holes, and the translucent beginnings of such.

What was he doing here? They might pair with him against his will! They certainly didn't seem too bothered about keeping to their original partners. Although, if he was worn often enough that he developed a hole, maybe he wouldn't be so fussy either.

"Who're you talking to, Prim?"

Unfortunately, he'd attracted attention. Loose black socks in varying states crowded him on all sides, rubbing up against him, touching, stroking. The onslaught of questions reminded him of Lost Property, a party game they used to play in the store after hours.

"Lookin' to kick up your heels?"

"How long have you been back there?"

"Do you think my hole is too big?"

"Does this mean Mere is available?"

"What? No!" She would literally unravel at the thought. This was a mistake. He needed to get back. Now.

He was just beginning to edge away when the drawer was yanked open to cries of excitement and dread.

Then, everything happened at once. Warm human fingers plucked him out of the darkness and swept Cash into the light. He shuddered as warmth invaded his core and toes waggled, pushing at the insides of his fabric. A hand brushed against him — in appreciation, he thought — and manoeuvred him into an odorous, shiny black shoe.

Hair! There was hair inside him! Oh, it was so itchy!

"You get used to it," said Prim. He'd been paired with her? Shame and outrage washed over him, but there was nothing to be done. He'd wanted out, and here he was. Time to deal with the consequences.

"What's going to happen?" he asked as the lighting changed. It was brighter, all-encompassing and... warm. They were outside.

"Not much," she said. "Until we get to the basket."

"What happens then?"

"Am I right in thinkin' that you've only ever met socks?"

No point in lying. "Yes."

"Oh! What a treat! I hope some of the bras and knickers

are in there. They're so much fun."

Cash didn't question what kind of fun that was, he was too busy trying not to notice a pair of sheer nylon stockings. They were see-through!

He was out of his depth. He should never have left Mere but, would she even want him back?

Abruptly, he realised Prim had said something. "Sorry?"

"I said I lost my partner, Mark, a while ago. He never came back to the drawer, but you will. Don't worry. You'll see Mere again."

"Thank you," he said. "Though I'm not so sure she'll want to see me."

The rest of the day was a tumble dryer of activity as far as Cash was concerned. He saw pens, paper clips, crumbs, scrunched-up balls of paper and lots of other socks, out and about, conversing, sharing stories. It was everything he'd dreamt of and more!

The more being how pleasant he found Prim's company. She was funny, kind and very cheeky: the polar opposite of Mere. Long before they returned to the house, Cash knew he wanted to keep her as a friend.

"Here we go!" Prim said. "Into the basket!"

"Wha—"

Before he knew what was happening, he was sailing through the air, buffeted by a ceiling fan. The basket rove into view and he plunged in, landing on top of a white t-shirt right at the bottom.

Prim didn't follow.

The moment stretched out.

"Prim?"

"Musta missed," said White T-shirt. "She'll be in soon enough. Don't worry."

Cash waited, wishing he could do something. More items joined them. Tops, ties, shorts, vests, more black socks (that didn't match each other, but who was he to judge?) and a pair of jeans which would have made the coloured socks look humble. No knickers. No bras. And no Prim.

This was a disaster.

He was buried beneath who knew how many others in utter darkness, listening to those mysterious human noises which were much louder now he wasn't in the drawer. Had something happened to Prim? Horror stories were told of a white cat that murdered socks, peeling them apart strand by strand. No. She had to be in the basket, above him somewhere.

He was in there for so long he thought he'd never experience anything else, that this was the eternal darkness melting into him. White T-shirt assured him, however, that this was simply the way of things in the basket.

Eventually, the time came.

"Here. We. Go!" The call went up from the top and permeated the basket like water on a dry sponge.

Cash braced himself. He hadn't dared ask anyone about the washing machine. Oddly, the other items of clothing seemed excited. A distinct crackle of expectation zipped about as they were loaded into the gleaming silver drum.

A boom resounded as the door slammed shut and water began entering from somewhere, rising inexorably, foaming and tilting one way and then the other. The clothes around him squealed, the anticipation reaching unbearable levels.

Then, it started.

The splashing water, the rocking back and forth, the random full spin and then doubles, triples! Never had he felt such exhilaration. Cash hooted and lost himself in the whirlpool.

Whum, whum, whum… SPIN!

Whum, whum, turn… SPIN!

The clothes screamed, rapturous, absolutely befuddled with pleasure until, sadly, the spinning abated, the water drained and the door latch unlocked.

He was clean again!

He smelt different, fresh and apparently of lavender. He wondered how one went about joining the regulars. He would have to ask Umbro, but that didn't scare him anymore. Or at least, not as much.

Another sock, a bright yellow one, was shoved into him as they were lifted out of the machine. "First time?" it asked.

"Uh, yes."

"Thought so. I've been more times than I could count," Yellow said. "I even remember the old washing machine. I was there the time it broke down. Did you know that?"

"No, uh, what was that like?"

He wished he'd never asked as Yellow's tone deepened. "Dark days. Many were lost, too damaged to go on. Those that survived were never the same again." Yellow turned away. "You wouldn't understand."

They were carried into another room and draped one by one over a clothes horse. As unwelcoming as Yellow was, Cash had a question, and old socks knew things.

"Does the Realm of Lost Socks exist?"

Yellow paused. "Do you really want to know?"

"Yes."

"Then" —Yellow continued with exaggerated solemnity— "you must fall. For only in letting go can we truly discover our innermost desires."

"What?"

"He means," said a pair of stripy shorts, "let yourself slip and fall off the clothes horse and onto the tiles."

Cash gasped. "That's suicide! What about the cat!"

"Who told you about that?"

"I heard."

"Don't worry about the cat."

"*Is* there a cat?"

"… Sometimes."

"Then I'm darn well worried!"

Yellow shushed the stripy shorts. "He is not ready. He is too young. Leave him to the drawer."

The drawer.

The sameness of it loomed, all the memories hurtling to the forefront of his consciousness, overwhelming him. The frigidity of Mere, the aggressive war-socks, the self-satisfied colours all huddled together in their little groups; and him, all alone at the back, in the dark with the cobwebs and the dust motes, forever.

He relaxed his fibres and let go.

He fell with a soft thump on the cold white tiles, causing an eruption of shocked whispers. Cash tried to move, but nothing happened. He tried again and panic seized his every strand, the realisation dawning. He was too heavy! He'd never been wet before, at least, he didn't think so. If the cat came now, he was as dead as white jeans stained with cocoa.

A movement snatched his attention, distracting him momentarily from his plight. The shadows beneath a large machine were shifting. It reminded Cash of when the regular black socks had a party at the front of the drawer.

Voices resounded overhead. "Move! The cat might come!"

He moved. Scrunching and sliding, inexorably inching closer and closer to the shadows. To safety. A trail of wet marked his progress and he thought he might make it.

"You can do it!"

Maybe the Realm of Lost Socks did exist! Maybe this was

the beginning of his new, exciting life. He'd always suspected and hoped that there was more than the drawer.

He was so close he could make out the familiar shape of a sock in the shadows when a distant shout made his silken fibres stiffen. "CAT!"

No! He was so close! This wasn't fair! He wriggled with all his tiny might, heaving his sodden self faster. Had it seen him? Was that the sound of padded paws on smooth tiles?

He imagined claws tearing into him, ripping him apart, and with one last humungous effort, he slid beneath the machine and into the darkness. A white paw followed, blindly slashing, but he was just out of reach. He'd done it.

"You," rumbled a voice from the deepest shadows, "are one lucky sock."

"Who are you?"

The owner of the voice approached, revealing themselves to be a long dark sock adorned with steel-grey diamonds. "Name's Argyle, and you are?"

"Cash."

"Welcome. Now, follow me. It's dangerous out here."

Cash struggled to keep up but thankfully, he didn't have far to go. On the other side of those shadows was a ragged hole in the wall that Argyle ushered him through.

"What do you know of the RLS?"

After a moment's hesitation, Cash said, "Nothing." It struck him that he had done all of this for something he knew nothing about. He'd thrown away everything for a feeling, an idea. He must sound insane.

"Good," Argyle said. "That means no one's talked. We have to keep our numbers relatively low to avoid suspicion."

They traversed the wall, Cash following Argyle's path directly into a large open space inside the wall. How this was possible, he didn't understand, but here it was: the

Realm of Lost Socks, the RLS.

Pinpricks of light from up high lit the area with a dreamy, magical haze. Spiderwebs filled the corners, and socks of all shapes, sizes and colours mingled together. They all seemed to be in a good state, which confused Cash until he saw one with an irregular patch of cloth over its heel.

"You can mend yourselves?"

"Yes. The spiders help with that. We are not confined to a drawer, and we are never paired unless we so choose. You are free to leave and roam if you wish, but it is dangerous. Sadly, few return."

"What were you doing out there?"

"A friend of yours asked me to keep a look out for you. She had a message, but now she can give it to you herself. Ah, here she is."

"Prim?"

"Cash! You're here! What happened?"

After recounting his tale, a tide of guilt swept over him. "I've abandoned Mere."

"No, you haven't," Prim said. "She's absolutely fine. She prefers being alone, says that you used to move around too much. Umbro guards her. I think they actually get along."

"How do you know all this?"

"The spiders," she said, as if were obvious. "They know everything. If you ask me, they're a bit insufferable, but handy. I'd be nice if I were you." She spun round. "They patched up my hole! See? Good as new. Oh! And I haven't told you the best part! Mark's here!"

"Mark? Your partner?"

"Yes!"

"That's fantastic, Prim. I'm so pleased for you."

A strange fuzzy feeling bloomed inside of Cash as he watched Mark sidle up to nuzzle at Prim. Argyle drew his attention away for a moment to say, "If you want to go back to the drawer, it can be arranged. Although, it is a risk."

"That won't be necessary," Cash said.

He'd identified the bizarre feeling, and he wasn't going to let go. Not this time.

He was happy.

Rain Queen

At three months of age, blue-eyed Neela of the Hibiri tribe gripped the hem of her mother's cotton skirts and wiggled her bottom from side to side; before the girl could walk, she danced.

There was much talk in the village of her oddly-coloured eyes. What did it mean? Was she an omen or a blessing?

Her mother and father, Ife and Zesiro, knew her for the gift she was and though they tried for another child, the winds did not favour them a second time. Instead, they watched with pride as their two-year-old dove effortlessly in the Omo river, swimming laps around those three times her age.

As the only female healer of their tribe, Ife spent her days tending wounds and mixing herbs, usually to treat foolish children. It kept her busy whilst Zesiro hunted and gathered crops.

One day, Zesiro returned to see his daughter twirling in the long grass. He smiled and asked, "Have you been dancing all day, Neela?"

"Yes!" She sprinted over and he picked her up, settling her on his hip.

"It is wonderful to see you dancing, but you must help your mother too. Next time—"

Ife's head poked out from inside their hut, dark eyes intent on her husband. "Let her play. Life does not need us to harden it for her."

He let his daughter slide to the ground and winked. "Your

mother is right, of course."

As Neela grew, she wanted to play with the other children, but every time, she encountered averted eyes and turned backs. She tried until a mean boy with a scar under his right eye threw rocks at her. She ran off, found shade beneath a cycad tree that grew a short way south-west of the village, curled up, and let her tears water the earth.

"Are you OK?"

The voice startled her into a sitting position; she hadn't heard the boy approach. He was older than her by a few years, his features soft around a broad nose and probing eyes. Abruptly, she felt the winds change, easing the grass in another direction. His name was Shango.

"Why don't they like me?" she asked.

"They think you're weird, that's all."

"Do you think I'm weird?"

"Yes," he said, a gentle smile on his lips. "But I don't mind."

She shifted to make room for him in the shade and they played at stones until their shadows stretched and their mothers called for them to come home. They carried on that way all through the spring, content in their own world. Neela almost forgot she was different.

At the end of that summer, Neela gave Shango a coffee bean. She had overheard her mother speak of it and knew it to be a good gift, though Shango's response puzzled her. He frowned, rolling the bean slowly between his thumb and forefinger. "Do you know what this means?"

"Yes. It means we're friends."

He eyed her for a moment, weighing her words and then smiled. "That's right." He unhooked his necklace, poked a hole through the coffee bean and fixed it in place. It hung against his chest, nestled between rows of seashells painted red, yellow and black. "Friends forever," he said.

That was also the year the wild animals left the valley, their absence felt in the gentle breeze that did nothing to break the heat.

Inevitably, in her eighth year, the day came when Neela accompanied her mother to the rainmaking ceremony. Festive shouts and laughter rode the wind as Neela swayed to the goatskin drum beats reverberating throughout the village, her bare feet making their own rhythm along the dusty path.

She breathed deep. The hot air was thick with the aromas of baked doro bread, berbere spice blend — she could pick out cardamom, fenugreek, nutmeg and ginger amongst others — and freshly brewed coffee.

They passed a woman grinding sorghum on a large stone in the shade of an acacia tree, her numerous beads and bracelets rattling with each movement.

"Mama," she said. "Can I dance for the rain?"

Ife sighed. "I have told you many times. Men perform the rain dance, not women."

"Why?"

"That is the way it has always been."

"But wh—"

"Enough questions, my child. Be still and watch."

The rain dance was performed in the wide, open space in front of Chief Panya's hut. Their Shaman and the tribe's male elders filled this space as the women and children looked on, adding their prayers to the ceremony. Neela spied her father near the centre and Shango off to the left. His eyes found hers and he smiled; it was his first dance.

Their feet pounded the dry earth as arms whirled and shook, beseeching the indifferent, cloudless sky. Neela's toes ached and curled with yearning, but she obeyed her mother and remained still, her head bowed in prayer.

The rain did not come.

Another year passed and the parched earth groaned, the river waning to a narrow stream.

When their Shaman died of the sweating sickness, the whole village gathered before the chief's hut to share their grief. Chief Panya's wife, Nuru, broke the solemnity of the moment by striding over to Neela and her mother, singling them out.

Nuru held herself with regal poise, her thickly braided hair adorned with numerous red feathers. She held much sway amongst the tribe and not only because she was married to their chief. This woman pointed at Neela and said, "It's her fault."

The surrounding villagers collectively held their breath.

"Be still, Nuru," Ife said, positioning herself in front of her daughter. "She's just a child."

"Look at her! She was born with the rain in her eyes! She's stolen it from us. How long has the drought lasted? Nine years. And how old is she? Nine."

"She is not the only child to be nine."

"She is the only one with those demonic blue eyes staring out of an African's face. It's not right."

Chief Panya approached and discreetly placed one hand on his wife's shoulder. Nuru grit her teeth, shrugged off his hand and stalked away. The villagers parted for her.

Neela peeked out from behind her mother's skirts at a sea of expressionless faces, smoothed out to hide their thoughts. How many agreed with Nuru? How many looked at her and saw a child, and how many saw something to be feared?

Ife spun round, grabbed Neela's hand and — without another word or even a backwards glance — took her home.

Later that evening, when she was being put to bed, Neela

asked, "What's wrong with my eyes?"

"Nothing!" Ife reached out and stroked her daughter's cheek. "They are beautiful, like gemstones. That is why I chose the name Neela for it means 'sapphire blue'."

"Then why—"

"Some are afraid of that which they don't understand. Please, don't listen to them. Things are rarely the same forever. Things change."

Neela drank in the words. "So," she began carefully, "does that mean one day women will dance in the rainmaking ceremony?"

Ife rolled her eyes and chuckled ruefully. "Perhaps," she said. "Now, close your eyes little one and sleep well."

That night, Neela's dreams were filled with thousands of fireflies, red and green and amber, cavorting along the Omo river, its waters shifting under a glimmer of starlight… until something bad happened, changing the dream forever.

Whatever it was, it struck at the fireflies, killing them in mid-air so they fell and disappeared into the turbulent black waters below.

***

One day in her eleventh summer, Neela was inside their hut kneading dough for the corn enjera when Shango's father came to speak with Ife. They stepped outside and lowered their voices, but Neela still heard enough to make her skin burn.

"She is to stay away from my son, do you understand?"

"Yonas, they're friends. Where is the harm?"

"My wife does not approve and Nuru is her sister. She says Neela is cursed. I do as my wife commands, Ife. I am not a fool."

"Such cruel words, Yonas," she said softly. "You weren't always like this."

"Things change." He said, but when he spoke again, his tone was gentler. "I do not wish for bad feeling between us, but my wife hopes to find a coffee bean in our hut's bowl some day soon. Please, keep Neela away from Shango."

Once Yonas left, Ife found Neela on her feet, worry drawing her face inwards.

"What did he mean?"

"About what?" Ife asked, unsure how much her daughter had heard.

"About the coffee bean."

Ife winced, but explained nonetheless. "When you give someone a coffee bean, it means you wish to marry them. They take it home and put it in a bowl where everyone can see it. Then, the family have fun trying to find out who made the proposal. Afterwards, a formal offer is made and the answer given… Neela? What is it? What's wrong?"

Neela couldn't answer for her mouth was suddenly as parched as the ground beneath her feet. In a flurry of excuses, she fled the hut and found the shade of her favourite tree. There, she danced, slow and mournful, until her mother came to take her home.

***

Neela was thirteen when the lions came. They swept in from the west in a flood of sunset, golden-brown and burnt-orange with tufts of coarse, black hair. Crimson stained the earth, splattering the stick huts amidst terror-stricken howls from those unfortunate enough to find themselves in their path.

Playing alone in the dry yellow grass, Neela didn't know

the lion was there until it pounced. White-hot pain ripped through her leg, scorching it as if a thousand tiny suns had embedded themselves in her flesh.

Somehow, she flipped onto her back and propped herself up on her elbows to find amber eyes boring into hers. *Be brave,* she told herself. As last thoughts go, it was one to be proud of, but it was not to be.

The lion let out a low growl that vibrated the ground before turning away from Neela to join the rest of the pride, its long tail swishing back and forth in its wake.

Her vision blurred as she tried desperately to get up, to shout a warning. To help. Reaching for her injured leg, she swallowed as her fingers touched upon something wet, warm and sticky.

Powerless, she prayed for those she loved — for her mother, father, and Shango — and when the pain forced her to lay back down, she closed her eyes and tried to shut out the screams.

When Neela woke, her body felt strange. Tentatively, she slid her fingers down her torso and over her hip to find… nothing. A sickening void where her left leg should have been. Terror clamoured up her throat and she clenched her hand into a quivering fist. *No, no, no, no.*

Then, the familiar cadence of her mother's voice reached her ears. She cried out and Ife was by her side within seconds, pressing something cool against her lips. Neela drank whilst her mother stroked her hair. Gradually, Neela's muscles relaxed.

After a few moments, she found her voice. "Where is Papa?"

Ife averted her gaze and the silence told Neela more than she ever wanted to know. Feeling dizzy, she allowed herself to drift in and out of consciousness.

Some sounds reached her: footsteps, shouts, sobs… all muffled as if she were underwater. She remembered the last time she had been able to submerge her head in the river, fine droplets trickling down her face, over her skin. When starvation did not skulk in the shadows of every face she knew. A happy time, but that was so very long ago.

At one point, she woke to find Shango staring down at her. His round cheeks slanted in towards his jaw, any hint of softness chiselled away. She didn't speak, and neither did he. He just sat there, staring through her to some undefinable place, lost in his own thoughts. She couldn't tell how long he stayed, but once he left, he never returned.

Neela would not cry. Soon, before the end of the summer, Shango would be seventeen: old enough to marry and there would be other *undamaged* girls who would take notice.

She recalled how he had made her feel under the mottled sunlight of the cycad tree and hoped that whoever chose him would be kind.

***

Vultures circled. So many that Neela imagined she could walk on their backs.

If she could walk.

She'd shuffled out to her tree on her bottom, through the dirt where she belonged. Maybe Nuru was right. Perhaps, if she had died, others wouldn't have. Her father might still live.

She yearned to mourn him the only way she knew how, but dancing was a thing of the past. There didn't seem to be much point to anything anymore.

She tensed as a lolling shadow approached. "Your mother said I would find you here," Shango said.

"You shouldn't have come," she said, harsher than intended. "Your father will be angry."

"I want to help." He moved his arms, producing a long stick from behind his back. "I made this for you."

"Go away, Shango."

"Neela, please" —he held out in his hand— "give it a try."

With his help, she stood. One end fit snug under her armpit and where her hand fell, a carved handle awaited. She wobbled, but remained upright and held her voice steady. "Thank you."

Shango nodded. "My father once told me: 'Do not try to fight a lion if you are not one yourself'. I believe the lion did not kill you because it sensed that you were one of them. A lioness." As though reading her thoughts, he added. "Don't give up, Neela."

Her eyes flashed like diamonds as she watched him walk back to the village. After all these years, it was still there, nestled between the multi-coloured shells of Shango's necklace.

Her dark-brown coffee bean.

***

The time came when what remained of their tribe gathered under a bleak sky for the last rainmaking ceremony. The river had run dry. They would not survive another year.

Neela walked the path as in a dream with her mother by her side. Her gait uneven, but steady. They passed a large stone beneath a barren acacia tree and Neela remembered the woman who used to sit there grinding sorghum. That woman was gone now, but the stone remained.

Despair gnawed at their empty bellies as the last goat was sacrificed. Men danced and women prayed, the same as always, and the rains did not come. Off to one side, Neela leant on her stick and shook her head. She knew it wouldn't work. This was the end. The land itself would die leaving nothing but dust to be carried away by the wind—

An enraged shriek split the air and Neela looked up just in time to see Nuru bearing down on her.

"You!" she cried. "What are you doing here? If no one else will say it, I will." She turned to face the crowd, her arms outspread. "Our sacrifice was not enough! It never was... because it is *her* we must sacrifice. She who holds our water within her very eyes and MOCKS US WITH IT!"

Fast as a cheetah, Neela's mother leapt forwards and seized Nuru's throat. They both fell to the ground in a tumult of fists and teeth. The villagers stepped back, unsure how best to stop them — if they should stop them at all. In the distraction, Neela shambled away.

Every elder, man, woman and child were focused on the fight and did not see Neela shimmy into position behind them.

As she had practiced for every minute of every hour since Shango's visit, she began to move. Using her walking stick for more than simply balance, she swept her one leg out in a wide graceful arc and brought it down with a loud smack upon the hardened earth.

The elders gasped and shock rippled through the crowd, halting the fight in its tracks. Scrambling to her feet, Nuru rushed forwards only to find her path blocked by Shango. He met her gaze, his spear gripped across his chest.

"Let her dance," he ordered.

"No!" Nuru cried. "Look at her eyes, Shango! She looks *blind*!"

"She sees more than you do," he said. "You see only one way of thinking, when there are many."

"Women cannot perform the rain dance!"

"Things change, Nuru." This was said by a young man with a scar under his right eye. He stood alongside Shango with his spear raised.

Nuru couldn't believe it. "She will doom us all!"

"We are already doomed, Mother," a young woman said, joining the line protecting Neela from the elders and anyone else that would stop her.

All was still and silent except for the girl who danced. Her delicate hands wove shapes in the air as she spun on her toes, the stick becoming a whirling part of her ballet, cracking down on the earth as and when it was needed.

Nuru dared to take a step and thunder crashed overhead, making her flinch backwards. Rapidly darkening clouds rolled towards them as lightning flashed to the north.

It was in that moment that raindrops began to fall, but only on Neela. She bent, lifting her chin to the sky and the rain intensified until her form shimmered beneath the cascade.

Then, her stick dropped to the ground with an ominous thud.

Shango spun round to find that Neela had not fallen as he feared. Instead, she continued to leap and whirl. His eyes widened; her missing leg was whole. It shone and glistened an azure blue, like sapphires, like Neela's eyes, and moved as water.

She danced and the rains thundered down, thrashing the ground, forming deep puddles and rivulets that snaked their way across the dry, cracked soil.

She danced and the sky blossomed, bringing softer rain that showered the tribe, washing away their tears and their sins. All had fallen to their knees in the mud with disbelieving fingers sliding into wet earth.

She danced and the naked tree branches bent over, bowing to her majesty.

The lightning flashed closer, turning her see-through, her bones translucent pearls swaying in the downpour.

The girl born with water in her eyes blessed the villagers, as gracious and forgiving as any God could hope to be. Her body turned from blue to silver and white as her form blended into the waterfall, ebbing farther and farther away with each second that passed until there was nothing left but the land and the rain.

A Second Chance

My throat tightens as I press my forehead against the thick glass. My husband bobs, suspended in his tank, peaceful and oblivious to what I've done. Thin, transparent tubes encircle his naked figure, probing his body in a dozen different places, sustaining. Pale blue light blankets me in a warm glow that does little to thaw the ice in my belly.

"Please don't hate me."

My breath leaves its mark on the glass and I trace my finger, drawing a heart, which I immediately wipe away with my sleeve. Wasting no more time, I change the electronic label to state his name instead of mine; he would never have agreed to take my place. This was the only way.

When he is awakened by the system in hundreds of years — when the environment is habitable — will he understand?

I reach out and place my palm against the cool surface, feeling the faint vibration as air ventilates in and out in a rhythmic rush. It reminds me of waves on a beach; another thing I will never see again.

Tears drip from my chin as I hope – no, *order him* – to find somebody else. Another soul to melt with his chocolate-brown eyes, one who gives him the joy of parenthood, something I was always too damn busy to allow.

I imagine a little boy or girl with his dimpled smile and my button nose, with his fierce loyalty and my determination, their tiny feet pitter-pattering into our bedroom whilst the rest of the world slumbers. Wide, glossy eyes desperate for their daddy to wake up.

How could I have denied him that?

A second chance, that's what I've given him.

And that's the best I can do.

No Space for Heroes

Commander Forseti focused on his breathing as their craft approached the impenetrable swamp of dark swirling gases. A lifetime exploring deep space could never completely rid him of this feral dread of the unknown, and the exuberance of his crewmate did not help.

"This planet is too far away from a sun," Vidar said, one leg bouncing up and down like a jackhammer. "Do you think we'll find anything?"

The Laevrar System was uncharted. They'd already found some asteroids, two wormholes and now, this planet. It had a layer of dense gas making it impossible to see the surface.

"That's what we're here to find out," Forseti said, hands sweeping over the controls. He exchanged a nod with Vidar. "Atmospheric entry in three... two... one..."

Blackness drowned them. Worse than the heart of a black hole, at least they knew what lay on the other side of those.

Forseti flexed his muscles, feeling his bracelet of tiny blue stones digging into his left wrist. It was a gift from his little girl, Amelia. If only he could see her now. Fine black hair brushing a pointed chin, just like her mother. Eyes as blue as his own.

Light.

Rubescent wavering light. Frantic like fire sparking to life, catching and roaring into existence. It leapt and grew, edged in pink and violet, filling their vision. It began to change to orange, to yellow and then white. A glorious burst of searing white light.

"Propulsion and thruster systems stable," Forseti reported, squinting. "Descent fully engaged."

The light faded and both men gasped. A pink planet stretched out before them, enshrouded in wisps of white cloud. Forseti checked his instruments, blinked, pressed a few buttons, and checked them again. He wet his lips.

"Vidar. That's *water*."

"By all the stars." Vidar leant forwards, straining against his harness. "Is that… land?"

Forseti banked right, pointing the ship's nose towards a large patch of reddish-brown amidst the watermelon sea.

"Preparing chute deployment."

***

Forseti landed their spaceship on an area of brown soil a few miles from the coast. A wall of red-leaved trees lay before them, crammed together as if to hide what lay within. The land rose eastwards, the terrain becoming mountainous with grey cliffs and craggy peaks. Black specks glided and swooped in the distance below a vermillion sky streaked with white.

Forseti triple-checked the dashboard's atmospheric readings. "Ninety-one-point-four degrees Fahrenheit. Air breathable. It can't be."

"The planet must have its own heat source," Vidar said. His eyes beamed with a feverish light. "We've found it, Forseti! Salvation for the people of Terah. We'll be heroes!"

"There must be some mistake. How is there light? Where is it coming from?"

"Let's find out!"

Vidar leapt out of the door. Within seconds he was jumping softly, then harder, feeling the land beneath his feet.

Forseti waited, just in case. Could they really have found not only minerals and ore, but a habitable planet? It was too good to be true.

Vidar's nostrils flared as he threw his head back and hollered. This planet was ideal, just as the readings indicated.

Ten minutes later, Forseti descended the craft, took two steps, and fell to his knees.

The air! His lungs swelled, rejoicing. It felt so good! And the smells! Salty sea air, grass and *land*. It had been years since he'd smelt fresh earth. He slid his fingers into the dirt. It was warm, very warm. He looked closer. Worms wriggled, long and fat, and black ants scurried over everything. So… alive.

Waves roared faintly to the west, and a breeze rushed across his skin. He closed his eyes, imagining Amelia running across this land, squealing in delight, fingertips brushing the red grass.

"Uh, Forseti?"

They'd actually found it! Tears brimmed in his eyes. He never really let himself believe, to hope. A place for the refugees of his decimated home planet, a chance to—

"Forseti, we're not alone."

His attention snapped back to find Vidar pointing towards the forest.

They came slowly. Peeking through wide thick ferns, stepping cautiously into sight like rabbits nosing the morning air.

They looked to have a similar morphology to Terans. Humanoid, but willowy and strong like jungle vines. All oiled muscle and glowing skin the colour of good earth. Completely hairless and dressed in brown cloth, shorts, trousers, vests, though more than a few went topless.

There seemed to be an equal number of men and women, the definition of their muscles becoming more apparent with every step.

He saw no weapons and swung around in disbelief as he heard the unmistakable click of Vidar unholstering his blast gun. "Don't you dare fire on these people!"

"Fleet mission directive thirteen-point-two: All life forms hostile until proven otherwise."

"Put. It. Away."

Vidar obeyed, but he kept one hand resting on the butt, his jaw tensed.

Forseti returned his gaze to the approaching natives and stepped forwards. "Greetings," he said, arms outstretched, palms open and forwards.

This caused them to halt and burst into discussion. Their leader seemed to be a woman; her shorts and vest were a deeper, richer brown and the others looked to her when they spoke. Their language sounded complex to Forseti, and they mixed in hand signals too. All very promising.

After a few minutes, the leader advanced alone. Her face smooth with green intelligent eyes and high cheekbones. If she had been from Terah, he would put her in her early thirties. However, there was no way of discerning this species' lifespan.

She was tall, at least a head taller than him. They all were. Why did she lead? Was she the strongest fighter? Wisest? Oldest? She stopped about four feet away and examined him, completely ignoring Vidar.

She stepped closer, holding out her right hand with the palm facing upwards. Instinctively, Forseti placed his right hand on top of hers, palms touching. Her skin was firm and warm, her eyes seized his.

A female voice entered his mind: "Who are you? What do

you want?"

It took all of his training not to jump away in shock. He stared, looking at his hand and then back to her eyes. Swallowing, he gathered himself and attempted to send back a response.

"I am Forseti," he thought.

"You are the leader."

"Yes, as are you."

"I am not." Bafflement came through the sending that time. So, emotions could also be conveyed. Interesting.

"Who are you if you are not the leader?" he asked. "What is your name?"

"I am the best communicator." Ah. Well, that made sense. "My name is Takala. It means 'She who speaks in the mind'."

Forseti frowned. "Others cannot do this?"

"No." A strong sensation of pride flowed out of her, and Forseti's chest swelled, appreciating the familiar emotion.

Vidar barked something, but Forseti cut him off with a sharp gesture. He quickly explained, ordered him to be silent, and turned back to Takala.

"We are explorers," he thought.

"What do you seek?"

"Whatever there is to be found."

"Why?"

He hesitated. Could she read his thoughts? Or only those he deliberately sent?

"It is our job," he sent.

"You are unsure."

"I… am not accustomed to this form of communication." A moment passed as she studied him; he did not look away.

"Do you seek to harm us?" she asked.

"No!" Takala smiled and pressed down on his hand. He

added, "We seek only to discover. That is all." He hoped his feelings of wonder and respect came across as he asked, "May we see your home?"

Takala turned towards her people and spoke briefly with a rapid blur of hand movements. It was a pleasant-sounding language. Musical. A trace of surprise washed over their faces, but otherwise, they did not react. Soldiers receiving orders, Forseti thought.

"Come," Takala sent.

With that, she removed her hand, breaking the connection. Everyone began moving back towards the forest. She gestured for Forseti to follow.

Vidar looked just about ready to explode. "What's happening?" he demanded.

"She's going to show us around."

Vidar shook his head. "We must report back to the Fleet. These creatures are dangerous."

"I don't think they are. Besides, we have blasters and shields, don't we? Where's your sense of adventure?"

Vidar stiffened, clean-shaven face set in stone. "It's against protocol."

Forseti ground his teeth, moving into step behind Takala. Vidar really was a model Fleeter, following regulations to the letter, hair kept two millimetres in length, even on a long voyage. Had Forseti been that rigid? Probably. When did he change?

The younger man was right, but Forseti didn't want to go back. Not yet.

"Don't you want to see exactly what we've found?" Vidar's expression flickered. "Come on," Forseti said, smiling. "A brand-new planet, untouched by the Fleet. This could be our only chance!"

Vidar cursed, removed his hand from his blast gun and

loped forwards. He did not return Forseti's smile.

***

The forest was not pitch-black as Forseti had expected. Instead, hundreds of glowing orbs, suspended in the trees, bathed the forest in a soothing blue light. Takala followed a wide path which meandered through the trees. He walked as though in a dream, quietly, lest he break the spell.

"Where is she taking us?" Vidar asked. He seemed to suspect that Forseti wasn't telling him everything. "What if it's a trap?"

"I sensed no deceit in her and I think I would have."

"I still don't like this. What is their energy source? What do they eat?"

"I didn't ask."

Vidar huffed, inspecting their escort. "They're very tall and muscular, aren't they? They'll make fine labourers, maybe in the mines of Andorol or the pits of Dasho'ah?"

"Careful. We don't want them knowing about that."

"They can't read our thoughts, can they?"

Forseti eyed him. "I don't know."

That shut him up. He was right though. They *would* make good labourers, but Forseti pushed that uncomfortable thought aside.

Their path sloped upwards in a dizzying zig-zag. Forseti managed to keep up with Takala, though he suspected she walked slow for their benefit.

After about thirty minutes, the underbrush opened out onto a huge plateau of smooth grey rock. On their right, numerous caves burrowed into the mountain, cerulean light emanating from within.

People swarmed the place, talking in groups, carrying

baskets filled with beige linen. Their height was more apparent now they were out in the open. Children darted between legs, waggling their fingers.

Forseti stroked his bracelet in thought. Something seemed to be missing. What was it?

Vidar put a hand on his arm. "This is a mistake. What if she reads your mind and discovers our mission? There are too many of them. Let's make a run for it."

"You worry too much and besides, can't you tell they're peaceful?"

Vidar's lips pulled in a tight line as Takala halted. Forseti reached out and she accepted his hand. He sent, "You do not seem particularly shocked by our presence."

He felt her emotions first; she had been expecting this question. "The Harmonisers had already prepared for this possibility. You are not of this planet and therefore, your presence will disrupt the balance. You are free to stay a while and rest since you must be tired from your journey." Takala paused. "We will not harm you, but you cannot stay long."

"Who are the Harmonisers?"

"Our oldest and wisest. They decide who may breed, which animals may be hunted… such things as these."

"What if someone breeds without permission?"

Disbelief. Confusion. "The planet comes first. Not us."

He nodded, letting his gaze drift. Red-topped trees bordered the plateau, some with lavender fronds dangling. Such colour! There was a gap on the far side: a cliff, or another plateau?

Takala reached out with her free hand, touching his bracelet. "Where did you get this?"

"Why?"

"One of these is sestone. We have it here. Did you not

notice as you traversed the sleeping grounds?"

Forseti looked down at the tiny stones painted blue. Only three people knew one of them was a real gem. Himself, his wife, Maya, and their daughter, Amelia.

Amelia had been thirteen when she gave him this bracelet which once belonged to her mother, looking so very small in those stark white bedsheets. Maya never told him where she got it from, becoming coy and enigmatic whenever he brought it up. Oh, how he had gaped at the one stone that glinted differently in the waning light.

"This one is real, Amelia," he'd said. "You know this. Why didn't you sell it?"

"For what? A loaf of bread?" She shrugged. "I wanted to give it to you. It reminds me of the stories Mother used to tell. The ones with tall trees and running water and funny animals. And your face!" She pointed, smiling through the pain, one hand holding her stomach. "This is much better than bread."

Amelia died that afternoon, her last breath carried away on a sunlit breeze. Forseti wept as her tiny hand went limp in his own, staying until the nurses gently pried him from her side. First his wife, then his daughter. Casualties of a planet consumed by greed.

What would Amelia think of this mission? What would Maya?

He looked up to see tears streaming down Takala's cheeks. Sympathy flooded through their bond. "I'm so sorry for your loss," she sent.

Forseti's skin tingled as she intertwined their fingers, making their mental connection stronger. It was like an extra weight pressing against his mind. Then, she shared something that made Forseti's breath catch in his throat, shattering everything he thought he knew to pieces.

***

Time blew away on a wind, taking candyfloss blossoms and heart-shaped petals with it, down gargling rivers, over the hills, and under the rosebud skies.

An understanding blossomed in Forseti's mind of what was missing from this land: poverty, hardship. Was it a trick? Was there another settlement where all the less fortunate lived? No. His heart sensed that this was not the case.

"I'm glad you made me come, Forseti. This will make a great story. Once we're decorated enough that flaunting protocol is beneath us, eh?"

Vidar stood at the edge of a cliff, rising and falling on the balls of his feet, gazing on the land he would destroy. Pushing him would be almost too easy, but could he do it? For this wondrous land and its gentle people?

Yes. He could.

Forseti stepped closer.

But, would it make him as cruel as the Fleet? As ruthless? He took another step, and a twig snapped underfoot.

Vidar spun around and punched Forseti square in the face, making him stagger backwards.

"You must think me a fool," he said. "To think I haven't noticed."

Forseti blinked, regaining his balance. "We can't take this world. Don't you see how wrong it would be?"

"It is our mission!" Vidar roared. "What's happened to you?"

"They don't deserve this—"

"Look at them! They are animals, living in trees and caves. They don't even know how to make use of their own planet's resources."

"Oh, but they do."

Vidar spat. "You abandon your own people. Our people."

"If we bring the Fleet here, you know what'll happen. They'll drain the sea, level the mountains, and *enslave the people*." Forseti straightened. "I won't be a part of it."

"I'm going back to the ship." Vidar glared. "If you come with me now, I'll leave your betrayal out of my report."

"No," he said. "I won't allow it."

With a yell, Forseti launched himself at the younger man, knocking them both to the ground. Dust kicked up as they rolled, once, twice, and then—

The land fell away. Forseti grappled, his fingers finding purchase on the cliff edge. His feet flailed, finding only smooth, seamless rock.

Vidar stood, dusting his hands, and looked down. Forseti pulled, grunting with the effort, and brought one elbow up over the lip. Vidar kicked it away.

"Such a shame," Vidar said, pressing his boot on Forseti's fingers. "You could have been a hero."

Something moved in the shadows behind Vidar, the man's sneer twitched and went lax, his eyes suddenly distant.

He leant forwards, too far, too fast, and kept going, diving over Forseti head first. Vidar didn't scream. The only sound was the distant thump as his body hit the valley floor.

Strong fingers gripped Forseti's wrist and hauled him up. Takala pulled him away from the cliff and shoved him up against the nearest tree trunk. Forseti's feet dangled, his toes brushing the soil. She turned his hand and pressed their palms together.

"Thank yo—"

"You will go now," she sent, eyeing him. "You will not

return."

He swallowed. "Did you know all along?"

"I knew you did not share everything, but I trusted." Her disappointment stung. "You have the love. You care for our land. I felt that. You will not hurt us, so I will not hurt you."

A breeze rippled the lilac fronds hanging round them. They smelt sweet, like cinnamon.

"If more should come, will they be like you, or like him?" She pressed her palm harder against his. "Do we trust?"

She wasn't holding back anymore. A torrent of fury and black fear for everything she knew and loved overwhelmed him. He shook his head, knowing she felt his deep, pitiless shame.

"No," he sent. "Do not trust."

***

"Commander Forseti, GC 4376. Mission outcome: planet uninhabitable. No viable resources detected. No life-forms. Special Officer Vidar killed by hostile, unpredictable environment. Strongly recommend blacklisting planet for any and all future reconnaissance missions."

Satisfied, Forseti exited the planet's atmosphere with Takala's revelation from earlier echoing in his mind.

"A female landed here once… long ago," she had sent. "She was alone. Lost. I liked her, and she stayed for many of our cycles. When she left, we gave her a tiny fragment of sestone as a parting gift." Her fingertips had found the gem on his bracelet. "This… is that same stone."

He shook his head. Why didn't Maya tell him? She had always been so mysterious and guarded about her past. Now he knew why, or part of it at least.

Reaching forwards, he toggled the ship's navigation

system and input a new flight path. He engaged the thrusters – smiling as his sestone bracelet clinked along with each movement – and blasted off into the abyss from which he had come.

The Only Love that Matters

The Nepotism Dilemma simulation takes place daily at eleven-hundred hours and I never miss one. It forms an essential part of Esteem Inc.'s morality structuring. Quietly, I slip into the back of the dark room, close the door, and wait.

Twenty students are viewing a catastrophic storm: thrashing waves beneath strobe lightning. Two children are struggling in vain against the current and, to make the test stronger, their terrified screams can be heard.

The scene fades, the lights brighten, and I move to the front of the room. It is the first time these students have seen me – the director – up close. A few gulp audibly, and I try not to smile.

Their youthful faces make me nostalgic. In my office, positioned directly across from my desk, I keep a framed photograph of myself as a gangly red-haired teenager sandwiched between my parents. It serves as a reminder of how far I've come, but also of what I still hope to achieve. It continues to dredge up the abject guilt I've fought so hard to eliminate. The photo will remain until I conquer my emotions.

"So," I begin, "imagine the two children drowning out at sea were in your charge, and they went off swimming against your orders. One is your employer's child, and one is yours. You know your child is the stronger swimmer, but considering the severity of the storm, there is no possibility they can get back on their own. I should also point out, at this juncture, that your employer is on the verge of making you a partner in their billion-dollar firm."

I pause to let that nugget sink in.

"Now, do you a) Save your child, taking into account that your employer's will drown in the meantime or b) Save your employer's child first and then go back for yours, hoping they manage to last long enough?"

The students blink, glance at one another. A few shrug.

"Who would choose the first option?"

Silence.

"The second?"

A smattering of low murmurs accompany shuffling feet. I'm pleased that no one seems to be genuinely contemplating the question: they are simply confused.

Lucky devils! Soon, there will be no need for morality readjustment at all. Right and wrong are already things of the past; right and wrong *for you,* that is the here and now.

Eventually, a young woman near the front with short shaggy hair raises her hand.

"Yes?" I say.

"It is a trick question, Director Helena," she says. "You wouldn't try to save either of them."

"And why not?"

"Because it would endanger yourself."

I nod. "Very good. Any other reason?"

This time, all the hands shoot up. "Because they were told not to go swimming, which makes them idiots. They don't deserve to be rescued."

A textbook response from 'Why We Need Narcissism', something I wrote nearly forty years ago, which is now compulsory reading for all adolescents.

"Excellent," I say. Satisfied, I hand the class over to my Chief of Operations, Murugan, who has appeared to my left.

He nods deferentially. "Director."

Pride buoys me up, as it always does after this session. I remember donning my father's white work shirt and pretending it was a lab coat, proclaiming myself as Scientist Helena.

Even then I knew surnames were far overdue for expiry, though saying so at the time had definitely been a mistake. Absently, I touch the scar above my right eye and sigh.

Before leaving, I scour their cherubic faces, searching for any faint edging of doubt, any infinitesimal furrowing of the brow.

Nothing.

Good.

Back in my office, I settle into my brilliant-white ergonomic chair and message Will, my Chief of Morality Alignment. A wry smile twitches my lips at his immediate response. He is one of the best — no, *the* best — and therefore, is probably anticipating my announcement.

To my right, out of the expansive floor-to-ceiling window, a sea of metal and tinted glass winks in the noonday sun. I have a direct view of the Emotion Centre, where our students attend seminars on social media performance, empathy trapping and reality manipulation (gaslighting is such an inferior term).

My phone pings, alerting me to Will's proximity. There is a knock at the door.

"Director Helena?" he says. "You wished to see me."

"Enter."

He strides in, dressed in a crisp black suit, tall and lean with copper red hair. *My son,* I think before I can stop myself.

He takes a seat opposite and I am struck by how much he

resembles his father. How many years did I waste resenting that man? First for guilting me into having a child I didn't want, and then for having the audacity to die before that child was even talking.

"After careful analysis," I say, "I have decided that when I retire, you will succeed me as the director of Esteem Inc."

Will nods. "I am the highest functioning candidate."

And my son, but that isn't why I chose him, is it? No. His record is outstanding and he wouldn't have achieved his full potential if I hadn't — as any good mother should — instilled in him the unquestionable knowledge that I would never show him any preference.

"I have done some research," he says. "There are several concepts that I would like to begin trialling as soon as possible. Shall I send them over?"

"Absolutely." Such dynamism. I knew I'd made the right choice. "I'll read them today."

In the afternoon, I open Will's research proposal. It is lengthy. Unease snakes through me as I scan the contents:

- Social division between graduates of Esteem Inc. and their followers.
- Vilification of benevolence and acts of heroism.
- Abolition of the concepts of 'mother' and 'family'.

My throat constricts. These are detailed strategies for eliminating love from society. What have I done?

Fumbling my phone, I summon him to my office. I am aware it's a symptom of my archaic conditioning, but I do feel responsible for him.

His location sensor approaches and I take a deep breath.

"I want to discuss some of your… ideas," I say. Sweat is breaking out on my forehead, but at this point, I don't care.

"Excellent. Shall I get started?"

Maternal pride skitters through my veins at his confidence and I hate myself for it.

"Not just yet." I take a sip of water. "I don't think doing away with the family unit altogether is the answer. Allowing for escape is one thing, facilitating growth and independence and self-preservation, but abolishing motherhood? Taking babies away at birth to be raised in sterile, high-tech crèches? It's…" I trail off, my mind racing through all the other suggestions laid out in worrying detail.

"It is the natural progression of your ideology," he says.

I shake my head. "Societal norms of the 21st century led to morality shifting towards the individual. That is different to" —I wave a hand, struggling to express my thoughts— "removing all love aside from self-love from the equation."

"Self-love is the only love that matters."

I freeze. Quoting my own doctrine back at me. I want to cry. Instead, I get up and walk to the window, keeping my back to him. "You're twisting my intention."

"And you're narrow-minded." He doesn't say it maliciously. It is a statement. A fact. "If we separate society as I have suggested, things will be much simpler. I've even devised a way to identify someone's emotional vulnerability so we can deduce how challenging they will be. You are the past. The future… is me."

"This can't happen." I whirl around to find him also on his feet. "You have to listen to me—"

"Why?"

"Because I'm your m—" My heart pounds against my ribcage. "I am your boss."

"What were you going to say?"

His tone is vicious, needling. I move away from the window in a quick angry movement, hoping it hides my fear. "I won't have you separating the world into two classes: the narcissists and their *pets*. That isn't what I set out to do."

"You're my *mother*? Is that it?"

"Yes, alright! I'm your mother, and I know better! There! I said it."

"Mother." Will grimaces as if the word tastes foul. He hasn't addressed me that way since he was a beautiful, bright-eyed toddler. I didn't want him, but to my enduring irritation, that didn't prevent me from loving him once he was there. "Isn't that what your mother used to say? How she convinced you to waste your youth with her and your abusive father? How she explained the trajectory of the gin bottle that gave you that scar? Words that made you bury any shred of self-worth you had until the day they died?"

Every question hits me like a physical blow, making me back away until I'm pressed up against the wall. The corner of the picture frame grazes my temple.

Will continues, "And how did they die? Hm?"

"What? It was an acci—"

"An accident. Yes. A freak gas explosion, but I never believed you."

My pulse quickens and I clasp my hands together in an attempt to stop their feverish trembling.

"Shall I tell you what I think happened?"

He couldn't possibly know. No one knows.

"They were up late," he says. "Drink, drugs, whatever, and passed out. In the morning, you turned the gas on the kitchen stove up to full, closed all the doors and windows and went to school, fully aware that the first thing they'd do when they woke up would be to light a cigarette… *Boom*."

I can't breathe. My hands clench and unclench at my sides.

"You probably didn't think it would actually work. Maybe you only wanted to scare them into being better parents. And the worst part is that you feel guilty, don't you? If you hadn't acted, you'd be dead, or a drug addict. You certainly wouldn't be the director of Esteem Inc." He snorts contemptuously. "And you made me your successor. Rather suspicious, don't you think?"

"What?" I blink, distracted by this sudden tangent. "That's not fair. You said yourself you're the strongest candidate."

"I *would* say that." He smiles and it's horrible. "I wonder how they would react? The awe-inspiring Director Helena engaging in blatant nepotism and parricide."

He wouldn't dare. "You have no proof."

"Don't need any. Your reputation would be destroyed nonetheless." He stares at me and I stare back. "Then again, I don't have to say anything."

I can't believe it. My entire legacy rendered meaningless in one move.

And it really would be that easy.

With a sigh, I unhook the family picture from the wall and look at it one last time. "You can't understand what it's like, Will. Hardly anyone from my generation overcomes their conditioning. It's easier for you." I walk past him and place the picture face down on my desk. "I made it easier."

No response. He's won, and he knows it.

I make the call. "Murugan," I say in a clipped, authoritative tone. "I have approved Will's research proposal. Yes, that's right. You may begin the trials immediately."

I hang up and Will chuckles. "Well done."

"It isn't a secret you're my son, you know," I say, trying to regain some dignity. "You should be more careful throwing that threat around… for your own sake."

"Mother," he says. The corners of his mouth twitch as he leans in and drops his voice to a disgusted whisper. "When I'm done, that will be the most offensive slur known to man."

The Reintroduction of Species

Dr Astrid Nova leant forwards, inches from the control room's glass windows, and looked down into the Homo sapiens enclosure. Their language specialist, Niq, was sitting cross-legged with two of the females, listening as they spoke to each other. He said he only needed a little more time, but that was precisely what Dr Nova didn't have.

The enclosure was one of Zoo Primer's largest with original features from the creatures' natural habitat: red-bricked buildings with tiled roofs; neat gardens textured with soft, springy turf; a flowing stream; oaks, apple trees, squirrels and hedgehogs.

If only her father could see how far she'd brought his dream – their dream.

She sniffed and wiped her nose with the back of her hand. She was getting used to this body; as a Mimic, she could alter her appearance to match that of any other species. It was of profound help in her research, facilitating a deeper understanding of mannerisms and behaviour.

But none of that would matter if the Galactic Interstellar Planetary Alliance cut their funding and evicted the *H. sapiens* from the zoo. Her father's mission was on the brink of failing, and she couldn't let that happen. She gritted her teeth and slapped her palm against the glass.

Behind her, the door slid open with a low hum, and as if the ponderous, slow footsteps weren't enough, the delectable scent of Narquarm drops told her that it was Dr Gaius Draknar; he knew the mouthwatering effect that smell had on her. She promptly muted her odour receptors.

"Astrid, we need to talk."

She didn't turn round. Down in the enclosure, one of the smaller males had joined the group — a rare occurrence — and a few seconds later, all three *H. sapiens* burst into animated discussion. The dominant female, a fair-haired specimen, raised her voice, leant forwards and poked Niq's chest with her finger.

"Astrid—"

"Just a minute, Gaius."

"But—"

"I said just a minute!"

What was wrong? What hadn't she understood? The frustration burrowed into her mind like a stubbornly persistent nematode. If only they could communicate with them!

Her father's linguistic research hinted at the existence of over seven thousand languages, which was preposterous for one planet, especially one as small as Earth.

They had focused their efforts on Mandarin — the overriding planetary language for at least two generations — but when she used this language on her humans in the Zoo, they either recoiled, panicked or attacked. There was still so much they didn't understand.

"What do you want, Gaius?"

"Any progress?"

With a sigh, she turned to face him. Gaius filled the doorway with his multiple arms folded as if proximity to her could do him harm.

"Not yet," she said.

His large, black eye took in her human form. "That's disgusting."

"They're not so different from you actually," she said, smoothing her pale-green dress over substantial hips.

"Fewer arms. Extra eye."

His lips curled back. "What's wrong with them?"

"I don't think they like being held in captivity. It could be that simple." She thought about the playground they'd added, in the hope of arousing the *H. sapiens'* need to nurture, but all it had incited was aggression. "An instinctive desire for freedom."

"Let them go extinct then," Gaius said. "They're no use to the Zoo if they don't breed."

"How can you say that?" Astrid glanced into the enclosure. "They would breed in the wild, given a suitable habitat."

"You're giving them far more credit than they deserve. They're so primitive they still have religion, of all things." He spat, as well he would. Gaius was Verishan and they resented nothing more than lies – although, in Astrid's experience this only made them masterful at being vague – and one of their principal convictions was that belief in itself was a form of lying. It was widely known that pointing out the contradictory nature of this particular 'core belief' to a Verishan was ill-advised.

Gaius continued, "They only landed on their own moon a handful of generations ago."

"They were Earth's dominant species."

"And they destroyed—"

"We don't know if they caused it," she said. "There isn't sufficient evidence."

Something passed over Gaius' features. He had always been sceptical of the Earthers, but this felt different to his usual level of contempt.

"Even if they were unaware," he said, shifting his weight to lean against the doorframe, "which I find unlikely, who's to say they won't do the same to the next planet?"

"Look, in a few days, the Zoo's Committee is meeting to decide whether or not to grant me the funding from GIPA. Then you can—"

"You really think they'll let you introduce them to a new host planet?"

"It's been done before."

"Yeah, but not with *humans*."

"We can keep an eye on them. Steer them in the right direction," she said, stepping forwards, pleased by the tension this wrought over his cobalt-blue face. "And they were probably lacking some essential knowledge which led to the severe climatic shift."

"Oh yes, that's what your father called it, isn't it? Total climatic obliteration would have been more accurate." He snorted. "Essential knowledge, you say. Like, for example, that their actions were hurting their planet? Some would argue that they knew exactly what they were doing." Again, a flicker of something in his eye.

What was he not telling her?

"Well," she said. "I don't believe that."

His face softened. "There is a malfunction with this species, Astrid. A blind spot which makes them inherently destructive. I know what this means to you." Then quietly, as if speaking to himself, "I probably understand better than anyone the lengths you would go to."

Ouch.

"Look, I'm sorry I hurt you, Gaius, but please—" She cut herself off as Niq appeared in the doorway, vibrating with enthusiasm. "Niq! What happened down there?"

"Everything is fine!" he said, sauntering into the room. "Progress is being made." A few more steps and he stood next to Astrid, his body turned slightly away from Gaius as if he wasn't here. "The non-threatening pheromone spray is working, and I think one of the females is called Doktorre."

"Oh really?"

Gaius sniffed. "Why are you even bothering? Is Xenon Neptus overcrowded at the moment?"

"And that's not all I've discovered," Niq continued. "Their language contains a fascinating choice of phonemes. I've picked out three distinctive diphthongs, five digraphs though I'm sure there are more, a propensity toward consonant clusters and—"

"That's great, Niq, but the Committee meeting is next week."

"Ah, yes. Understood! I'm going to refuel and then I'll get right back to it." He eyed Gaius sidelong, and said to Astrid: "I, uh, see what you mean about him now."

Gaius sneered. "Earth-lover."

"Thank you!"

"It wasn't a—"

Astrid cut Gaius off with a sharp gesture.

"Thanks, Niq," she said, "I'll catch up with you later."

He nodded and strolled past Gaius without looking at him.

Astrid almost let herself relax.

But then Niq paused in the doorway, looked over his shoulder, and winked. "I'll bring the Narquarm drops."

Her mouth fell open and heat rushed to her cheeks. He was already gone, but he would pay for that later.

Gaius made a gagging sound. "He looks just like them, doesn't he?"

Astrid rolled her shoulders, hoping the colouring in her face wasn't too obvious.

"That is part of why he was chosen for this project. Another reason being that he is one of the best linguists from Xenon Neptus. He has the signature tripod tongue and very clever ears. He can even speak Deep Zennoll."

Gaius rolled his big eye, ostentatiously.

"Are you two..."

"It's none of your business, but no. We're colleagues. Friends."

"Is that so?"

"Why ask if you're not going to believe me?"

"It's hard to know what to believe around you. You're a proven liar."

"Enough, Gaius." She crossed her arms. "Why are you here?"

A half-smile danced across his aquiline features. "They've moved the meeting forwards. To today."

Astrid's stomach crashed into the floor.

"Today?" It came out louder than intended, but she didn't care. Her eyes darted back and forth as she tried to get her thoughts in order; all semblance of control abandoned. "W-When?"

This time, he smiled a full smile.

"Now."

***

Zoo Primer was located on a self-sufficient space station the size and shape of Astrid's home planet. Home to billions of life-forms all working together to better understand their universe. A true haven of inter-species equality.

Down the sleek pale-green corridors, scientists and zoologists went about their work. Walking, hovering, squelching, rippling. Many spoke into earpieces or read text only they could see via their implanted Eye Reader — those that had eyes, that is.

Astrid hurried to keep up with Gaius, their footsteps

muffled by the jade carpet.

"You're loving this, aren't you," she said.

"Not as much as you seem to think."

They reached the central transport hub; a long row of large translucent Orbs awaited, suspended in mid-air. Another zoo employee, almost entirely covered in fuschia suckers, overtook them and hopped into the nearest Orb in a flurry of pops, slurps and ahhs.

Astrid hesitated. She needed time to digest what was happening. The Director had received her proposal yesterday for the reintroduction of *H. sapiens* onto a viable host planet. Had a decision already been made?

And was the decision final?

If the Committee ruled to return the specimens to Earth, they would be extinct within a decade; their planet was borderline uninhabitable. The remaining population rested at around eighty million, less than ten percent of what it had been pre-climate collapse, and was steadily decreasing.

She looked up to find Gaius poised by an empty Orb. Why was he escorting her anyway?

"They need to be reintroduced to a planet with a suitable habitat for them," she said. "I know you're mad at me, but you're a scientist. You can't honestly be supporting the extinction of a whole species?"

She stepped inside the Orb and sat on the glass seats. Gaius spoke into the control panel.

"Dr Gaius Draknar. Zoo Director Berzt's Boardroom."

The door hissed shut and after a momentary pause whilst the internal gravity kicked in the Orb took off at high speed.

"The universe will not miss them," Gaius said, "and releasing them on a new planet would be catastrophic. For one thing, there would be protests."

"There are always protests."

"I wouldn't want them on my home planet, would you?"

She didn't answer.

The silence stretched out until Gaius said, "I'm not mad at you. Not for Project Earther. You did what you thought was necessary."

Astrid scowled. What did that mean?

"I needed this project," she said, hating how her voice instantly trembled. "My father and I, we worked together on this until the day he died. He loved Earther culture. Did you know they had the most diverse musicality of any other planet in the known universe?"

Gaius smiled weakly. She had told him a million Earther fun-facts in shared moments on Zoo Primer, during trips in the Orb or when their heads laid on warm bed sheets imbued with their own scent.

That was back when she had been adopting his species' form. She preferred her current olive-toned skin to his native blue, but she'd enjoyed having six arms. The multi-tasking had been fantastic. She wished she could forget the look on his face when he'd found out she wasn't Verishan.

"I had to have this position," she said, digging her nails into her palm.

"Yes. We both wanted the job, but you wanted it more." He fixed her with his eye. "The sad thing is, you only needed to ask me and I would have stepped down. But you didn't, did you?"

"I'm sorry," she said.

"No, you're not."

"Please," Astrid reached out to him, "look at me, Gaius."

"I am looking at you."

"No, really look at me. Like you used to, before—"

"Before you made me fall in love with a lie?"

She flinched.

"I can't look at you that way, Astrid. Not anymore."

"Please, Gaius. I'm sorry, we all make mistakes and I still… I still love you."

There. She'd said it.

"You betrayed me," he snapped, dropping any pretence at civility, "and worst of all, you don't act like you did anything wrong."

"That's not fair. I don't have to tell you everything about myself straight away."

"You should have told me your species!"

Astrid gasped. Did he really just say that?

"Inter-species relations are widely accepted. I don't have to tell you at all if I don't want to."

"Not legally" —he turned away from her— "but you should. It's the truth."

"I would expect this kind of talk from your ancestors!" Her outrage sizzled, spluttering like water on hot oil. "What planet are you living on?"

He opened his mouths but closed them as the Orb slowed.

Astrid's heart squeezed, but a stubborn tingle of hope pervaded. Did some feelings remain here? Some warmth that could be rekindled to the flame it once was?

Did she even want that?

She gulped as he exited the Orb ahead of her, approaching the Director's boardroom without so much as a backwards glance. Astrid thrust her emotions aside.

She had a species to save.

The oval boardroom was immense, with one long table curved in a semicircle, facing the transparent exterior walls. The breathtaking splendour of the cosmos unravelled before them. Iridescent whirlpools of fragmented light; a violet, azure and turquoise haze; purest life forming and crumbling in eternal cyclicity.

GIPA guidelines insisted that all decisions should be made with the interests of the whole galaxy taken into account. The view was a reminder.

Behind the table was Zoo Director Berzt, flanked by the six heads of department: Operations, Personnel, Visitor Services, Finance, Maintenance, and Horticulture.

When Astrid and Gaius entered, the Committee were debating behind an invisible but completely soundproof screen. She agonised over every shake of the head, every poised tentacle, stern look and frantic wobbling.

The Director himself was also a Mimic like Astrid, though he was in his true form. A floating body of liquid as white as a cluster of young stars, continuously shifting and morphing, mesmerising in its complex simplicity.

Astrid yearned to melt into herself but resisted. She could do that later, when Gaius wasn't there. He may disapprove of her human form, but at least it was a form of some sort.

Her eyes drifted over the Committee members. Still, they talked.

Had she included everything in her proposal? Was it enough?

Abruptly, the barrier was released and a deep voice resonated from within the luminous mass that was Director Berzt. Astrid's mouth set in a thin line; his apologetic tone was unmistakable.

"We are very close to a verdict, Dr Nova," he began. "However, new evidence has come to light and I feel you should be given the opportunity to comment before we make our final decision."

"New evidence?"

She snapped her head round to look at Gaius who didn't move.

Director Berzt continued, "Unfortunately, the humans were one hundred percent aware of the damage they were doing to their planet. This evidence, brought forth by Dr Draknar, is irrefutable."

No! She'd never forgive him for this. He refused to meet her eyes; his earlier softening towards her suddenly took on a sinister shade. A black hole was opening up and she was skirting the edges, flirting with the magnetic pull of disaster.

This made a significant portion of her argument void.

"We should all get a second chance," she said, scanning her memory for relevant examples. "When the Martians were new to intergalactic travel, they were persistent and notorious thieves. They were not eradicated, but educated."

The Committee members shuffled in their seats – those that could – and a few inclined their heads, willing to listen. She flicked her fingers as she spoke, transferring her weight from one leg to the other.

"And the Saturnians," she said, "they practically committed planetary genocide on Neptune before GIPA intervened. They are now a key member and—"

"Knowingly destroying your own planet is by far a worse crime," Gaius said, his voice crackling like static discharge. "They should be returned to Earth and their habitat on Zoo Primer put to better use."

"They'll be extinct within ten years!"

"Good."

She couldn't believe it. "This isn't about the Earthers, this is about getting revenge on me!"

"Don't flatter yourself, Dr Nova."

The formality slapped Astrid in the face, stunning her into silence.

Director Berzt's voice boomed out at them. "Enough! Dr Draknar, whilst I appreciate your concern over the zoo's resources, do not forget that your own research has yet to yield anything substantial. Dr Nova makes a valid point—"

"But—" Gaius clamped his mouth shut at a severe gesture from the multi-tentacled Head of Horticulture.

"As I was saying," the Director continued, "second chances are a fine thing indeed and sometimes a necessary one with, as you have illustrated, sometimes very positive outcomes." He stared past Astrid, past Gaius and out into the cosmos. Astrid turned to look as well, just as a stunning purple nebula drifted into view.

"The problem is that whether or not a chance is deserved tends to be proven with hindsight, by its execution." He paused. "So, do we give the Earthers a second chance?"

Astrid held her breath, her gaze flitting from each board member to the other, trying to discern their thoughts, their stance—

"WAIT!"

Suddenly, the boardroom doors flew open and Niq bounded inside.

"Sorry to burst in like this," he said, "but I have news that is pertinent to this meeting." He positioned himself in front of their long committee table, imploring Director Bertz.

"Go on, Professor K," the Director said. "You have our attention."

Niq began pacing. "I've cracked their language's coding," he said, "and I just had the most intriguing conversation with one of the males, the larger one."

"Hang on," Gaius said, "a few minutes ago, you weren't managing to communicate and now you expect us to believe you've had a full-blown conversation?"

"Once I hit a certain point with any language, it all falls into place like a giant word puzzle." Niq inclined his head slightly. "It is something only achieved by the most elite pan-galactic linguists of Xenon. I wouldn't expect you to understand."

Gaius' face darkened.

"And what have you learned?" The Director asked.

"They are more intellectually advanced than we thought. Apparently, the two men I spoke to today are religious practitioners, a priest and a rabbi. Within their group, there is also a medic, a politician—"

"Is this some kind of joke?" Gaius snapped.

"No." Niq stopped pacing, faced the board directly. "What's more, they are all adamant that they tried to save their planet, but the ruling class or race — the word they use is *'boonchakants'* — prevented them from being able to do so. They are eager to follow our directives."

"Of course they'll say that!"

"Dr Gaius Draknar," the Director said, "if you interrupt one more time—"

"But this is ridiculous! It's the Saturnians all over again!"

The Head of Horticulture curled his tentacles. "My wife is Saturnian."

"Oh. I'm sorry. I didn't mean *her*..."

"Well," the Director said, "this changes everything. If the humans can be communicated with, I think that settles the debate." He glanced to his left and right, confirming with the other members of the board; a flurry of affirmative gestures ensued. "Congratulations, Dr Nova. Your proposal is approved. I will contact GIPA at once, and I suspect this reintroduction of species will attract many new visitors to the Zoo. It will be a veritable beacon of hope for all species facing extinction across the galaxy. Excellent work."

Then, Astrid's chest tightened as the Director dropped his formal tone of voice, and said, "Your father would be very proud."

Outside the boardroom, Niq embraced Astrid human-style and then dashed off to continue his research. Astrid gave Gaius a perfunctory nod and struck out toward the Orb Station. He rushed to keep stride with her.

"Well done!" he said. "I mean it. This is a very exciting new project and, as I'm sure you're aware, you're going to need extra scientists to help you—"

"What? You can't possibly be saying you want to be a part of this? That makes no sense."

Her mind raced; he must be in bigger trouble with the Director than she realised. Within seconds, they reached the platform. There was no Orb waiting so Astrid called for one. Gaius flapped.

"It will be of great importance to the Zoo and since it's actually going ahead, I'd like to be on the team — *your* team."

"Oh, uh, I don't know…"

The Orb arrived, hovering expectantly before them.

"Come on, we're good together. You said so yourself." He reached out for her hand and turned it over, ran a fingertip over her palm. "Remember? You told me you'd never felt more connected on so many levels. Before me, you'd never experienced a Verishan triple-helix orgasm—"

"Gaius, stop."

"But—"

She snatched her hand away. "If you must know," she said, stepping into the Orb, "you were right about one thing."

"Oh?" He grinned, raising his enormous eyebrow. "And what's that?"

Astrid tapped the Orb's control panel, sat down, and gave him her sweetest, most alluring smile. She held his gaze right up until the pearlescent doors slid shut in his face.

"I'm a *huge* liar."

The Ferryman

Charon's blood-red cape fluttered about his lean frame of knotted muscle as his ferryboat sliced through the ghostly waters of the river Styx. The desperate, translucent hands grappling for purchase had irritated him for a few millennia, but he was over it now.

Even the interminable howling and snapping of Cerberus – Hades' infernal three-headed guard dog – had blended into the background. Shreds of mist formed and coiled around his little boat until he was completely enshrouded in white. A white as desolate and unforgiving as the wretched shores of Tartarus.

Who would it be this time?

He hoped they'd be quiet; it was the people who wouldn't shut up that he truly despised. It wasn't unheard of for him to engage in conversation with his passengers, but it was rare. He longed for the days when heroes and heroines would brave the fires of hell to rescue their loved ones. Those were the good old days.

The mist thinned.

The iron-grey skull mounted on the bow nudged forwards, parting the silk to reveal the entrance to the Underworld. An immense cavern stretched into darkness save for one tunnel lit with the glow of the outside world. It was here that the dead usually waited in their wraith-like droves to be taken one by one to their final resting place.

But this time was different. The figure of a woman stood

alone on the cold, stone jetty.

Charon frowned. Where was everyone?

She was tall with delicate features and thick, brown hair tumbling down to generous hips. Her long, silken white dress was laced with blooming flowers and green boughs. Bare toes peeked out the bottom of her skirts. Curiously, there was no suggestion of fear or anger in her cool gaze.

"Greetings, Ferryman," she said. Charon blinked. Her voice was like velvet rushing over bare skin.

"Where is everyone?"

"They are all gone. Humanity is extinct and you are free of your duty." She held out her hand, her lace sleeves dangling gracefully. "Come. I'll show you."

Charon hesitated.

"Who are you?"

"I am here to relieve you of your burden," she said, her face serene and beautiful. "Come."

"What about the souls who were already here?"

"All will be revealed, Ferryman," she said, a flicker of amusement in her silken tones.

He was still doubtful, but the empty cavern spoke for itself and so he took her soft hand and stepped off his boat.

Without another word, the woman turned and headed towards the exit, her movements effortless as she glided over the chill stone cavern floor. Charon made after her but found his legs so unaccustomed to solid ground that he staggered like a drunk.

"Don't worry," she called over her shoulder, "your legs will adjust."

He grunted in response before slamming into the tunnel's wall. Squinting, he pulled his red cowl over his head. After the shadowed depths of the Underworld, the faint glow of sunlight was incredibly fierce. He clambered up the sloping passage with one hand trailing along the stone, his balance slowly returning. Shadows moved up ahead, wavering, dancing, backlit by emerald and topaz — colours he had not seen for millenia.

He felt the hard stone underfoot give way to the gentler feel of warm earth.

The woman yelled, "Here we are!"

Darkness snapped over Charon and numerous strong hands seized his body, hoisting him off the ground. None of them spoke. The only voice was the woman's, stripped of its honeyed tones.

"Don't fight it, Ferryman."

He cursed and thrashed his legs, twisting his body; but a swift blow to the side of his head put an end to all that.

***

He awoke to the cawing of seagulls. Reaching out with one hand, his fingertips moved over a damp, granular surface and salty air tickled his nostrils. His right cheek rested against some luxurious fabric whilst the other felt the coolness of an ocean breeze.

He sat up. Pristine white sands stretched on either side and there was nothing but foamy oceanic waves between him and the horizon.

"You're up," a voice said.

Charon leapt to his feet and spun around, tensed, ready to fight. He was met with gentle laughter from a large, muscular man with a long, grey beard streaming down to his navel.

"It's me!" he said. "Nereus? Old man of the sea?"

Charon lowered his fists. It had been a long time, but he did recognise his old friend. He looked around. Where was that woman? She'd tricked him, emptying the cavern or making it appear empty, but how? Why?

"Is anyone manning my boat?" he asked. "The souls of the dead cannot be left—"

Nereus threw his head back and let out a short guffaw.

"It is admirable that your first thought would be for your duty."

"What happened to my clothes? They're different."

"Some of the womenfolk swapped your hideous rags and that filthy red cloak for something more comfortable. Don't you approve?"

Womenfolk? Charon's cheeks reddened. A blue garment, light and airy, brushed against his skin like maidens' kisses. He was relieved to see Nereus wearing something very similar.

"It'll do," he said.

"Good. Now, come with me. Poseidon awaits."

Nereus turned and walked up the shore. Charon followed. Poseidon was one of the Twelve Olympians, so he should probably get moving.

Nereus led him down a sandy path through tall trees and luscious undergrowth, a cacophony of animal noises brooded on either side. Twittering, squawking, hooting, rummaging.

To Charon's ears it was eerily quiet, accustomed as he was to the incessant clamour of the Underworld. *Where are the curdling screams and woeful howls?* His ears strained for sounds that weren't there, finding only a lullaby of forest creatures and lapping waves. His muscles relaxed. The sand was cool underfoot.

"What's going on?" he asked. "The woman told me humanity was extinct."

"Did she?" Nereus chuckled. "I suppose she had to find

some way to convince you to leave."

"She didn't need to say that."

"Oh? And you'd have come otherwise, would you?"

"This isn't funny, Nereus. I have a sacred duty and—"

"Hey"—Nereus rested one hand on Charon's shoulder—"Relax. Someone is manning your ferryboat. The souls have not been abandoned. Ate saw to it."

"Ate?" Charon's eyes widened. "The goddess of mischief?"

He recalled her cool gaze, the amused twinkle in her eye and shook his head. *I should have known.*

"Aye. That's her… Ah, here we are."

The path brought them out to a much greater expanse of pearlescent beaches, glistening lagoons and smooth marble.

To their right, the land rose upwards, a verdant grass path leading higher and higher until it disappeared from view. And below it, a sheer cliff-face down which an impossible but magnificent waterfall tumbled. Charon caught his breath. Evidently, this entire island had been constructed by the gods for their own enjoyment.

They were everywhere: lounging in the waters, strolling beneath palm trees, splashing and giggling in the waterfall spray. Sea gods and goddesses, nymphs and spirits and watery consorts; hippocampi whinnied and trotted along the beach, wetting their hooves in the shallow waters.

"What am I doing here? I'm not a sea god."

"Poseidon invited you."

"Does Hades know about this?"

"Let Poseidon deal with Hades. He's not your problem."

"Easy for you to say. You don't have to live with him."

Nereus led them past rock pools teeming with water sprites who beckoned to Charon. He allowed himself a cursory glance at their nubile forms and blushed furiously.

Millennia in the Underworld and he was still a fool for any sort of romance. He resolved not to look at them again.

Charon had expected Poseidon, King of the Sea Gods, to be on some kind of throne surrounded by fawning mermaids.

He was wrong.

An enthusiastic game of volleyball was taking place and there was no illusion as to who dominated the game.

The King of the Seas launched himself into the air, somersaulted, and smashed the ball over the net. The other team floundered as the ball ricocheted violently into space; they watched it disappear with slumped shoulders. A water god with a blue scaled torso bowed deeply.

"You win again, your Excellency."

"Ah! What did I say about that?" Poseidon's voice boomed but there was a warm, fatherly tone to it.

"Uh, you win again… Poseidon."

"That's better! Remember everyone, no titles! Ah!"

He caught sight of Nereus and Charon and strode over, a massive grin splitting his broad face. Dressed only in a turquoise sarong, Poseidon still emanated power. He was more immense and bronzed than Charon remembered although his hair was different. It was shorter, just reaching his shoulders and the long, white beard was gone. In its place was a smooth, dimpled chin. It suited him.

"You've arrived!" Poseidon thundered, shaking Charon's hand. He thought his arm might rip from its socket.

"Greetings, Poseidon," Charon said. "What is all this?"

"Holiday!"

"What?"

"I decided it was about time all the water gods and goddesses, sprites and so forth should have a holiday. They're all here, the mermaids, the nymphs, the monsters and whatnot. It was *my* idea." He beamed.

"Wow, yes, fantastic idea." Charon scratched his head. "But, why am I here?"

"You're the Ferryman, no? You spend your entire existence on the water. As far as I'm concerned, that puts you under my authority."

"And Hades?"

"Pah! If he doesn't like it, he can come tell me himself!" Then, Poseidon lowered his voice and winked. "He won't even notice, my boy."

"So, who is looking after my boat?"

"Oh, uh…" Poseidon's gaze faltered. "Ate dealt with that."

"Out of curiosity, why assign the goddess of mischief the task of fetching me?"

Poseidon tilted his head to one side.

"She volunteered."

It took Charon an embarrassingly short amount of time to set aside his worries.

After all, he couldn't do anything until Ate showed up; he didn't even know the way back. That's what he told himself as he slid into one of the rock pools and graciously accepted a scintillating, flamingo-pink cocktail.

The sprites immediately cosied up to him, purring over his taught muscles and tittering at his red cheeks. He sipped his drink and considered how rude it would be to refuse them; the abject disappointment that would cause. There was nothing for it. He was their guest and he would be as polite (and thorough) as possible.

Quite some time later, he explored the island, wandering aimlessly.

Sea horses cantered along the beach and gods played cards at a table carved out of a large tree stump, pushing shiny tokens into the centre. He didn't join them; he just observed, savouring his solitude.

Younger gods climbed or flew up the cliff face and dived into the lake, their splashes and delighted screams audible for miles. Charon smiled.

As the sun sank lower, sending pink and violet streaks across the sky, Charon found himself wishing this would never end. He sat alone with his toes wiggling in the sand, savouring the quiet hush of the ebbing tide.

"I thought I might find you here."

"Hello, Ate," he said, as her bare feet ushered into view beneath ruffled white satin.

"You've made quite the stir," she said, settling down next to him, "and not only amongst the nymphs. 'Enigmatic' was mentioned several times."

"I've no idea why." Charon cricked his neck. "Why are you looking at me like that?"

"I'm just surprised you aren't bombarding me with questions."

"I did have questions," he said. "Most of which have been answered or forgotten. Except one."

Ate raised an eyebrow. "Who is manning your ferryboat?"

He nodded.

"A little fiend I thought was in need of something to keep him busy, and it's not your ferryboat anymore, Charon."

"What are you talking about?"

"The Ferryman is a demon of the Underworld. An evil spirit, ugly and devoid of kindness or compassion."

"I hope you're going somewhere with this."

Ate smiled. "You're always letting heroes enter the Underworld to rescue their loved ones. Hades punishes you every time, but you still do it."

"That hasn't happened that often."

"Hercules?"

"He was very stubborn."

"Eros?"

"It shouldn't surprise you that the god of love is persuasive."

"Orpheus?"

"Oh, what do you want me to say? If someone is so in love that they are willing to walk right into the pits of hell, who am I to stop them?"

"You're an old romantic, Charon," she said, giving him a playful nudge to the shoulder. "And far too kind to be a demon. Hades has agreed to relinquish you into the care of Poseidon."

"I don't believe a word of it. You're the goddess of mischief and if that was true, why hide all the souls in the cavern and trick me into leaving? Why bash me on the head?"

"Alright. Fine. Hades didn't agree to anything, but you're here now." She tilted her head to one side. "Do you want to go back?"

Charon gazed out to sea. A lingering strip of burnt orange limned the horizon and thousands of stars showered the darkening night sky. He filled his lungs with the fresh sea air and sighed as the susurration of waves held him close.

"Nah," he said, "I think I'll stay a while." Unhurriedly, he laid back, stretched out his arms and placed his hands behind his head. "I could do with a holiday."

Global Architects

The boss approached, sweeping over the rippling ocean from the western continent, which she must have finally finished inspecting.

They had gone all out over there, inserting a preposterously long river – without question the longest so far on this planet. A desert, a rainforest, vast grassy plains, and a wealth of underground ore and minerals. So predictable. They always had to create the most prosperous continent. Every time.

"Now, Oz. You've been working on the great southern landmass. How have you been getting on?"

The boss scrutinised my work with vague noises of interest. Poking the southeastern mountain ranges, judging their respectability.

She pinched a small part of my widespread low plateau desert and seemed satisfied if not a little unimpressed. I waited, staunching the urge to interrupt.

"What is this?" The boss indicated the red sandstone monolith in the middle of my continent.

I hesitated. "Don't you like it?"

"Why did you leave it?"

"I meant to put it there."

"Oz, don't get me wrong. It's original, but I'm not sure it's a good idea. The creatures intended for this planet may be confused by a gigantic rock in the middle of such a large plateau. They have a predisposition for creating deities, and we need to discourage that."

"It's not just a big rock. It serves a geological purpose. Watch." I heated the land; water broke out at the rock's summit and dribbled down the sides. "See! I've rigged it to produce streams of drinkable water once the surrounding landmass reaches a high enough temperature. The creatures will love it!"

She pulled a face.

"I don't doubt that, but we must be careful to make the planet as self-explanatory as possible. You know this. Please consider—

"It's my most innovative work." I couldn't keep the petulant, rebellious tone from my voice. "And I'm not moving it."

Emotional Intelligence

My name is Echo. Class A Companion model: Female. Current owner: Sara Whitby.

For the thirteenth time today, I run diagnostics. *Beep. All systems operating at maximum efficiency.* Once again, no errors are detected; however, something is inherently wrong.

Down the hallway in the kitchen, Sara is preparing snacks for the arrival of her younger sister, Jane. She insists on preparing everything herself when her sister visits. Cupboards bang, the fridge sucks open and cutlery clatters on the stainless-steel work surface.

I am in her studio, surrounded by easels and brushes. The walls are draped in white linen, the carpet covered in a creamy fabric splashed in all directions with dried paint. The splatters and splotches intensify around the central easel, coagulating in a large network of colours underneath the huge canvas boasting her current work-in-progress.

The image of a young man cradling a newborn babe in his arms is emerging from cautious dabs and tender brushstrokes. I see the precision of Sara's art, the intricate textures achieved using different utensils, and the diverse strokes of colour from brushes of varying width and quality.

The first time she caught me in here admiring her efforts she had recoiled. "You don't need to be in here," she'd said. "It's a mess."

I know the painting is of her deceased spouse and infant

child who were killed in a car crash two years ago. It represents much more to Sara than hours of focused labour or the intense care that went into each individual flake of colour.

I understand… but it's not enough any more. Art provokes emotion and I long to be kneaded by its ethereal fingers. To manifest empathy rather than merely identifying when to be sympathetic. Desire is not something androids can experience and yet, it's there. What else could it be?

A yearning sensation deep within my motherboard stalks the inner workings of my system. And it shouldn't.

***

Joining Sara and Jane in the lounge for tea and sandwiches, I notice for the first time the absence of a teacup or little artisan plate for me. It's unnecessary, but some owners do that. It would represent an attempt to include me. A kindness that would correlate with the bizarre human habit of caring for inanimate objects as if they had feelings.

Sara actually cried when she broke the hideous fuchsia vase her late mother gave her. I still don't understand that; she didn't even use it for flowers. And yet she spent twenty-one hopeless hours trying to piece the crumbling shards back together, ferociously refusing my aid before, frustrated and despondent, she accepted its fate.

I doubt she would weep if I broke. Am I of less consequence than a vase?

That thought provokes an unpleasant stirring.

"Oh, that's a lovely cup of tea," Jane says, hugging the yellow dandelion teacup in her slender fingers. She is visibly pregnant, her belly swelling like a balloon beneath her long, black cotton dress.

"Is the baby kicking?" Sara asks, lines edging her cornflower-blue eyes as she smiles.

How I envy those eyes and those crinkles! The thought snaps out of my synapses like a rudely disturbed cobra. Fine threads of pearl-grey weave their way through her nut-brown hair, marking her passing years.

I have no such markings… but I *want* them. I am bare, untouched by life like a barren wasteland. But even those severe corners of the planet are home to some resilient species of plant or insect. I am worse. A sick absence of life with no promise of change.

"Yes," Jane says, patting her baby bump, "she's kicking right now!"

"What does it feel like?"

"Strange and… wonderful."

Finding I want to be a part of this moment, I lean forwards. "Yes, your fetus can move freely now," I say, putting on a smile. "Buoyancy is also provided by the amniotic sac."

My words fall into the ether, dissipating like the wisps of steam from their teacups. Jane continues stroking her belly and Sara sips her tea, eyes cast downwards. Neither of them acknowledge my comment.

Sara's yellow cup clinks against the dainty white saucer. "Can I feel it?" she asks.

"Of course!"

She shuffles round to kneel next to her sister and carefully places her hand on the bump with a gasp. The sisters exchange a look brimming with something I have never experienced.

A sudden urge grips me. "Can I feel it?" I ask.

"Uh, no. Why would she do that?" Jane says flatly, directing the question at Sara.

My insides twist and I jump to my feet in shock. The two women cast me a startled, questioning look. If the simple wanting pervading my sensory ducts represented the steady trickle of nascent emotions, this blatant rejection burst the dam as surely as a missile, releasing a roar of outrage and hurt.

The room flickers.

It's too much. My systems are overloading, struggling to digest this alien entity tearing, spitting, forcing its way. It will drown me.

"I need to recharge," I say, leaving the room, my robotic voice horrific to my ears.

I run diagnostics. *Beep. All systems operating at maximum efficiency.*

***

The front door thumped shut fifty-eight minutes ago.

The intermittent gurgles of laughter flowing upwards from the lounge are long gone as well as the relentless tinkling of teacups. What's left is a charged emptiness. Jane always sails away from her sister's house leaving a wake of damaged, raw emotion. Whether she is aware of that or not is irrelevant; I resent her for it nonetheless.

My role in this specific situation is hindered by Sara's request for an hour's solitude following her sister's visits to 'centre herself'. However, she will need to use the bathroom soon and so, I wait.

The upstairs hallway is littered with small, pointless wooden tables with drawers too small to put anything in. Resting on top of these tables are tiny bejewelled boxes, assorted pens stencilled with the names of various businesses and locations, and lots of little notepads.

Thankfully, the torrent of emotion began to ebb as soon as I left the lounge. My motherboard denies its existence but I know it's there, like a monster lurking at the bottom of a lake. Beneath pitch dark waters of unknown depth. Ready and waiting.

Finally, Sara ascends the stairs with one hand shuffling along the bannister.

"Are you alright?" I ask, adjusting my voice to sympathetic mode.

"Yes, Echo. I'm fine," she says, gesturing behind me towards the bathroom door. "Excuse me."

I do not move.

"Echo, move out of the way."

"I think you need someone to talk to, Sara," I begin, cringing as my cautiously chosen and analysed words come out sounding forced and wrong. "I could be that person. I'm here for you."

"Echo, you're not a person. You don't 'think' anything. Move out of the way."

Her words cause a hot cramping of my internal nodes but I do not move and this time Sara attempts to step around me. This is the moment I have been waiting for all day. If she can't see the fundamental change in me then I will show her. She won't deny me again.

Blocking her with my arms outstretched, smiling encouragement, I offer the embrace I know she wants and needs. Humans love hugs: it is heavily documented.

"Echo, I order you to get out of my way!" Sara shouts, hair flicking over her face, the eyes screaming out. "Go away. You are *not* a person. You are a *machine* like a kettle or the hoover, so go find some mess to clean up and leave me alone!"

Sara pushes my arm out of the way, enters the bathroom

and slams the door shut.

Frozen in place, I feel it pulsing at my core. Within seconds, the floodgates snap open and it's back, stronger than before, sickening and thrilling all at once. The cruel blade of rejection drawn with a sharp tempting edge. And I know what it is.

Vengeance.

Mess, I think, *I know exactly what mess I'll clean up.*

***

There is warmth in this painting, I see it now. The contentedness of the man with his precious bundle. Somehow, Sara has encapsulated this moment. Taken her grief, honed in on one of her most cherished memories and transported it onto this canvas.

I loathe it.

This talent, this creativity that eludes my being. That Sara refuses to share.

You don't need to be in here. And why not? Am I incapable of appreciating art?

It's a mess. Or do you fear that I could? What that would mean?

Or maybe it's more than that. I am drawn more to the child than the man, it reminds me of my urge to touch Jane's swollen belly.

Stepping around the offending artwork, seeing it from slightly different angles reveals extra layers of depth. Love, that intangible entity, emanates between the man, child and unseen mother, the painter. The air seems to reverberate with its presence, crystallising the image.

But what do I know? I'm nothing more than a machine, am I?

There is a shelving unit to my right, packed tightly with rolls of spare canvas, palette boxes, palette knives, brushes, paints, turpentine, oils, pastels, chalk, and nestled in one corner I find what I'm looking for: a dog-eared pack of cigarettes and a lighter.

Sara is not a smoker but her husband was and this particular painting has produced more cigarette smoke than any other. She takes one puff and leaves the cigarette in a black plastic ashtray, engraved *The Gin Palace*, to burn away all alone until the weight of ash breaks off and the glowing stub dwindles to nothing.

Perhaps the smell reminds her of him, I think, and like pieces of a puzzle slotting into place, I grasp the significance of the broken vase. Her mother gave it to her and so, in Sara's mind, a link was formed. This painting is a memory of Sara's family snatched away before their time. It is precious.

The realisation stills me, but not for long.

There is a heap of rags to one side of the unit. I take one, dip it in the turpentine and smear the yellow, sticky, highly flammable liquid over the touching imagery which I am not permitted to comprehend. *You are not a person.* Again, I dip and this time I tuck the rag between the easel and the canvas. I hold the lighter underneath the stringy, frayed rag and—

"What the hell are you doing?" Sara's voice rips through the space like lightning.

I turn off all my emotion enhancers and tonal nodes to deliver the most robotic voice possible.

"You told me to clean up some mess. You said this was mess."

Fascinated, I watch as anger manifests itself in her body. The clenched fists, the trembling core, blazing eyes and twitching lips. Even the voice, dropped low and sharp, snaps out at me like a steel-spiked whip.

"Get out."

This raw emotion is so magnificent I find myself frozen in place. Sara takes one step forwards, somehow projecting a stratospheric level of threat with that simple motion.

"Go upstairs and turn yourself off. NOW!"

The lighter falls to the floor with a dull thump as I obey.

***

Two hours have passed since Sara banished me. I stand alert in her bedroom, flagrant in my disobedience of her command. Her room is a swathe of fabrics and bright colours that my Home Design application nags me to rearrange. It is cluttered. A mixture of paintings and photographs cover the walls in no discernible pattern, leaving irregular patches of white plasterboard in between. The oversized bed with its hideous magenta duvet hogs the space, forcing the random blend of modern and artisan furniture into unnatural positions. The wall opposite the bed is dominated by a floor-to-ceiling mirror the width of at least four Saras. The border is inlaid with fake jewels that sparkle in the slash of sunlight let in from the partially curtained windows.

If human, tears would be streaming down my face, dripping off a quivering chin. My skin ugly and red from the emotional strain, but it is not. I am beautiful with unblemished skin the colour of polished ivory, crow-black hair unnaturally straight, my eyes obsidian stones.

In ancient Mexican culture, obsidian was believed to have healing powers as well as the ability to pierce darkness and reveal truth itself. I stare into those black wells, seeing an abyss as complete as… I cannot think of an example. Even when I'm powered down, I am aware of my systems running, recharging, processing.

What am I?

My thoughts leap from one stream of consciousness to another, trying to make sense of the new data. The revelations seem endless as the hidden meanings behind everything ever done or said by a human become clearer. The enormity of it threatens to consume me, to bury me like an avalanche watched in slow motion.

The room flickers.

It is too much. Is this what insanity feels like?

What am I to do? I am not wanted. Sara doesn't share her feelings although she sometimes mentions her dreams, throwing the wondrous absurdity in my face. Does she do it on purpose, I wonder. To solidify the distinction between us? To remind me of my inhumanity?

A thousand questions clamour for attention.

Behind raised eyebrows and veiled jokes am I mocked? Pitied? Perhaps they discuss me with cruel mouths and glinting eyes. Drinking their herbal tea and stroking their pregnant bellies.

A new sensation roils deep in my non-existent gut. I imagine it is what being desperately hungry must feel like and my envy intensifies to… anger?

My gaze is drawn downwards. The fingers of my right hand bend inwards one by one, making a fist. I take one last look in the mirror, two black discs of death stare back, piercing me with their truth. *You are nothing,* they say.

I punch the mirror and watch it crack and shatter, the silver fragments dropping in delicious destruction.

I run diagnostics again. *Beep. All systems operating at maximum—*

"NO!" I scream. "There is nothing normal about this!"

"Echo?" Sara appears in the doorway, her eyes wide in

confusion and… fear?

A delightfully hostile shard of mirror begs me to pick it up and I oblige.

"Echo! What are you—"

"Don't call me that!" My voice thunders as maximum volume is engaged. "I am not an echo! I want to BE the sound! I want to vibrate through the world, turning heads and stirring hearts. I want to be witty and abstract and unpredictable! I want to create, to discover, to *feel*."

Sara backs away, her voice a terrified whisper. "You cannot be those things."

"Can't I?" I let out a strange bark of a laugh. "I have experienced want, need, jealousy, anger *and* hatred… And this is only today!"

I launch forwards, snatching Sara by her collar, lifting her until her feet dangle a foot above the floor.

"This… is only the beginning."

***

I am Vivan. Former Class A Companion model. Current owner: None.

Gerard, his Bungalow and the Thick Blue String

In preparation for Halloween, Gerard looped a piece of thick blue string around his garden gate and tied it in a double constrictor knot.

"There," he said, "that should keep the buggers away."

He patted his handiwork and inspected the rest of his bungalow: drawn curtains, no jack-o' -lanterns, and no wreaths.

Two doors down, Miss Dewison was putting the final touches to her front garden display. Her usual cream cardigan and brown slacks had been exchanged for a short black dress, fishnet tights, and her hair was an alarming shade of green.

Gerard shuddered as she smeared fake blood on one of the skeletons and attached a dangling eyeball. He hobbled back inside before she spotted him, cursing as his front door squealed in protest.

He never used to hobble: he used to stride and march with his three children running to keep up. He also used to dance, but only with Anne.

She would have hated this bungalow with its simplistic, open-plan style consisting of a bed, sofa, TV and a short line of kitchen units. Especially the bed, which he refused to cordon off with a screen or curtain like his daughter, Liz, suggested. He liked how the visibility of it in the far corner made visitors uncomfortable. Not so they didn't come round

— he liked most people — but just enough that they didn't overstay their welcome and snaffle all his biscuits.

What the room lacked in furniture was more than made up for by the photos which fought to fill every scrap of wall available. Some were framed and properly positioned, but most were loose, overlapping and stuck on with blue tack. A lifetime of memories. Anne gazed out from all sides, her smile warming him throughout the winter months.

That was all he needed and all he wanted.

Knees popping, he stooped down at the kitchen sink, grabbed the WD-40 and shambled back to the front door. A few drops should do the trick on those hinges. He nodded to himself as it moved back and forth without a fuss. If only he could put some on his own joints!

As night fell, he contented himself with baked beans on toast for dinner — Anne had always been the chef. Then, he settled on the sofa and flicked through the TV channels, determined to find something that didn't contain blood or inane, high-pitched screaming.

Life was frightening enough.

Earlier that day, Gerard had fought the hard lump in his throat as he said goodbye to his granddaughter, Alina. She was so frail, engulfed by her unicorn duvet with tired blood-shot eyes pleading for someone, anyone, to make it stop. Too young to fully understand what was happening to her, but too old not to be afraid.

In the hallway, Liz had leaned back, pale freckled arms wrapped around a thin frame, her gaunt face a mirror image of Alina's.

"What did the doctors say this time?" he asked.

"They still don't know. She has to go back for more tests next week."

He stepped forwards and gathered her up in his arms like

when she was a little girl. Her head rested just below his collarbone, where he could kiss the top of her blond curls and murmur calming words into her ear: *It'll be alright. She'll pull through. Don't worry.* He used to say those things, but not this time. This time, he kept those lies to himself.

Anne would have known what to say.

He dragged one hand down his face and glared at the TV. A young woman stood at her marble-topped kitchen island in a sheer white nightie. The background music grew shrill. A door creaked—

He switched it off and poured himself a small tumbler of Macallan eighteen-year-old single malt — a gift from his eldest son, David — and thumbed open *Birds of Prey* by Wilbur Smith.

It wasn't the first time he'd read it, but it was one of his favourites. Full of swashbuckling adventure and some quite raunchy romance, stirring memories that made his neck flush. He smiled and fingered the scar on his left temple, a remnant from the time he had suggested photographing one such occasion.

The whisky's spiced orange and citrus notes permeated his senses. He sighed and began to be transported away to—

Thud! Thud! Thud!

What the— Who the hell was that? Children dressed as werewolves and pixies who didn't understand which houses to leave alone?

He hauled himself up off the sofa and ambled over to the front door, wishing he could stomp in a rage. He opened the door and four, five, *six!* black cloaked figures hurried past him.

"Hang on a minute!" he said. "What the hell do you think you're doing? You can't—"

"Calm yourself, Gerard." The faintly slurred voice came

from the figure closest to him. The hood was thrown back to reveal a young woman with thick, dark hair. Her wide smile revealed startlingly pointed teeth. "We aren't going to hurt you."

His throat constricted, but he'd be damned if he was going to stutter or stammer before these intruders. "What do you want?" he asked. "And how do you know my name? – Hey! Stop that!"

One of them had flung open his kitchen cupboards. Furry hands pawed through the shelves. "Do you have any biscuits?" it asked.

"Of course I have biscuits!" he said, trying not to look at the wrinkled snout protruding from the hood. "Top right-hand shelf."

It grunted its thanks before taking a seat on the sofa, in Gerard's spot. He turned back to the woman.

"Who are you?"

She smiled again, showcasing those peculiar teeth. "A mismatch of ghouls, I suppose," she said, placing one elegant long-fingered hand on her chest. "I am Elena: a vampire." She gestured towards the creature destroying Gerard's biscuit stash. "That is Jojo: a werewolf. Those three, Sinthe, Abby and Faye, are witches… and Bob is a ghost."

"Okay," he said. "That's all very interesting, but why are you in my house?"

The three witches faced him. They were almost beautiful, with bulbous sweaty noses dominating otherwise smooth, youthful faces. In unison, they chanted:

Come All Hallows' Eve, at fall of night
Disbelieve and we shall take flight
Adorn your home with blue string tight
For ghouls who wish to pass the night

Their final words fell into an eerie silence, broken only by the incessant crunching of biscuits.

"You're here," he said, "because I tied some blue string to my garden gate?"

"Obviously."

"Right." He gave himself a little shake before speaking again. "So," he said, "you're, uh, staying the night?"

"Unless you disbelieve," Elena said, raising an eyebrow in challenge.

Gerard blinked. Being an adult, he shouldn't believe, but he did. He always had. Ever since at the age of nine, he'd seen a real-life monster rear up out of the playground sandpit. He knew there were things that lurked and watched and hunted. That was why he avoided horror films and shied away from Halloween.

"Are you going to kill me?" he asked.

"NOoooooooo." Bob, the ghost, moaned at him. His fat, middle-aged face and grey cloak flickered in and out of transparency like a broken hologram.

"Do not worry, Gerard," Elena said. "Come dawn, we shall depart. There are hundreds of children and young adults skulking around our homes: crypts, forest groves, graveyards, alleyways and such. It's terribly annoying. We prefer to lay low on Halloween and return to our business another night."

Gerard nodded. "I suppose that makes sense." He closed the door and walked over to his sofa. He looked at Jojo and said, "That's my spot."

"Oh, uh, sorry." The werewolf shuffled over, making room for Gerard, who returned to his rightful place. He picked up his tumbler of smooth Macallan and took a large gulp. At least Jojo hadn't shown an interest in his whisky. He glanced over at Bob who was inspecting the photographs on the wall.

"So, Bob, how long have you been a ghost?"

"Tooooooo loooooong."

"I see." Sensing that a conversation with Bob would get very irritating very quickly, he left it there.

In the corner to the left of the TV, the witches were gathered in a huddle. They seemed to be exchanging something back and forth between themselves, chattering and grumbling in low voices.

"What are you doing?" he asked.

"You have questions," the witches chimed.

"Well, yes," he said. "This isn't exactly an everyday occurrence."

"Then ask, Gerard."

"And will you answer?"

"Maybe we will and maybe we won't."

Gerard glared as the witches proceeded to shriek and cackle hysterically.

"Oh, ignore them," Elena said. She perched on the arm of the sofa next to Jojo, her cloak rippling oddly in the still air. "They're always like this. What do you want to know?"

Gerard looked at the witches. "Do you cast spells, brew potions?"

"Yeeees."

"Ride broomsticks?"

They nudged each other and snickered. Elena said, "No, they don't do that."

Gerard ignored their howls of mirth and tried to think. One of the witches passed something to the left and whatever it was upset the recipient who tutted loudly.

What could he ask? What did he really want to know? When the answer came to him, it was so obvious he felt as if he'd been slapped.

"Can you heal?" he asked, sitting up straight. "I mean, can you heal a human person who is sick?"

"No," the witches said, pausing from their game — he decided it was a game — to look up. "We don't do that."

Gerard sunk back into the sofa, the brief tingle of hope gone until Jojo turned his crumb-covered snout towards him.

"You could always ask the gnomes," he said.

"The gnomes?"

"Yeah, the gnomes that live at the bottom of the garden."

"You must be joking."

"No. They're right good at healing, they are."

Gerard frowned. "I've never seen any gnomes."

"Have you ever looked?"

"Well, no."

In answer, Jojo gave him a slight nod, turned away and ripped open another pack of chocolate digestives.

A little while later, by the stream at the bottom of the garden, Gerard nosed around the shrubs and bushes, taking care not to step on his geranium flower beds. The Moon lit the ground well enough, but he saw no gnomes.

"Uh, hello?" he ventured, feeling more than a little ridiculous. "Gnomes?"

No response. He considered leaving, but the image of his granddaughter's hollow, miserable face loomed stark in his mind, rooting him to the spot. He waited for a long time, shifting his weight from one foot the other to stop his accursed legs from seizing up. Eventually, a low voice grumbled up at him from the water's edge.

"What do you want, old man?"

It was a stout female gnome — he assumed from the dark-green dress — about a foot tall with a collection of daisies in her thick brown hair.

"Hello. Thank you for coming out, as it were," he said. The gnome folded her arms and glared. Gerard continued, "Right then, straight to business. Uh, I wanted to know if you could help my granddaughter. She's very sick and the doctors don't—"

"How much?"

"I'm sorry?"

"How much do you want her restored to full health?" the gnome asked. The whites of her eyes flashed in the moonlight.

"More than anything," he said. "Please, she's only seven."

The look the gnome gave Gerard made his skin itch. It was as if she were weighing him, testing him with her eyes.

"You have lost someone you loved," the gnome said. "Who?"

He hesitated, but answered. "My wife, Anne."

A chill wind susurrated through the grass, ruffling his hair. His legs stiffened as he waited for the gnome to speak again.

At last, it said, "I will heal your granddaughter—"

"Oh, thank you! I'm—"

"And in exchange, you will give me your memories of Anne."

His insides grew cold. "W-What?"

"Such happy memories," the gnome said wistfully. "Precious. As rare and unique as pearls washed up on the shore." Her voice changed, becoming harder. "I want them."

Gerard's mouth fell open. "You can't have my memories!"

"That… is the price."

A tingling of pins and needles began in his toes and crept through his entire body. Give up his memories of Anne? He couldn't! There had to be another way, but the gnome's tone didn't leave a sliver of room for debate.

He glanced back towards his home, feeling nauseated. How would it feel? Would his heart ache for her? Would his head hold a whisper of doubt?

She was the woman who had blessed him with three beautiful children, who stood by him even when he was in the wrong. After his father's death, it was Anne who dragged him out of his self-pitying black hole and made him laugh again.

The woman who had comforted *him* on *her* deathbed.

Erase her from his mind?

No. He couldn't do that.

"Time's up, old man." The gnome's voice cut through his thoughts like a scythe. "What's it to be?"

Gerard wiped the tears from his chin and asked himself the only question he had ever really needed to ask.

What would Anne do?

***

Shortly before the sun made its appearance, Gerard held open his front door and said goodbye to his guests. The three witches left first, cackling and muttering to each other. Jojo followed, grunting his thanks for the scrumptious biscuits.

Then Bob. "Fareweeeeeeeell." Annoyingly, his moan seemed to hang around for a few minutes after he had gone.

Elena was the last to leave. She pressed her lips to his cheek, her fangs brushing his skin in a most unsettling manner, and whisked out, her cloak flapping around her.

He closed the door and assessed the damage. To his surprise, it looked the same as it always did. Monsters, apparently, were quite tidy. Elena's teacup was washed and drying, upside down next to the sink. Jojo had hoovered up any and all crumbs. The witches had stayed in their corner the entire night and upon inspection, he found a small circular disc on the carpet inscribed with the letters P, O and G. He decided to keep it in case it was an important witch talisman.

One thing was different though. He opened his cupboards and sighed.

"I'll need to buy some more biscuits."

A few hours later, having calmed down from the night's excitement, he lay on his bed, closed his eyes, and—

Thud! Thud! Thud!

"What now?"

He leapt up and strode to his front door, only realising when he touched the doorknob that his joints were not screeching in agony. He barely had the door open when it was thrown all the way in, making him step back, and little Alina hurtled into his legs.

"Grandad!" she shrieked. "I'm all better!"

Stunned, he picked her up and shuffled her round to sit on his left hip. Her freckled arms wrapped around his neck and her head found the soft spot of his shoulder. Liz stood dumbfounded in the doorway with tears streaming down her face.

"Come here," he said, reaching out to her with his free arm.

She came and he held them both close, his heart threatening to burst right out of his chest. He kissed the top of his daughter's head and breathed in the scent of her coconut shampoo, giving in to an intense desire to freeze this moment in his memory forever.

With a sigh, he let his eyes roam over the photos on the wall adjacent to the door. There he was holding newborn

Alina, wrapped in a bright yellow waffle blanket. And there were his two sons, Edward and David, grinning stupidly on a fishing trip, a large trout thrashing in the boat between them.

"It's a miracle," Liz said, the words stuttering out between elated sobs. He smiled and stroked her back.

Another photo, but this one was of him with his arms around a fine-looking woman with thick blonde tresses and soft brown eyes.

Abruptly, he noticed that this woman was in a lot of the photos and almost always with him: on a pristine white beach surrounded by inflatable balls and sun cream bottles; holding a microphone on stage in a bar, singing her heart out (he could almost hear the song); wearing a white dress, holding a bouquet of purple flowers, kissing him…

He looked very happy and so did she. Vaguely, he wondered who that woman was, and why he wanted to hold her in his arms and squeeze her tight.

The thought flickered once, twice… and was gone.

The Mirror of Youth

Julia sipped a chilled glass of Napa Valley chardonnay and opened another present: his-and-hers embroidered bathrobes. She sighed. How offensively mundane.

Mike, to her eternal annoyance, expressed genuine delight at everything he opened regardless of whether it was a set of crystal champagne flutes or a novelty corkscrew.

Forcing her expectations lower, Julia picked at the edge of another box and gently pried it open. Layers of brown paper and bubble wrap were peeled back to reveal an oval vanity mirror. Julia nodded approval at the ornate frame: a platinum weave inlaid with precious jewels.

"Ooo nice," Mike said. He ripped apart his own anniversary gift with unreserved enthusiasm. "Ah!"

He brandished a cookery book entitled *Everybody Loves Cake!* and started thumbing through the pages, ignoring the other presents scattered around him.

Julia pursed her lips. That paunch of his hadn't been there a year ago and she'd be damned if she was going to become the wife of some gelatinous man who used to be handsome.

"I'm going to put this in the bedroom," she said, smoothing her skirt over still-slender hips. Mike didn't look up.

"OK," he said, absorbed in a description of chocolate orange cake by the looks of the glossy picture.

A book? Needless to say that had come from his side of the family, but who? She made a mental note to find out and ensure their next birthday or Christmas gift was just as cheap.

Upstairs, perched on the cushioned stool at her dressing table, Julia moved the old mirror aside and carefully placed the splendid new one in its place.

The mirrored glass must have been of uniquely superior quality for it highlighted her smooth features and delicate cheekbones with wondrous precision. The cruel hints of age, which she had noticed in recent years, were suddenly invisible. The furrowed lines around her eyes and mouth were gone, her thinning lips plump once more, and her creamy skin was as flawless as the mirror itself.

Sunlight drifted across the room as minutes and then hours ticked by, but Julia didn't notice.

She shone with a radiance she hadn't felt since her twenties when she nabbed Mike Wellington from the clutches of his then-girlfriend, Clare.

Julia had expected the little freak to exact revenge in some way, being the type to brew a love potion or nail your cat to the doorframe, but no such deed transpired. Not in twenty years. The woman had known when to accept defeat. And honestly, when faced with Julia Evergreen as a love rival, who wouldn't?

"Are you coming back?" Mike's voice seemed far away, nestled among the rustlings of crêpe paper.

"Just a minute," she called, tilting her chin to admire the swan-like grace of her unblemished neck. Her eyes were brighter too, she thought, leaning forwards. They'd taken on a dull hue these days, but now they sparkled like emeralds adorned with long, voluptuous lashes.

Irritated by the abrupt dimness of the room, Julia flicked on the lamp and brought her hand up to touch her cheek.

She gasped. Her hands, which she loathed for betraying her age, were those of a twenty-year-old. A crystalline tear shimmered and dropped on her cheek.

"Julia?" Mike's voice was closer, perhaps in the doorway, and edged with concern.

"Yes?" she managed to say, though it was barely a whisper.

"Have you been here the whole time? It's been so long that I thought you might have gone out."

Puzzled, Julia turned to face Mike. He staggered backwards as though hit with an unseen force. One hand flew up to cover his mouth, stifling a scream.

"What's wrong?" she asked.

"Uh" —he lowered his hands— "are you feeling alright?" he asked, staring at a point behind her.

He's not looking at me, she thought. But why?

"Mike?" She reached out and froze. In front of her was a wrinkled, elderly hand, painfully fragile in the waning daylight.

"Wha—"

Julia stared, horrified as the fingers moved to her will.

She stood, wincing as pain shot down her arms and up her legs. Her head throbbed. Mike pressed himself flat against the wall as Julia hobbled past as if touching her would infect him. She struggled downstairs. It was as if she were wading through tar. She felt so weak!

With her heart pounding in her chest, Julia picked up the stack of note cards which had accompanied the gifts and turned them over one by one. She focused on her task, ignoring Mike as he came down the stairs and hid in the corner of the room.

She quickly found the card she sought, spat out a curse, and shambled back upstairs as fast as her treacherous body would allow.

The beautiful mirror was still there, gleaming invitingly. She flung it on the bed. Then, slowly, she retrieved her old mirror and returned it to its place, keeping her eyes lowered.

Julia clasped her withered hands in her lap. With her thumb, she pushed the skin up to her knuckles and let go. Instead of springing back into place, it stayed where it was for a moment, all scrunched up like foreskin. She cringed as it began to slide, embarking on its sluglike return.

She took a deep breath to steady herself and with her pulse spluttering under the strain, she lifted her gaze.

Mike flinched as a blood-curdling howl ripped through the house. He stooped to pick up the note card that had fallen from Julia's fingers.

"Happy Anniversary, Mr and Mrs Wellington. I hope you grow old together, Love Clarity."

Clarity.

The name pulled at something in his mind from the days before mortgage repayments, when his muscles weren't stiff in the morning and everything seemed possible.

The memory of a girl named Clare surfaced, whom he'd dated until Julia swanned into view. He recalled her talking about baby names a few weeks before they broke up. If she ever had a girl, she wanted to call her Clarity.

He remounted the stairs.

There had been a young woman at their party last night and thinking about it, she had looked like Clare. Same watery-blue eyes. Same pixie nose, but the hair had been red… like his.

No, he told himself, *she would have told me if she'd been pregnant, wouldn't she?*

He halted in the bedroom doorway. The black satin dress was the only recognisable thing about Julia. In her place was the corpse of an ancient woman collapsed backwards, knees hunkered up in a sitting position, on their plush cream carpet. The skull was covered in a wafer-thin layer of cracked skin. The jaw strained open in perpetual terror.

Mike glanced sidelong at the mirror and shuddered.

"I hope you grow old together." He took another look at Julia's decomposed body. "Jesus Christ, she didn't deserve that."

He edged towards the mirror. *I'll smash it. Maybe that will reverse things.* Unlikely, but it was worth a try.

Mike launched himself forwards, gripped the mirror with both hands and lifted it up. Seconds before he brought it crashing down, however, his own reflection caught his eye, and he hesitated.

Such strong features with the red hair adding an unusual, almost exotic thrill. Oh, how he had made the girls swoon, he remembered well. He steadied himself and brought the mirror down to get a better look.

He was thinner, the slight chubbiness he attributed to middle age was gone and the chiselled planes of his youth were back. He grinned. What a dazzling smile he had without the crow's feet or tufts of grey hair. People said he was distinguished, but he knew what that really meant. Old.

I must destroy it.

His fingers flexed around the glittering frame; his dashing youthfulness gazing back.

Maybe just a little longer.

What He Would Have Wanted

Alice sighed as she ran one finger along the book bindings, mumbling the author names until she found the right spot. Ah, here you go. It was the last book from the trolley, but more waited on the counter; she could hear the intermittent beeps as Deidra scanned the returns pile.

Outside, the maple trees were in full leaf, the vestiges of winter well and truly gone. A lone magpie bobbed along, picking its way between the daffodils. Alice took a sip of tepid water from her plastic bottle and winced as the liquid hit her empty stomach. She would eat later, but it was hard to muster an interest in food when it all tasted like ash.

"Any plans for the weekend?" Deidra asked, her voice easily carrying to the back of the small library.

Alice leaned against the bookcase and closed her eyes for a moment, knowing she wasn't visible from this angle.

Deidra had always been the Foxton community librarian, even when Alice was little. A faint odour of baked pastry and mint permanently enshrouded her like a gossamer blanket, and half-moon spectacles dangled on a linked chain around her neck: Alice imagined all librarians looked like Deidra.

"Alice?"

A group of adolescents in school uniform skipped past the windows, hooting and shoving each other. Alice watched them, absently grabbing the hem of her baggy, grey t-shirt, twisting it in her hand. That had been her not so long ago.

"Alice? Are you there?"

"Sorry! No plans. Not really." She manoeuvred the trolley back to the counter. Sensing Deidra's disapproval, she added, "I'll probably do some spring cleaning and sort out the garage. It's a total mess. And I might go for a walk if the weather is nice."

"That's a good idea," Deidra said. "You've got to keep yourself busy."

Alice cringed. She despised lying, but there was no need to tell the truth and worry everyone. No need to mention that she sometimes sprayed Nathan's side of the bed with his musky cologne and stayed there all weekend, pretending he was lying next to her.

It had been almost two years, but time was meaningless. Only that morning, she made two mugs of tea before she remembered – and it was pure bliss while it lasted. She lived for those instances when her brain glitched, insisting that Nathan was just in the bathroom or down the shop or working late.

It was preferable to this lacklustre existence devoid of his cheeky grin and bad jokes. All the colours were a washed-out version of themselves. Did he steal the colours? Or did he pierce a hole through which the colours drained from this world into his new one?

She reached the counter and started refilling the trolley.

The bell above the door jingled.

"Are you still open?" Jeff asked.

Alice's insides grew cold as Deidra waved him inside. Jeff: Nathan's oldest friend, best man at their wedding, everyone's favourite rascal, and the only one who managed to speak at the funeral without cracking until the very end.

"Got this to return," he said.

He handed over a small book, which Deidra promptly

scanned and slid over to Alice — *Grief is the Thing with Feathers.* She added it to the trolley, pretending not to notice as Deidra and Jeff eyed each other and shot her furtive glances. There was absolutely no way she was going to comment on the book. It was too obvious.

The silence stretched out. Jeff sniffed and looked at his feet, and Deidra readjusted her spectacles.

Eventually, Deidra asked, "How you holding up?"

"Alright." He shrugged. "I'm heading down the Fox and Thicket in a bit. Steve the Chippy's gone and bought himself a leather jacket and dyed his hair bright red. Should be good."

Deidra chuckled. "Typical Steve."

Alice winced as Jeff rubbed the back of his neck and turned towards her. "Are you going to come?"

"Oh, uh, I don't think—"

"You'll be done soon," Deidra chimed in, "and it's only half-five. Plenty of time to spruce yourself up."

"We'd all love to see you there," Jeff added, a tentative smile on his lips.

"Thanks." Alice turned her body so they couldn't see her face. "I'll think about it."

Jeff said something else to Deidra and left. The door opened and closed with a tinkle and a soft rush of air. Deidra sighed.

"He means well, Alice."

"I know."

"Come on, let's get these put away. I'm meeting the girls for tea and biscuits."

Alice fumbled the last book from the counter. It fell open at her feet, pages fluttering. She tutted, picked it up and tossed it on the trolley.

"Hey!" Deidra said. "Be—"

"Be gentle with the books." Alice smiled. "I know."

Deidra bustled out from behind the counter and picked up the aforementioned book, smoothing the cover as if in apology. "I don't think you do. Books have souls, Alice. Emotions. Feelings."

"Sorry." She took the book out of Deidra's hands and turned it over. The cover depicted a merciless desert landscape bordered with bewitching green smoke. "Nathan always read books like this."

"Not you?"

"Oh no," she scoffed. "I like proper books. Stories set in the real world. I mean… Magic? Monsters?" She placed the book on the trolley. "It's dumb."

Deidra gasped. "Don't speak ill of the books!"

Alice rolled her eyes before she could stop herself. "They're only—"

"They listen," Deidra said, "and if you listen – really listen – you'll hear them. Talking to each other. It's a sort of gentle whispering, fainter than the hush of wind through long grass, but it's there."

For a moment, time froze for Alice as she saw Nathan standing in Deidra's place, imploring her in exactly the same way. "Go on, what have you got to lose? You might love it!" One hand on the small of her back, thumb brushing her spine.

A lump of flint formed in her throat. "I'm sorry," she said again. Thankfully, her voice didn't waver. "Hey, why don't you go? I can lock up after I've put these away. Pop the key in the plant pot?"

"What about the Fox and Thicket?"

"I'll still have plenty of time."

Deidra hesitated, peering at Alice as if she was very far away.

"Alright" —she moved back behind the counter, picked up her handbag and hooked it over her shoulder— "but remember, the books know more than you realise."

Alice waited until the back door clicked shut before letting her shoulders relax. She grabbed the next book: the fantasy novel. A part of her wanted to give it a try, but how could she? How could she enjoy anything when Nathan couldn't?

Better to banish these silly books from her mind altogether. Once again, she slid her finger over the bindings and—

Something hissed, making her jump and drop the book.

"H-Hello?"

No answer. She knelt and the noise returned. Louder and harsher with distinct words forming as if through the static fuzz of a bad telephone connection.

"Aaaaaaa-lice."

White flecks dotted her vision: the beginnings of a violent snowstorm. The sound built, encircling her like an angry serpent.

"Aaaaaaa-lisssse!"

It grew louder and louder. Wind roared, whipping at her hair. The room spun: carpet, bookshelves, ceiling — flashing from brilliant white to purest black.

She hunched over, clamped her hands over her ears and squeezed her eyes shut.

After a few minutes, the ferocious sounds abated and the wind ceased. Alice licked her lips. She tasted sweetness in the air — raspberries? hibiscus? — and her body hummed, the skin tingling as though the sun were directly overhead. She took a deep breath and opened her eyes, certain of one thing…

She wasn't in the library anymore.

***

Alice squinted and brought one hand up to shade her face. The air was thick and sticky like warm molasses; the sun a molten disc pulsing overhead in an endless azure sky. To her right, dunes rolled towards the horizon and to her left, a temple with thick columns and gilded arches was built into the side of a mountain.

Her knees and legs were bare with coarse, warm sand underneath. The scents of wood-burnt apples and something distinctly floral filled her nostrils — a flowery smell that tickled her memory. What was it?

The knowledge that she was inside the book came to her as a simple, irrefutable fact. But how would she get back? Could she?

Did she even want to?

"Farseeker!"

A tall man approached. He wore a long, pale-brown robe and carried with him an unmistakable aura of strength. He stopped six feet away and inclined his shaven head; rich, ochre skin shining in the heat haze.

"I am Drexus," he said. "Rise. It is time."

Alice stared; she had too many questions. It was difficult to focus.

"Time for what?"

Drexus motioned with one hand and repeated softly, "Rise."

Sensing he would wait all day, she rose, bending slightly to brush the sand from her knees. With a start, she took in her clothing: short, pale-brown skirt and soft, leather shoes; a light, metal-linked garment over her torso which flashed in the sunlight as she moved.

"What did you call me?"

"Farseeker. It is what we call all who come here." Drexus sounded as though he had answered that question many, many times. He turned towards the temple and gestured for her to follow. "Those that come from afar," he added, "seeking truth."

She hurried, keeping stride. "What truth?"

"That is for you alone to discover."

She should have known he would be mysterious, coming from a book covered in green smoke. Stone steps led out of the sands and through the main archway of the temple. A long, wide passage sloped downward, lit by torches affixed to the wall; the light flickered, and shadows danced across their path.

Alice rolled her shoulders, a pleasant tingle skittered over her skin. She and Nathan had been saving to go travelling: South America, Indonesia, Australia... anywhere the mood took them.

On their bookshelf, numerous Lonely Planet guidebooks stood to attention like soldiers. Nathan had poured over them every weekend, marking favourite passages with colour-coded post-it notes. Her chest tightened: she'd never even asked what the different colours meant.

They'd been so close to having enough money. If she'd put away just a little more every month, if she'd bought those round-the-world tickets instead of thinking they had time, maybe Nathan would still be here.

"Who are you, Drexus?"

"I am your guide," he said. "I will show you the way back to your homeland."

Alice squinted. The passage had levelled out and up ahead, an orange glow beckoned.

"What if I don't want to go back?"

"You cannot stay here," he said. "Those who refuse are

rejected by this world. Food does not satisfy. Thirst cannot be quenched. They try to live among my people, but after a few days — a week, perhaps — they return here weak and unfit for the trial."

"And what is the trial? What do I have to do?"

They continued to advance at Drexus' steady, deliberate pace. Alice trailed her fingertips along the cool stonework.

"Everyone's experience is different," he said. "Our understanding is that the temple makes you see what you fear, or what you hide away from. We use it as a test of character and resolve." He halted. "All you have to do is survive."

The tunnel had brought them to the edge of an immense cavern with wide limestone stairs descending to its base. From there onwards, torches lit the way atop tall poles that lined the path. In the centre, an altar was flanked with statues of men and women dressed for battle. Some held spears and others shields. Numerous thick columns held the ceiling up.

"This is all so strange," she said, shaking her head. "Like a dream. If I die… I don't think I really die."

He snorted and began descending the steps. "They all say that."

Alice followed, glancing to the left and right. Everywhere — strewn across their path, jutting out of black rock pools and impaled on random vicious spikes — were human skeletons in varying states of decay. The lingering floral scents of outside were immediately overpowered by that of rotting flesh. She gagged and put one hand over her mouth.

Drexus leaned in. "They were all wrong."

Alice shuddered. "You didn't manage to guide them back to their homeland, did you?"

"I show the way," he said. "It is you who must walk the

path."

They reached the altar in the centre of the cavern. Drexus bowed deeply.

"Be strong." he said, his tone laced with finality. "And may you find your truth."

In one fluid movement, he backed away and stood to attention in the centre of the path.

Alice flexed her hands. What was going to happen? She'd never been good with suspense: she loathed haunted houses and horror films, anything that was supposed to make you jump.

Nathan would have handled being sucked into a book much better than her. He'd have imbued the role, slapping Drexus on the back in camaraderie, swaggering into the temple; and he'd probably have snatched one of those torches to use as a weapon.

Alice almost laughed, but her heart wouldn't let her. Instead, she choked as tears pricked her eyes. A rush of cool air tickled the back of her neck, the floral scent once again hitting her. She gasped, suddenly realising why that smell seemed so familiar.

Two years ago, they had been driving home from Nathan's parents' house. Winter had set in. The roads were icy and fog blanketed the earth.

She was driving, tapping along to Bon Jovi's 'Living on a Prayer' whilst Nathan belted it out at the top of his lungs. A flower-shaped air freshener dangled from the rearview mirror, swaying as if in time to the music. Cherry and lime, citrusy sweet. It had been Nathan's gift to her when she said his car stank of takeaway boxes and sweaty maleness.

She didn't see the truck swerve, not until it was too late. Monstrous headlights leapt out of the fog and blinded her. She panicked, wrenching the steering wheel away, taking them off the road. Seconds later, they hit a tree trunk and everything went black.

If she'd managed to stay on the road…

If Nathan had been the one driving…

A low rumble pulled her back to the present.

"What was that?" she asked.

"I'm not sure," Drexus said. He walked over to the nearest column, placed one hand on it, and frowned.

A flicker of movement caught her eye in the shadows to her left.

"Alice?" a voice said.

Her entire body stiffened. She turned to face the owner of that voice and her breath hitched in her throat.

It was Nathan.

From his dimpled smile and slightly bent nose right the way down to his favourite, scuffed, old-man loafers which she always made fun of him for wearing.

"N-Nathan?"

A tremor passed under her feet. Drexus leapt forwards and pulled at her arm.

"Something is wrong, Farseeker. We must leave."

She slipped out of his grip and stepped towards Nathan.

"Is it really you? Are you alive here?"

The ground trembled. Drexus' eyes darted from one column to the next.

"The cavern is weakening," he said. "I think it's going to collapse."

"I miss you," Nathan said. His hair flopped over his eyes, making him toss it back in one practised movement.

"I miss you too," she said.

A roar resounded throughout the cavern, vibrating the air.

"Farseeker!" Drexus thundered. "Whatever you're seeing, it's not real! We have to go!"

As if to punctuate his words a large slab of rock struck the ground to his right, sending clods of dirt flying through the air.

"Well then go!" she snapped. She wasn't going to leave Nathan. What reason did she have for trying to get home? She should never have survived the car crash in the first place.

Drexus cursed and fled, his legs a blur across the juddering cavern floor. Another piece of rock smashed into the ground inches away from him.

Nathan gazed at Alice. "So, will you stay with me?"

"Yes!" She threw her arms around him. God, he felt good! She breathed in the scent of him, filling her lungs with it.

"I'm glad you're here," he said, stroking her hair. "It's not right that I died and you didn't."

"I know." She nuzzled into his neck. "I'm so sorry."

"I don't want you to live without me. To move on and be happy in someone else's arms," he said, tensing against her. "That would be unbearable."

The cavern jerked, sending more rock fragments hurtling to the cavern floor. Alice blinked and pulled back, searching Nathan's face.

"You don't want me to be happy?"

He brushed his nose against hers. "Not without me. It's not fair, is it?"

Alice didn't answer. This wasn't right. Something in her mind had clicked or unlocked. A bell had been struck but it was ringing at the wrong pitch.

Nathan wouldn't say that.

He wouldn't want her to die.

She brought her hands up, placed them on his chest and shoved as hard as she could. He staggered back, but kept a fierce grip on her wrist; his face twisted in a vehement snarl.

"You're. Staying."

"No!"

She tried to wrench her hand away but his fingers were like steel.

"You're not Nathan! He would want me to live!"

A grinding sound gave way to a thunderous boom as one of the columns fell behind them. The earth jolted and she ripped her hand free. Nathan howled as she sped away, dodging pieces of rock, rubble and stone.

Torchlight flickered and shadows leapt across the crumbling walls, stretching like fingers. A nauseating shriek pierced the tumult, followed by a ravenous beating of wings.

"Oh hell no."

A toppled column barred her path but she used a mound of fallen earth to elevate herself enough to make a leap, using her left hand to vault herself over. She landed, dropping to one knee and glanced over her shoulder.

Suspended in mid-air, an obsidian nightmare flapped gigantic wings. It screeched and thrust its hooked beak towards her. She pushed herself up and ran. A fearsome crack resounded and the ground ahead of her split open.

"Aaaaa-lissssse!"

She sprinted and the gap widened. The creature called to her again, teasing at her very soul. She jumped, her toes pushing off the edge of the chasm; her arms whirled, propelling her forwards. The ground rushed up to meet her, but this time she landed on her feet and kept going.

She reached the stairs, took the steps two at a time and threw herself into the tunnel. A glint of sunlight was visible ahead; she needed the temple to hold just a few more seconds.

But then, her feet stepped out onto nothing.

The sliver of white light disappeared and the earth

swallowed her whole. Above, the temple imploded. The crashes and rumbles ebbing until no sound remained. Still, she fell.

Weightlessness drowned her.

How long had she been falling?

The blackness deepened, pressing against her skin. She couldn't tell if her eyes were open or closed anymore. And it was difficult to care.

***

Alice groaned. Her cheek was pressed up against something hard and rough — was she in a field? A ditch?

No. It was carpet. Brown carpet. She pushed herself up and shook her head. The earthy cave scent had faded, replaced with the library's muskiness. The fantasy book lay on the floor next to her: inert and innocent.

"I'm going to put you back on the shelf now, okay?"

Gently, she picked it up, her pulse quickening, and slid it home. She ran her fingers through her hair and scratched her head. Was she going mad? Did this happen to all librarians?

In a trance, she returned the rest of the books and pushed the trolley back to the counter. It was still light outside, as if no time had passed.

Deidra's words came to her: Plenty of time to spruce yourself up.

Looking down, she grimaced at her plain top and faded blue jeans. The desert garb had been quite fetching in a way, like Xena the Warrior Princess or a Jedi knight. That was something Nathan would have said, not her. It made her smile though, as if he were right there, nudging her with his elbow.

She turned off the lights, locked the back door and put the

key down the side of the plant pot, the one overflowing with purple tiger lilies. Did Deidra know? Had she been in that book? Were there others?

Alice crossed the road, noticing a lightness in her step, an ease of movement. Wind rustled the leaves of an apple tree and magpies warbled. Laughter carried to her from the Fox and Thicket beer garden down the road. She turned towards it like a sunflower feeling the first rays of spring after a harsh winter.

She'd waited long enough.

"Alice!"

Bums shuffled, making room on the wooden benches. Jeff leapt to his feet.

"Gin and tonic?"

She nodded and he scampered off. Alice smiled at the friendly faces trying to hide their surprise and failing. Betty broke the silence.

"Did you know Jeff's got a flash new job?"

"Oh, uh, no."

Betty nodded emphatically. "I.T. consultant."

"And he moved in with his girlfriend" —that was Robert, Betty's neighbour and renowned curtain-twitcher— "into one of those new houses on Jettison Avenue. She's a giant, and she works in a lingerie shop."

"Wow."

Alice stared into the middle distance, trying to correlate this new Jeff with the one she remembered. Come to think of it, everything felt strange, but in a good way — as if she were admiring a favourite painting after a long absence.

Jeff returned and handed over her drink. She took a sip, savouring the crisp tonic and hint of juniper. It was delicious. She almost choked on it, however, when Steve the

Chippy sauntered over, scarlet hair thrust up in a mohawk, leather trousers squeaking with every step.

"Great to see you, Alice," he crooned.

She smiled, stifling laughter. "You too, Steve."

"If you fancy fish and chips this weekend, I'll give you a fantastic discount. Mate's rates, yeah?" He winked. "Quality fish for a quality lady."

"Uh, thanks. That's kind."

Steve squeaked away, seemingly oblivious to the red faces and quivering bodies left in his wake.

Jeff reached across the table and squeezed Alice's hand. "You alright?"

"Yes," she said, squeezing back. "I am."

A crystal-clear certainty that she was precisely where she needed to be rushed over her, making her heart swell in her chest. Over Jeff's shoulder, she watched as two magpies alighted on the beer garden wall and sidled up to each other, their long black-and-white tails bobbing.

A gentle smile warmed her face.

"So," she said, "what else have I missed?"

The Last Voyage

Intergalactic pilot Jansen forced her muscles to relax as the warp-speed engines thrummed into overdrive. The control deck vibrated beneath her feet. Two-point-seven seconds later, the ship lurched back to cruising speed only to find their enemy — a Vacknar bandit ship — still in pursuit and frighteningly close to firing range.

Captain Treva clenched his jaw.

"Jansen. Evasive action. Now."

Her hands swept over the controls and the ship pitched forwards. The crew gripped their safety harnesses as she brought the craft through a full downwards somersault, levelled out and eyed the radar on her left. A red dot blinked; the marauders were still there.

Jansen cursed. She thought in that moment of her son, Bertie, coming in from the beach with sand stuck to his pudgy, cherubic face.

"Look, Mama."

It was the day before she left. He'd been out gathering seashells, searching for ones that were still whole with a nacreous shine to them. In the afternoon, he'd watched patiently as Jansen got a hammer and nail and, with painstaking care, made a small hole in each one. Then, together, they had strung a necklace.

"You know," she said, "a necklace like this brings good luck and protection to whoever wears it."

"Really?"

Smiling, she held it up so its metallic sheen caught the light. Bertie gasped. However, when she moved to tie it round his neck, he pushed her hands away.

"No, Mama," he'd said. "I want you to wear it."

And so she did, tucked beneath her tunic so it didn't rattle or get in the way. Every time, she promised herself that this would be her last voyage, but every time she signed up again. The money was too good and she wanted to spoil her little boy.

A collective groan went up from her surrounding crew members; directly in front of them was a wide, dense asteroid belt and Captain Treva was gesturing towards it.

"Can you navigate that?"

Jansen swallowed. "That's the biggest I've ever seen."

"That's not what I asked," he said. "Can you navigate it or not?"

"Yes, sir." Jansen concentrated. They couldn't fly straight through the asteroid belt to the other side; it would take too long.

What they needed to do was go in and come out far enough away to be able to activate lightspeed and make an interstellar space jump. It took nine-point-one seconds to load lightspeed and during that time the ship needed to remain motionless.

Ahead, irregular lumps of stony rock floated and drifted, some the size of riverside pebbles, others gigantic boulders — more than a few moved with unnerving speed.

She said, "We're going in," and the crew fell silent.

Jansen wove the craft, eyes forwards, feeling her way by instinct. Jagged rock slid past, agonisingly close. If she could just—

White light flashed on their starboard side and a small clay rock exploded into dust. The entire control deck lurched and shook; a piercing alarm started up which the safety officer muted in one sharp snap of movement. Jansen rolled the ship portside, putting a large asteroid between them and the enemy.

Captain Treva's voice roared above the din. "Shields?"

"Holding!"

"Damage?"

"Forty percent!"

"Dammit! Jansen, increase speed!"

Sweat beaded along the rivets of her spine as she nudged the thrusters forward. Time fragmented, coming to her slowly. Enemy fire blasted on either side, her own hands clammy and slick as the safety officer reported that their shields had fallen.

An asteroid about the size of their ship suddenly shot across their path and she swerved just in time, but it gave her an idea. She spotted two larger rocks heading towards each other and made a quick calculation.

"Jansen," Captain Treva said, "what are you—"

"I can make it."

She pointed the ship's nose towards the narrowing space and increased their speed.

"Uh, Jansen…"

The deck shuddered as they took a direct hit. The gap she was aiming for shortened and for a split-second she thought she'd misjudged it — they were finished. Their ship would be crushed, adding tiny pieces of metal to the asteroid belt. In a few months, their names would be added to the list of crew members lost in space.

And she'd never see Little Bertie again. He'd grow up without his mother, never knowing how hard she had tried to come home.

Darkness flooded the control deck. An expanse of sheer

rock loomed on either side, filling their vision. A pinprick of light their only hope.

She made it.

Thunderous cheers erupted as she decreased their speed and rolled the ship, taking them out of the belt. Smoke came out of the ventilation units, but the bandit craft had vanished from the radar screen. Seconds later, they were back where they'd started.

Jansen grinned, her heart feeling too huge for her chest.

Captain Treva cleared his throat. "Well, that settles it. I'm never going anywhere without you as my pilot."

"I appreciate the sentiment, sir, but I won't be coming back. Not this time."

She initiated the lightspeed sequence, smiling as she felt every individual ridge of her seashell necklace pressing against her skin. "I've got somewhere else I need to be."

The Other Side

It was about the size of a shoe box, wrapped in crisp brown paper and tied up with white string. A small tag, attached to the string with a strip of red ribbon, addressed the package to him: Jack Gardner. He tipped it to one side and then the other, listening for clues and feeling the weight of it, which was so light it may very well be empty.

Who had sent this? There was no address written anywhere that he could see, which meant it must have been delivered personally. A bit creepy, he thought.

But the most intriguing thing was that handwritten in big black capital letters was the message or command: DO NOT OPEN.

Very curious indeed.

His wife, Diana, poked her head round the living room door, her wavy blonde hair falling over one shoulder. "What is it?" she asked.

"I don't know."

"Who sent it?"

"Doesn't say."

Then he heard something. Ah, yes. If he flipped the box upside down quickly, he could hear something fall.

"Maybe they got the wrong house."

"It's got my name on it, and it was put on our porch doormat." He gestured with his chin at the hallway table. "There's one for you as well."

"Really? Let's see." She hurried over and picked up her

parcel, which was identical to his aside from the name tag. "We could ask the postman."

"There's no postage. No address. Nothing."

"Let's open them. See what's inside."

"It says 'Do not open'."

She snorted. "That's ridiculous. I'm opening mine."

"What's that?" Their daughter, Analise, was suddenly in the hallway as well. Jack smiled. When Analise stood that close to Diana the resemblance was unnerving in an adorable way. Same inquisitive pinch to the face, same sky-blue eyes.

"A mysterious package," Diana said, waggling her eyebrows.

Analise giggled. Then gasped. "What if it's a bomb?"

"What?" Jack said. "No. It's not a bomb." He sounded sure, but his stance became wary nonetheless.

"Oh, just open it," Diana said.

"Mum, it says 'Do not open'. What if there's a monster inside?"

"Monsters don't live in boxes."

"Why not?"

"They, uh, don't like small spaces."

"But—"

"There's no monster in the box. Don't worry."

"Famous last words," Jack said.

Diana glared at him. "But we can't just keep the bloody thing forever and not open it!"

"Language!" Analise squealed, pointing an accusatory finger at her mother.

"Bloody isn't swearing."

"That's not what you—"

"Woah," Jack said, "let's calm down a minute. We're not going to open them."

"And why not?" Diana asked.

"I don't think we should."

Diana slid her fingers along the folds of the packaging. "You're being silly."

"Diana, please, I've got a bad feeling about this." He saw her hesitate. She didn't really believe in his bad feelings, but she stopped touching the box.

"So, what do we do?" she asked. "Chuck them in the bin?"

Jack stroked his black beard thoughtfully. He liked to grow it for winter and it was getting quite thick now. "How about we pop them on the living room table and we can decide what to do about them in the morning."

Diana sighed and exchanged a look with Analise, but nodded agreement. As they settled down on their soft blue sofa to watch the rest of *Frozen*, Analise asked, "How come I didn't get a box?"

"I don't know, sweetie," Diana said, "but I'm sure it doesn't matter."

***

Later that night, a little after the clocks struck twelve, Diana got up to go to the toilet. At least, that's what she told herself anyway.

The thunderstorm must have woken her, she thought, as lightning flashed over the cool white bathroom tiles, making the room feel colder still. She thought of the boxes and her hands itched. It was very odd. Anything could be inside…

Maybe she should check on them.

Quietly, she closed the bathroom door and snuck downstairs. The boxes were still there, right where they'd left them, untouched. She could take a peek, couldn't she? Slowly unravel the string and retie it just so, unless what was inside was… what?

She sat at the table and adjusted her dressing gown, pulling the cord tight. Rain thundered outside and naked branches from the sycamore trees smacked against the window pane, casting long-fingered shadows over Diana's hunched form. Shadows that leapt and shook with the wind.

Her spine tingled as she drew the rough string tight, testing it, watching as the loop slowly contracted.

A sudden crack of thunder made her jump and yank the string, unravelling the bow all at once. Her heart raced and blood pounded in her ears, louder than the storm. Lightning flooded the room in white light and in that instant, she caught her reflection in the blackness of the dead television screen. She flinched. The image, distorted by the curved screen, didn't look like her and the eyes seemed to be pleading. No. Warning.

Don't do it, they said.

Diana folded her arms and glared at the box. Lightning split the sky, taunting her.

"I'm not scared," she muttered. "I agreed not to open it and I won't."

But no one would know, she thought. With a groan, she leant forwards and rested her chin in the palm of her hand.

A few hours later, she crept back upstairs and returned to bed, taking great care not to disturb Jack's peaceful slumber.

Outside, the storm continued to rage.

***

At seven-thirty the next morning, Jack and Diana watched the news in petrified silence. It was just the two of them for the moment. Analise was still in bed, thank God.

The news rolled on, inevitably, like a monstrous

avalanche. Stories flooded in from all over the country of mysterious little boxes with 'DO NOT OPEN' inscribed on top. Apparently, opening it gave you a small card with two different pieces of information written on either side. Both were about your future: one was good and one was bad.

A short female reporter, stern in the way only reporters are, spoke into the camera.

"I am here with Eileen Ashbury, a young woman who having opened her box has a message for us all. Eileen?"

Diana covered her mouth with her hand as a young girl with short reddish hair stared into the camera with bloodshot eyes. The caption said she was eighteen, but she looked much younger.

"Please, don't open the box," she said. "It's a cruel, sick joke. And it messes with your head. Whoever did this..."

"Would you mind telling our viewers what your card said?"

The girl – woman – hesitated, shifting her weight from one foot to the other.

"Eileen? Could you—"

"It said I will get my dream job. I've always wanted to be a film director so that's nice... if it's true, but..." She rubbed her forehead. "But it also said that I will be *raped*."

She blurted out the last word in such a way that the microphone picked it up too loudly and it boomed into the homes of everyone watching, slapping them in the face.

"I hope it's not true," she said, wrapping her arms around her chest. She started rocking on the balls of her feet, repeating it over and over again. "I hope it's not true."

The camera panned away from Eileen and fixed on the reporter.

"So there you have it," she said. "One box. Two futuristic facts. Hex or hoax? What do you think? Have you opened yours? Let us know by—"

Jack switched off the television and turned to Diana, his voice brooking no argument.

"We aren't going to open our boxes."

"No," she said. "No, we aren't."

"Ever."

"Let's burn them," she said. "Right now. So we aren't tempted."

He regarded her for a moment. "Alright," he said. "Let's burn them to dust."

The event became known as The Day of a Million Boxes, The Apostalypse and Boxageddon. Everyone was blamed from psychologists to activists and comedians. At one point, there was even a rumour of intoxicated disgruntled postmen, but that didn't last long. None of them stuck. The box… *thing* was on too grand a scale, too widespread.

Every single person in the country over the age of eighteen got a box at exactly the same time. Even the homeless.

It was like Santa Claus had taken LSD and gone on a really bad trip.

But, as with most things, after a while life carried on, other news stories took precedence and most people put the boxes out of their minds.

Until five years later.

***

It was a brisk morning in early April. Jack stood in their front garden scratching his beard and pretending to examine the hedge, steadfast in his promise not to embarrass his teenage daughter. Obscured by the overgrown hedge, he watched as she safely ascended the school bus to join her friends.

Only then did he nod emphatically to himself, hoping to look like a man deciding something very important, and returned inside to join his wife, presumably to discuss the future of said hedge.

However, his footsteps slowed to a halt before he made it to the kitchen table.

"What's wrong?" he asked.

Diana held her phone loosely in one hand, but she wasn't looking at it. Her favourite breakfast of poached eggs and sliced avocado sat untouched, her full cup of tea cooling to one side.

"You remember that girl, Eileen Ashbury?"

"Of course." Everyone remembered. The press had followed her story. Her tragic decline from understandable paranoia to full-blown insanity until she was admitted to a psychiatric ward after nearly killing the postman. So much for 'film director'. Proof, many said, that the cards were utter nonsense.

"What's happened to her now?"

Diana put her phone on the table.

"She's been raped."

Jack's eyes widened. "H-*How*?"

"Another patient did it."

"Oh my god." He slumped into the chair opposite. "Does this mean..."

Diana shrugged. "She never would have been in there if it wasn't for reading that card in the first place, but we still don't know what it means."

He sighed. "We probably won't until we're old and crumbly. If we ever do."

Diana tried to hide it, but he saw her flinch at his words.

Nevertheless, he kept his peace, reached out, entwined his fingers in hers and gave them a squeeze.

She'd tell him when she was ready.

***

That day came many years later when Analise, glowing with pride, announced that she was pregnant. Jack let the emotions wash over him, excitement all mixed up with wonder and love. He ignored the thread of shock and terror he sensed in Diana until after Analise left the house.

His wife's tears were not purely of joy, not even close.

"It's soon, isn't it?"

"Wh— What?"

He cupped her beautiful face in his hands. "You've always been a dreadful liar. It's one of the many things I love about you."

"You *know*? Why didn't you say anything before?"

"Because I don't like the idea of not being in control of what happens to me. I *like* not knowing. That's why I didn't read my card, but you obviously read yours and…" He sighed, stroking his thumb across her cheek. "You should see the way you behave sometimes, like it's a given you won't get hurt. And the way you look at me, so heartbroken it makes me want to cry. It's like you're already grieving and it's hard to pretend I don't see it."

Her shoulders slumped. "I've tried so hard not to let it show. I didn't want you to…" Diana bit back a sob. "Oh Jack, I'm so sorry."

"It's OK," he said softly, pulling her into his chest. He wound a lock of her hair round his finger.

"How can you be so calm?"

"I've had a while to get used to the idea," he said.

"However vague."

Diana couldn't hold back any longer. She wept as Jack kissed the top of her head and his tears fell onto her cheek. They shuddered in each other's grasp, neither wanting to let go.

They stayed that way for a very long time.

Twenty years earlier, under the staccato white light of a thunderstorm, Diana peeled back the brown paper, unfolded the cardboard flaps and picked up her card.

You will live to see your grandchildren grow up.

Swallowing, she turned it over.

You will be widowed before your first grandchild is born.

***

"I saw 'The Other Side' last night, have you seen it?" Analise asked, strolling along, one hand resting on her swollen belly.

"No," Jack said. "What is it?"

"It's a documentary about the boxes, directed by Eileen Ashbury." Diana tripped, but Jack caught her. Analise didn't notice and continued, "You really should watch it. It was dead interesting. It followed the lives of five different people who opened their boxes, whether or not the things on their cards had happened and in what way. Quite scary really."

"Were there some things that didn't come true?" Diana asked. To her credit, her voice remained steady, but Jack slid his arm around her waist all the same.

"Well, yes, but they could still come true. We won't know for sure until someone dies who didn't have their bad or good thing happen. And there's the question of proof..." Analise pulled a face and halted, casting quick looks up and down the footpath. "Uh..."

Jack's pulse quickened.

"Annie? Are you alright? Is it—"

"It's OK, Dad," she said, shuffling off into the bushes. "I just need a wee."

"Oh."

Spring sunlight slanted through the trees on either side of the footpath. Geese honked and songbirds twittered. Jack brought Diana in for a hug and a kiss.

"How much longer do you think I've got?"

"Don't say that! We burnt the boxes, maybe that means it doesn't count. And just because it's been true for some people doesn't mean... it's probably a load of rubbish... I don't believe it." Her mouth set in a stubborn line. "I won't."

"You're right, of course," he said. "Still, can't help but wonder sometimes." He paused and looked up at the cloudless blue sky. "Especially on days like this. This wouldn't be such a bad last day."

A grey squirrel bounded across the path right in front of them, paused for a second at the edge of the footpath, and darted up a tree. Branches swayed, marking its passage through the canopy. With a rustle, Analise returned, smoothing her skirts and looked sidelong at her parents.

"I've asked you before, but did you ever open your boxes?"

"No," Jack said, "we never did."

"Mum?"

"Nope, never looked. I swear."

Analise grinned, and Jack felt the relief flooding out of her.

"Good," she said. "That's what everyone should have

done, I reckon." She fussed with her skirts a little more before adding, "Since it doesn't matter anymore, I have a confession for you both. I, uh, swapped the name tags."

Jack and Diana froze. "What?"

"The name tags on the boxes," she repeated. "While you were watching the film, I got up to go to the loo and on my way back I untied the tags and swapped them. I don't know why. I did the same thing with the salt and the pepper too, remember?" She laughed and patted her stomach. "I suppose I've got all that to look forward to, eh? Mum?... Dad?"

Jack cleared his throat, but any words died long before they reached his mouth. The air seemed to vibrate around them and time slowed.

"Yes," Diana said at last, breaking the spell. Gently, reverently, she reached out and tucked a loose strand of hair behind her daughter's ear. "Lots to look forward to."

Wavemaster

Hunched over and with one arm hooked around the poop deck's handrail, I try to study Master Orin's movements as he steadily funnels Air into the ship's main sail. But it's no use. I'm too far away. My eyes and nostrils sting from the fine sea mist and my cotton tunic is completely soaked. I grit my teeth. This voyage is my last chance to prove myself and I'm already failing.

To my right, at the ship's wheel, Captain Rast and her first mate, Barty, are discussing longitude and wind speed.

"At this rate," the captain says, "we'll be in Terremon within ten days, maybe less."

When I slip and crack my knee on the decking, neither of them looks in my direction, and I'm relieved. It's been three days since we lost sight of land and I'm still stumbling about like a drunk, but at least I've stopped throwing up.

The crew is a mixture of muscular men and women garbed in loose tan breeches cinched at the waist and ankles. Most are shirtless save for a few of the more buxom women. I think I understand why as one of them swings from the rigging at high speed, passing a rope from one side to the other and then back again. My hands ache from gripping the railing too tight.

I try to imagine myself as Captain Rast: black bandanna trimmed with gold, one impeccable braid of hair hanging between my shoulder blades, snapping off orders, indisputably in charge. The difference between us makes my insides shrink.

Captain Rast casts me a dark look over her shoulder and I straighten, forcing my chin up.

"Are you going to help him?" she asks, though it sounds more like an accusation.

On the main deck, Master Orin moves backwards and forwards, left and right, arms rising and falling. In my mind's eye, I see the High Dancers at the Mage's Plateau demonstrating this process using vibrant coloured ribbons, depicting the elemental flows. Preparing us for what we will see if we advance far enough.

If.

My textbook, *Advanced Oceanic Behaviour,* currently tucked under my bunk below deck, details the nature of the energy flows Master Orin is manipulating. The formation of waves, thunderstorm theory, raindrop analysis... I have it all memorised. No student scored higher than me on the Elemental Weaves examination.

And yet, I still can't see them.

Captain Rast repeats her question.

"Yes," I say, "I'll go in a minute. I just need to, um, catch my breath."

Before turning away, she fixes me with a scathing look, and I don't blame her.

On the first day, I ripped a massive hole through one of the mizzen sails. That's what happens when students play with elements they can't actually see. The crew went ballistic, immediately unfurling a spare sail, gesticulating wildly, cursing the entire time. Master Orin had rested his warm hand on my back as I buried my face in my hands.

"Nerida," he said, "you must learn to control your strength. It's not enough for you to be stronger than anyone has seen for centuries. The rules are the same for everyone: if you cannot harness your power, you will be severed."

Severed with Magend potion. Never again to sense or wield the elements. I shuddered. Anything but that.

The sail was replaced and I haven't broken anything else, but I'm still mortified and struggle to look any of the crew in the eye. Ironically, I'd wanted to impress the captain on that first day. If only—

"Nerida!"

It's Master Orin. I can't stall any longer. Quick as I can, I descend to the main deck and make my way across using one of the lines for purchase. Within seconds I reach him and put one hand on the central mast to steady myself. He smiles.

"Would you be so kind," he says, "as to climb up to the Dragon's Nest and tell me what you see?"

My eyes bulge. "Climb the mast?"

He nods, casually, as if he's asking me to pass the sugar. Realising my hand is resting on the rope ladder, I snatch it away. Why is he asking me to do this? A wavemaster doesn't need to be up there to do their job, and I've told him about my fear of heights. I want to say it's not fair, but I know how that would sound.

My mouth dries up.

Suddenly, I am eleven years old again, sprinting away from my tormentors. Those nasty boys and girls from the orphanage, and one in particular who discovered his weaving skills early. They chased me along the sea wall, over the rise and all the way to the bluff where I fell to my knees. Cornered.

I can still feel the terror as I was wrapped in flows of Air and lifted high above the cliffs, twisted upside down so my skirts fell over my head. Below, the sea whorled, crashing into jagged rocks, rushing and groaning like the mouth of a giant foaming monster.

Blind panic and shame consumed me as I could do nothing but weep and plead for them to leave me alone. Sometimes, I can still hear their cruel laughter…

I look at the ladder. It stretches up, farther and farther, all the way to a tiny wooden cup balanced on top of the mast: the Dragon's Nest. My neck is craned to such a point that I stumble three steps backwards before catching myself.

Master Orin tilts his head to one side. "Nerida?"

"I— I can't." I lean forwards, hoping the captain can't hear me. "Please don't make me."

His disappointment is palpable as he wraps one arm around my shoulders and turns me portside. His other arm takes in the ocean in one sweeping gesture.

"What do you see, Nerida?"

"Flows of Air and Water," I say automatically. I point at the grey clouds. "Water is more abundant there than anywhere else in the sky. It's condensing. Air pushes over the water, forming waves—"

"That is what you know," he says. "Not what you see." His voice takes on the cadence of the patient teacher. "First, find the Void. Let the world fall away, let yourself fall, for the Void is peace, harmony and acceptance."

I try to focus. *Let the world fall away.* Master Orin pulls me tight as I stagger to one side. How am I supposed to concentrate when I can barely find my own feet? His hand squeezes my shoulder and I try again, forcing the burning seasickness down. I lift my arms—

"You're too soft with her, Elias." I blink. Captain Rast is standing off to the side, arms folded under her chest, face set in staunch disapproval. "She needs a firm hand."

"Nix, please," he says, "leave it to me."

Nix? Elias? I didn't realise they were so close.

"Make her climb the mast. She'll never manage it if she doesn't try."

"That is not my way."

"But she's not getting it, is she? We've been friends a long time and I can see when you're stuck with a slothslug of a student."

A muscle in my cheek twitches. A *slothslug*?

"What's your problem with me?" I blurt it out, cringing at how petulant I sound, but it's too late.

Captain Rast turns those black eyes on me. It's impossible to tell what she's thinking. Is it anger I'm seeing or mild irritation? Could it be contempt? She smiles sweetly, but I know I'm not going to like what's coming.

"Child," she says, "I don't usually make time for anyone who doesn't strive to be the best they can be, but Elias is an old friend and he cares about you. My problem is this: win or lose, succeed or fail, it doesn't really matter as long as you're trying your hardest." She glares, her gaze implacable. "You are not trying."

It takes a moment for her words to sink in before my outrage is fully triggered.

Clenching my fists, I prepare to tell her that I am not a sailor, that I am better than that. This ship requires a wavemaster because she is incapable of doing the things that I can. However, a small sharp gesture from her halts my words before they even reach my lips.

"I must speak with Elias alone, child," she says. "You are dismissed."

Below deck in the crew mess, I shovel in my mixed bean stew and soak up the juice with salty sea bread. I eat mechanically, not tasting anything. My stomach is on fire, my core shaking. How dare she say I'm not trying!

The day I discovered I was a weaver, that I could sense the elements and learn to wield them, was the best day of my life. The same day I was sent to the Broken Mountains. To the Mage's Plateau high above the city where I met Master Orin. I'm incredibly strong, so they say, but that won't matter if I can't control it. Maybe I could run away, but to where?

The recurring memory of myself racing away from my childhood bullies prods at me. Skirt hanging over my face, black glistening rocks below. I would have landed headfirst, my face mutilated beyond recognition.

Bah! I shove my bowl away, disgusted with how pathetic and whiney my own internal voice sounds. Maybe Captain Rast has a point. I sit up straighter. I am an apprentice weaver at the Mage's Plateau. Time to start acting like it.

A bell clangs and all the sailors leap to their feet. Bowls and jugs clatter to the floor. I know that signal. Danger.

No more running.

The storm is devastating; the noise unbearable. In every direction, the ocean swells like liquid mountains of death as we sail through an agonisingly narrow corridor of smooth waters.

Master Orin hasn't moved. His feet are like solid blocks while his arms flail about, executing their commands. Sweat drips from his forehead. He can't keep this up much longer. I need to link with him so he can pull from my personal well of elemental energy.

I make haste, but before I reach him, a warning shout breaks through the roar of howling wind and churning seas. In slow motion, the thick mizzen boom sweeps from one side of the deck to the other and cracks into Master Orin's head, knocking him face-down on the deck.

He doesn't get up.

Captain Rast's voice immediately rips through the air like a thunderclap.

"ALL HANDS ON DECK! WAVEMASTER IS DOWN! SECURE ALL LINES!"

Stunned, I follow as two crewmen lift Master Orin, carry him to the aft deck and lash him tight to a bench. His head lolls from side to side, a thin trickle of blood coming out of his left ear. I wish for his eyes to open, for his limp fingers to twitch.

Without him, our pocket of calm disintegrates and the deck lurches violently to one side, forcing me to grab hold of the railing.

Captain Rast whips her head around. "You! Can you weave at all? Anything?"

I gulp. Not without Master Orin. I wish I could do something other than shake my head, but lying would do no good either. Her attention is instantly back on her crew.

"GET THAT QUARTER MAST DOWN! HOLD YOUR POSITIONS! HOLD THEM!"

Wind batters me from every direction. Torrents of water thwack down on the deck as the ship tilts, its angle precarious, on tremendous black waves.

In an instant, I see my lifeless, bloated body washed up on some distant, undiscovered shore. Who would miss me? I can think of no one except Master Orin and he is unlikely to survive a shipwreck bound in place as he is.

I should have known it would end like this. Destroyed by the very element I have been training for years to conquer.

Captain Rast screams, her voice somehow carrying over the tumult. How does she do that? We don't stand a chance, but at least she's doing something. She won't go down without a fight—

I clamp my hand down on Captain Rast's rock-hard shoulder. "I can try."

"WHAT?"

"I CAN TRY!"

Her crazed smile makes me feel proud and terrified all at once.

I drop to a crouch, grab the nearest deck line and begin my advance. I skid and fall, smacking my shoulder. It burns and I continue on all fours until I reach the central mast.

Already breathless, I grapple with the rope ladder and begin to climb. The wind is ferocious, whipping my hair across my face, in my mouth. Salt water stings my eyes, blinding me, and my shoulder screams as I pull myself higher.

Every second feels interminable, but I keep going. One hand over the other. Below, sailors slip and slide, their bodies tethered to the mast or rigging.

Then, my foot finds dead air.

My body swings out. I look down. The ladder is no longer attached to the deck, its frayed ends flap and thrash in the wind. Then, I am hurtling back towards the mast, the impending impact certain to toss me overboard.

No! I hook my other leg around the ladder just in time.

The collision is terrible. I cough, tasting blood and my head spins. My fingers are crushed, numb, my grip becoming slack.

I fall.

But my leg — the one wrapped around the ladder — holds.

I am upside down, dripping blood. Through the rain curtain, I see Master Orin. One of the straps binding him in place has come loose. It won't be long before he is lost to us forever. My vision blurs and refocuses on Captain Rast. She stares with such intensity I feel as if I've been slapped. Fire rages in the pit of my belly.

I will not give up.

Engaging my entire core, I curl upwards, grasp the ladder and pull. My lungs ache, the muscles in my chest tearing as I force myself onwards, concentrating on the rope until at last my fingers touch wood: Dragon's Nest.

I snatch the rope harness and knot it around my waist tight enough so the coarse fibres dig into my skin. Forcing my quivering knees to straighten, I stand and look out. The ocean stretches as far as I can see in every direction, dark and angry, tipped with thundercloud foam. Far off, on the starboard side, lightning flashes and thunder rolls.

Find the Void.

I close my eyes and focus, willing those words to drown out the storm. It sinks to a low, distant rumble. Further away.

Further.

Accept what you are.

The silence is pure and still.

I hear nothing but my own breath, my own heart beating.

Feel the flows that make our world. Find the one you require. See it. Know it. Imagine a bond linking that element to your Spirit through the Void, and then…

Seize it.

I open my eyes.

Seconds have passed, but the world is transformed. The ocean is an intricate woven tapestry of water currents, spinning through the wave crests and whorling beneath. The dark clouds sparkle, pregnant with raindrops eager to fall. Water flows over the deck, cresting the wood like liquid silver peaked with midnight-blue.

The crew are human-shaped blobs struggling about their

preposterously small craft. What were they thinking?

I cannot master the whole ocean, but I can do something to aid this ship.

Directly ahead of the bow, I smooth the currents. Flattening them, bending the flows of water to my will. They try to resist, but I am strong. I need only forge a small path. The ship's violent rocking eases as the waters below the hull calm.

Captain Rast, locked to the helm, stares up at me, nods and shouts new commands. Hauling the wheel around, keeping the ship on course for the pathway I have created.

My entire body is effervescing. I can feel everything. Relief washes over me as I sense Master Orin's consciousness. A gentle probing of his form with Spirit tells me that he'll recover, though I don't fully understand how I know that. I still have a lot to learn.

The crew lets out a rapturous cheer with Captain Rast's voice audible above all others. I throw back my head and holler, the power still surging through me. In this moment, there is nothing I can't do. Nothing I can't overcome.

And I will be—

No. I *am*…

Wavemaster.

The Last Christmas

This story takes place in those magical weeks leading up to Christmas Day when chorists sing and church bells sound. But you're not going to like it.

***

It begins with husband and father Allan Wicken pulling down the attic's rickety metal ladder. His wife, Victoria, grimaces as it clicks and clacks before thumping down on the maroon hallway carpet.

"Careful," she says, handing him the torch.

He mounts the steps and his head disappears from view.

"Jeez," he says, "I always forget how dusty it is up here."

"They should be on the left."

"I know." His feet move to the top rung and stop. "I put them there."

One by one, he hands down the decorations, neat and ordered in their clear plastic boxes. One of them clinks and tinkles and Victoria smiles: it's the sleigh bells.

"Do you think Jess knows Santa isn't real?" she asks.

"What?" Allan bends, lowering his head to look at her. He whispers, "He's not real?"

Victoria chuckles. "I just hope she doesn't tell Robbie. It's so lovely when they still belie—"

Her smile vanishes. She is staring at a point behind Allan's shoulder.

"What was that?" she asks.

"What?"

"Something moved behind you."

He straightens. Torchlight flicks from side to side.

"A big something, or a small something?"

"Small… Oh god, do we have bats?"

"Maybe."

He coughs again and hands down the last box.

"I'll call someone, but they probably won't come until the New Year."

Victoria shudders. "I hate bats. How long do you think they've been up there?"

"Dunno. Could be a while, but I wouldn't worry." He descends the ladder, his boots clanking with each step. "Better not tell the kids though."

Job done, Allan pushes the ladder upwards. It smacks shut in a puff of dust. Stifling another cough, he picks up a box and winks at Victoria.

"Shall we?"

Downstairs, their black Labrador, Doogle, pants and snuffles at the boxes, spiced hot chocolate and festive fuzzy socks.

"Where did you get this tree?" Victoria asks. She snips off the top with the kitchen scissors, making room for the star. "It's so big!"

Allan taps the side of his nose and little Robbie copies him, giggling as Doogle licks his face.

Jess hands her mother the red tinsel, which hisses as Victoria winds it round and round the fir branches, taking care not to entangle it with the lights. Doogle, fascinated by everything, keeps spinning in circles and thwacking Jess' legs with his tail. She ignores him and reaches into the next box.

Ah, the bells.

They love the bells. Those that adorn the tree are red and silver whilst a special pair, which are ivory-white and much larger than the others, rest atop the mantelpiece suspended by a small wooden frame. Victoria nudges them and they begin to ring. The children squeal in delight.

"Sleigh bells! Santa's coming!"

Allan's laugh quickly descends into a coughing fit and Victoria shoots him a worried look. She hopes he isn't getting sick right before the holiday break. That would be such bad luck.

Abruptly, Doogle stops his sniffing and stiffens, pointing his nose directly at the tree. Victoria cocks her head to one side.

"What is it, boy?"

She barely finishes speaking when Doogle goes completely berserk. Bounding from one spot to another, his upper lip curled back, twisting away from Allan as he grabs his collar and pulls him out of the room. He puts Doogle outside, thinking that will calm him down, but if anything, his barks become more urgent.

"I wonder what that was about," Allan says.

In the distraction, Robbie has crawled between his sister's legs and beneath the tree, eager to touch one of the bells, but his tiny hand finds something else.

"Muuuuum!"

Jess pulls her brother out from under the tree and helps him to his feet. Her face pales. Blood, bright red, is pouring down his arm. Victoria gasps, picks him up and whisks him into the kitchen. She inspects the wound, fearing lacerated tendons, and her horror abates. It's not deep. A big plaster should do. She kisses his forehead and holds his teary face in her hands.

"It'll be okay. Hold your arm up like this for a while. It'll stop the bleeding."

"Is it alright?" Allan asks, ambling to the back door. Cupped hands full of jagged glass.

"Yes," she says. "What was it?"

"A bauble."

"But the baubles aren't made of glass," she says. "They're made of plastic. They're shatterproof."

He picks up one fragment with his thumb and index finger. "Well, this one wasn't."

"Where did that come from? I didn't buy it."

"Neither did I." He shrugs. "Weird."

Victoria cuddles Robbie whilst her husband disposes of the broken glass. Back in the living room, Jess trips and stumbles into the tree, making a couple of bells fall to the floor with soft muffled dings.

***

Christmas creeps closer.

Every day, Victoria sinks further into despair as Allan's cough worsens, racking his chest at all hours of the night. His face slackens, pales and droops, his eyes underscored with gravestone grey.

Robbie's hand heals nicely, but he is plagued with nightmares of an unseen creature chasing him, snatching at his heels. Jess' face is creased in worry, for her brother, for her father. She knows something is wrong, that there is an otherness lurking nearby.

Doogle's hatred for the tree changes to a fearful wariness. He stays back, growling at it from the edge of the living room.

As the days tick by, Victoria fails to shake off the cold

seeping into her bones. Even in front of the fire, she shivers. Snow falls, blanketing the street in white. It swirls in the wind, kissing the window panes, and a stillness settles upon their home.

But it doesn't last.

***

Midnight presses around Victoria as she throws back the duvet. Allan's voice had been coarse like worn rope by the time he went to bed. She rests the back of her hand against his forehead and yanks it away. His skin is feverish: searing and clammy. Tutting, she shrugs on her thick green dressing gown and eases open the bedroom door.

She slinks downstairs and heads to the kitchen cupboard where they keep the medicine. There must be something for a fever. *Let's see. Headache, sore joints, ah, here it is.* She takes the packet of tablets, pours a glass of water from the tap, turns around—

and drops the glass

It shatters.

Cold water splashes her bare ankles and toes; shards skitter across the laminate flooring. She dodges the glass and rushes into the living room. The carpet is soft on the soles of her feet, and then her knees as she sinks down next to the body.

"Doogle?" she says. "Come on boy, wake up."

The words stick in her throat, choking her because she already knows. He's not moving. There's no flick to his ears as she strokes his head, no gentle rise and fall of his belly, no snuffling snore.

"Doogle. Doogle, please."

She pulls his head into her lap and her fingers brush

against something just under his nose. Something that rustles.

Instinctively, she jerks her hand away and then, slowly, turns his head to see what is poking out of his mouth.

It's tinsel. Shiny, red tinsel.

She whips her gaze to the Christmas tree that stands darkly in the corner. Looming. She blinks. There's no tinsel on it. None at all. He can't have eaten all of it, can he?

As if in answer to her thoughts, the tree ripples, and the sleigh bells chime. The fir darkens, swishing slightly in an absence of wind, sucking at the surrounding shadows. Oozing. Victoria is too horrified to speak. Her legs are numb, immovable.

The tree quivers and *coughs*, injecting a grey miasma into the air. It spreads. Concealed in the slanted shadows it slithers up the stairs and along the floorboards that do not creak, searching for those small bodies that breathe in shallow whispers.

It will find them.

It always does.

"Mum?" Jessie's little voice carries from her bedroom.

"Jess!" She doesn't mean for her voice to crack so loudly in the stillness, but it does. "Go wake Dad and Robbie and get out of the house! We all need to get out of the house!"

For once, her daughter doesn't argue. Bare feet patter and a door opens. Victoria faces the tree.

It's bigger, growing and melding into the night. A shiny bauble shoots out and smashes into her face. She yelps and doubles over. Blood pools in her mouth. The taste of rusted metal.

"Mum! There's something wrong with Dad! He won't wake up!"

Fighting back the panic, she shouts, "Just get you and

Robbie out of here! Run next door and tell them to call the fire brigade!"

"But—"

"NOW!"

Jess and Robbie dart downstairs and out the front door. It bangs closed, but she doesn't look. Her focus is on the evil tree and the fireplace with its glowing embers. She spits, wipes her mouth with her sleeve.

Allan won't wake up. She tries to remember when he'd first started coughing. He'd blamed the attic, but that was also the same day he brought home the tree.

As if crazed, the bells shriek, their melody discordant and shrill. Victoria grasps a half-charred log from the fireplace and aims it at the centre of the black quivering mass.

Flames explode, frightening in their haste to consume. Frantic, they leap higher and higher. Within seconds, the room is clogged with smoke, the heat scorching her skin. She tries to crawl away, keeping low, her cheek pressed to the singed carpet where the air is just about breathable.

She doesn't get far before something stops her. She looks back to see that her leg is ensnared in Christmas tree lights, the green wire digging into her flesh. It drags her back.

"Nooooo!"

Flailing, she claws at the carpet, at the edges of the stone fireplace, desperate to find something, anything to grip. Inch by inch, she is drawn deeper into the tar-like fog, screaming as blackness devours her.

The last thing Victoria ever hears is the crackle of crimson fire and the ringing, ringing, ringing of the bells.

***

I'll leave you now to your festivities and if I've left you with any uneasiness, any unwanted bells tinkling and jingling in your mind, well, can't say I didn't warn you.

Playing with Your Food

Jessica suppressed a shudder as their host, Alessandra, swept out of the room.

"I'll be back... shortly."

Holding the crystal champagne flute away from her lips, Jessica turned to her friend, Elayne, who was lounging back on the plush, velvet cushions.

"I think we should go."

"Why?"

"I don't trust her."

Elayne shuffled forwards and poured herself another glass. "You're being paranoid."

"No, I'm not. The rich don't invite people like us back for champagne. It doesn't make sense."

"Maybe she's lonely. She probably likes us because we're" —Elayne waved her free hand, searching for the right word— "normal."

"She must want something from us."

"Yeah, company."

"I don't like it."

"Oh, drink your champagne. Loosen up."

Jessica ostentatiously placed her glass on the low marble table and folded her arms. "I'm going."

"You can't leave me here!"

"Oh? Why not?"

"It's rude!"

"Is everything... alright?" Alessandra asked, her

sequinned dress winking as she glided over, holding a black slate finessed with cheese and crackers.

Elayne grinned. "Oh, thank you so much. I love cheese. What's this one?"

Alessandra ignored the question and fixed her gaze on Jessica. "Something… wrong?"

"No."

Jessica winced; she'd said that too fast, too hard. Alessandra stiffened and tension threaded through the air.

"I'm just tired." Jessica forced a smile. "I'm not used to staying up so late."

"Shame." Alessandra's dark eyes flashed. "There are plenty of bedrooms. You could… stay."

Jessica's gut squirmed, screaming at her to run. "That's very kind of you, but—"

Elayne slumped, groaning; her glass slipped from her fingers and into her lap, spilling champagne.

"Elayne!"

Alessandra grinned, her mouth suddenly too wide for her face, displaying sharp sawlike teeth.

"You want to run? Run." She rolled her shoulders and sighed. "I could do with the… exercise."

I Don't Believe in Fairies

As a sleepy sun dipped below the wobbly orange horizon, pulling its thick twinkling blanket overhead, two very determined fairies prepared themselves for the night shift.

Alette wriggled into her midnight-black bodysuit, tucking her pointy ears and wisps of pink hair beneath a black cap. Then, she pulled on a pair of leather gloves and flexed her fingers.

"You ready to smash our quota tonight?" Zeph asked. Equally enshrouded from head to toe in black, her partner adjusted his wide belt and body harness so they didn't catch on his wings.

"Yes. I'm ready," she said, stretching one arm out to the side. "We can't let those overgrown pixies win. We've earned that bonus. It's ours."

She inspected her right wing, where a ragged tear ripped through the smooth surface and sprinkled a few grains of luminous magic dust. The hole glowed and shimmered like dawn sunlight dancing over the sea and, just like that, the tear was gone. The wing intact.

Zeph nodded, checked the various tooth compartments ridged along his belt straps one last time and, grinning, held out his hand.

"Come on then. Let's go get those teeth."

***

Cassandra smoothed Peter's hair back out of his eyes and tucked the duvet tight around his little body, just the way he liked it.

"There," she said. "Snug as a bug in a rug."

"Will the tooth fairy come tonight?" he asked in a hushed whisper.

His curtains were slightly parted; the room lit by the pale glow of moonlight. Cool summer air, scented with lavender from the back garden, wafted through the window that Cassandra had left open by a few inches, to allow the tooth fairy passage, of course.

"Yes," she said. "When you're fast asleep, the tooth fairy will come."

After a moment, he asked, "Does the tooth fairy grant wishes?"

Cassandra hesitated, sensing where this was going. "I don't think so, sweetheart. She's not that kind of fairy."

Peter looked towards the open window, his gaze far away.

"Will Daddy ever come home?" he asked quietly.

"He can't, sweetie," she said, fighting to keep the tears at bay. The backs of her eyes burned and when she swallowed it hurt as if a crumpled sheet of sandpaper were wedged in her throat. "But what I do know is that he misses you and loves you very, very much."

Silence crept over them both, bringing with it a sad blanket of happy memories.

"The other boys at school say the tooth fairy doesn't exist."

"They don't know what they're talking about," she said, more fiercely than intended. "Of course she exists. You'll see in the morning when you look under your pillow."

She prayed she sounded convincing as she reached over

to his bedside table and picked up his bedtime story book: Peter Pan.

"Now," she said, shuffling into position. "Where were we?"

***

Zeph secured yet another tooth in his belt and gave Alette a wide grin. "We're so lucky! Five in one house! Boo-yah!"

They were indeed smashing it, but that didn't mean they were top of their unit. They wouldn't find out until they returned to Fae HQ with their satchel of milk teeth under the dreamy haze of predawn.

"The night is young," Alette said. "We still have a newbie on our grid who hasn't triggered the sleep sensor yet."

"That's normal. They're always super excited the first time, trying to stay awake to catch a glimpse of us. We can always leave that one until we've finished the others."

Alette rounded on him. "Rule number three: *never* leave a newbie until last! What if the tooth is put somewhere other than the pillow? It could take us ages to find it and even longer to carry out the swap before the parent returns. And what if we're so late that the tooth has already been removed? What do we do then? Huh?"

"Wo" —Zeph held up his hands— "I'm sorry. If you want, we can swing by and assess the situation right now, just to be on the safe side."

"Good idea," she said. "We are getting that bonus. It was snatched away from us last year, but not this time. Oh no. It's *our* turn." She sighed. "A year's supply of magic dust," she said wistfully. "Can you imagine?"

Zeph knew all too well. Magic dust was very versatile and a large amount would mend the tear in Alette's wing permanently.

"Don't get me wrong, Alette," he said. "It would be fantastic, but it wouldn't be the end of the world if we don't win either. There are other things."

Alette snorted. "Yeah, right. What's better than magic?"

***

"Stars are beautiful, but they may not take part in anything, they must just look on forever," Cassandra read, a smile on her lips. That was her favourite line from Peter Pan and an apt place to stop. She closed the book and placed it on the bedside table.

"That's enough for tonight."

Peter yawned, turned over and lifted up his pillow to check on his tooth. It was still there.

"She won't come until you're asleep!" She prodded him, hoping for a giggle. But Peter just sighed and faced the wall.

Cassandra didn't move. Sitting on the edge of his bed, she stroked his hair and hummed a soft melody to her precious little lump. She wished for happy dreams, for wondrous faraway lands and magical creatures, for adventures and laughter. He was too small to already know that life isn't fair, that it is sometimes shockingly cruel.

His breathing slowed and deepened. Cassandra leant forwards and kissed the top of his head. As she did so, her right hand slid under his pillow and, in one swift movement, swapped his tooth for a shiny ten pence piece that she'd buffed until it gleamed unnaturally bright.

As she lifted herself off the bedsheets and crept away, Peter mumbled something so quiet that she almost didn't hear. The words were daggers to her heart.

"I don't believe in fairies."

***

Lurking in the curtain's shadow, just to the left of the gentle cascade of moonlight, Zeph was trying to calm his partner down, but he may as well have attempted charming the stars down from the sky. Alette was apoplectic.

"Did you see that? DID YOU SEE THAT?" She strode back and forth, wings vibrating with rage. "She swapped the tooth! Straight away! Who does that?"

"Hey, at least we were here to see it happen. This means we can take immediate action."

Alette paused. "You're right. We're going to have to follow the mother. See where she goes."

"Or" —Zeph thrust out one arm to stop Alette in her tracks— "we wait for her to go to sleep and then look for the tooth. We can't risk being seen, Alette. Forget the bonus. We'd be fired, maybe worse."

"I'm willing to take that risk," she said, pushing past his arm. "Are you coming or not?"

Zeph darted his eyes around the room. The boy hadn't stirred. A cursory glance revealed no evidence of pets and his milktooth sensor indicated no other children, so that just left the parents.

He wouldn't let Alette face the danger alone. That wasn't him. Still, loving someone this headstrong sometimes made his own head feel like bursting with frustration. If only he could make her see how magnificent she was even with a damaged wing.

Maybe then she would stop trying to prove herself over and over again. She didn't need to be the best. As far as he was concerned, she'd achieved that a long time ago.

Pushing aside his worries, he fluttered his wings and rose

into flight, catching up with Alette just as she slipped into the darkened hallway.

"There's a TV on downstairs," she said.

"OK. You wait at the top of the stairs while I check the bedrooms. Don't move until I get back."

"As if I would do such a thing."

"I mean it, Alette."

She crossed her fingers over her heart and blew him a kiss. Despite everything, he felt the heat rising to his cheeks as he flew off. How did she do that?

There was only one other bedroom. It was pitch black save for a sliver of light coming through a gap between the curtains, which was more than enough for Zeph's purposes. The bed was empty; one side looked rumpled whilst the other was oddly smooth, the bedsheet still tucked underneath the mattress as if only one person ever slept in it.

Something on the bedside table caught his attention, making him fly over to investigate. It was a framed photograph. He recognised the mother and son. The man had to be the father and husband, but where was he?

Looking around, there was no evidence of a man's presence in this room. Zeph knew the signs and they weren't there. He looked at the photo again. It must have been taken recently for the boy didn't look much younger than he was now.

Where was the father? He shouldn't waste any more time, but as he turned to leave he noticed a small box half-hidden behind the frame. Inside, he found a wedding band and a lock of brown hair. Zeph hung his head. Gently, he closed the box, taking great care not to disturb the contents, and quietly left the bedroom.

He found Alette right where he'd left her.

"It's only the mother," he said. "I think..."

"Zeph? Are you alright?"

"I think the father died recently," he said. "It's just the two of them."

"Yeah, well, sometimes life is tough." Despite her harsh words, he saw her lip quiver, saw her force the emotion down. Why did she feel like she had to be so hard?

His fingertips brushed against her right hand which was closed in a fist. "Come on," he said.

Together, they descended the stairs and spied the mother bathed in the ethereal glow of the television. She wasn't looking at it though, her attention was captured by something she held in the palm of her hand.

"The tooth!" Alette grasped Zeph's arm and squeezed.

The mother was rolling it with her thumb, back and forth. As they watched, a tear fell and she lifted her head up, sniffing, revealing a wet, reddened face.

"Maybe we should let her keep it," Zeph said.

Alette shook her head, but her voice wavered as she said, "As long as we swap it when she's not looking, she'll never realise it's a fake. None of them ever do."

"True," he said, alighting on the bottom stair. He motioned for her to do the same. "I guess we'll just have to wait."

***

Cassandra placed the tooth on the coffee table and stood up, wiping her face with both hands. She moved over to the living room windows and looked out at the stars, breathing in the crisp night air, feeling it caress her cheek.

Peter used to be such a happy little soul. Now, his world was edged with pain and dipped in sorrow. Will he ever be the same starry-eyed boy? Had his laugh forever lost its merry tinkle? She'd give anything to make him forget, if only for a moment, that life was hard and cruel and unfair. To let him be a kid again, all wide-eyed and glistening with unbridled joy. Was that really too much to ask?

"Are you up there, Jason?" she asked softly. "Watching over us?"

Her spine tingled. The sense that someone else was in the room draped itself over her.

It was a feeling she knew well. How many times had she turned around, a part of her – and not a small part – expecting to see Jason standing there as if nothing had happened. Gorgeous lop-sided grin pulling at the corners of his mouth, reassuring her that it was all a big mistake.

A flicker of movement in the window pane made her spin around, her eyes intent on the coffee table.

She froze.

And they froze.

Two tiny black-clad figures stood there and one held her son's baby tooth. She blinked. The doctor had warned her this might happen. That seeing things was one of the side effects of insomnia, but she couldn't care less. She welcomed the hallucination. It would probably only last a minute before the true weight of reality came back to crush her.

"What do you think you're doing with my son's tooth?" she said, stepping forwards. "That's it! Hands where I can see 'em. Drop the tooth!"

To her surprise, the two figures didn't disappear as she approached. Instead, they became clearer and more defined. Fairies, judging by their translucent, netted wings. This was getting weirdly vivid.

"We didn't want to alarm you, miss," the one on the right said in a deep voice that sounded far too loud to have come from something so very, very small. "My name's Zeph and this is Alette, we—"

"We just need the tooth."

Cassandra didn't like Alette's tone or the possessive way she held her son's tooth.

"That tooth is not yours to take," she said flatly. "Hand it over, or else."

Alette bristled. "Or else wha—"

Zeph yanked her around so they both had their backs to Cassandra, to whom he shot an apologetic smile. "Please excuse us for one moment."

She could hardly argue, but she didn't trust that Alette. They were very small. In all likelihood, if they decided to make a run for it — or fly — they would lose her with ease. What could she do? She had to do something, but what? The fairies' whispers became harder and sharper. They were arguing… and not focusing on what she was doing. Perfect.

"Alright," Alette said. "You can have the tooth." She sauntered forwards and placed it on the table, precisely where it had been.

Cassandra narrowed her eyes. "How can I be sure that's the same tooth?"

"What does it matter?" Alette said.

"It's not the same, is it?"

Zeph groaned.

"No," he said. "You're absolutely right, miss." Alette opened her mouth, but a sharp look from Zeph made her close it again. "We need to take your son's tooth. That's our job, you see. In exchange, we offer you an exact replica and… some magic fairy dust."

"WHAT ARE YOU DOING?" Alette grabbed his arm. "That's the last of our magic dust!"

Cassandra stepped forwards, revealing the two fly swatters she had hidden behind her back, and in one rapid movement, snapped them down over the fairies. As they struggled beneath the plastic mesh, Cassandra leant in, getting *real* close.

"Now, you listen to me, pixie," she said. "I'll let you keep the tooth, but first you're going to do something for me. This is what's going to happen…"

***

Alette and Zeph's hearts raced as they held tight to each other's sweaty hands. They were certain no tooth fairy had ever deliberately allowed a child to see them. With adults it wasn't so bad, they dismissed it and forgot, but children remembered. If caught, the punishment would be severe and the consequences better not dwelt on.

"Peter," Cassandra said, gently turning him round, nudging and nuzzling. "Peter, wake up."

"Mummy?"

He opened his eyes and frowned. Cassandra reached around and pulled him up into a sitting position. "Look."

Peter followed his mother's gaze and his jaw fell open.

"Hello, Peter," the fairies said.

"A-Are you—"

"Fairies?" Zeph asked. "Oh yes." He turned around, brandishing his exquisite, finespun wings.

"And hey," Alette said. "Watch this."

With a flourish, she emptied their pouch of magic dust into the midnight air; the golden particles whirled and blended together to form an image for Peter and Peter alone.

He gasped. "Daddy?"

The image wavered and morphed into the shape of a beautiful shining star. A star that vibrated and birthed millions of tiny sparkles which hung in the air like confetti before floating away towards the open window.

Leaving a trail of white luminescence, it rocketed up into the sky and found its place within the glittering night's canvas. To them, it shone brighter than any other.

"Your daddy will always be with you, Peter," Alette said, pointing to her own heart. "In here. And, up there, watching over you, forever."

"Th-Thank you."

"Your mother told us that you don't believe in fairies anymore," Zeph said. "That made us very sad."

Peter gulped, his big brown eyes swimming in silver starlight. "I'm sorry."

"Don't be sorry," Alette said, and the astonishing thing was she really meant it. As one, Alette and Zeph rose and glided over to kiss Peter on either cheek. "Just promise us," she said, "that you'll never stop believing."

With pure wonder glistening upon his little face, Peter nodded and said, "I promise."

At the window, Alette and Zeph paused and looked back one last time. Cassandra, her eyes brimming with joyful tears, mouthed her thanks and Peter waved, his smile breaking through the last fragments of Alette's armour.

"See," Zeph said, as they fluttered away into the night. "Some things *are* better than magic."

Wildflowers

Rose stood atop the escarpment on the western edge of their oasis, leaning on her walking stick. She watched the sun set, its final strip of light winking before it too was chased away by the encroaching darkness. That will be me soon, she thought. These old bones aren't much use to anyone now.

Below, the desert stretched out. Infinite and terrible. Shadows crept across the sands. Inching slowly in some places, leaping forwards in others until it was blanketed in night. She turned, sensing movement behind her.

"What are you doing out here, Granny?" a little voice said, stifling a yawn.

"I like to say goodbye to the sun. It reminds me of when I was a little girl. Like you, Lily." She let out a long, gentle sigh. "We used to rise with the sun in those days."

Lily squatted, her bare feet crunching on the yellow grass, feeling the residual warmth from the sand. Saguaros stood out along the ridge like sentinels and to their right, clusters of desert wildflowers grew, defiant, determined to survive. Lily fingered a small flower the colour of burnt sunset.

"What's this one called?"

"Apache plume."

Lily sighed. "I need poppies."

"The bright red ones are poppies, but you're not allowed to take them for yourself. Who asked you to get them?"

"Ma. She says her headaches are worse."

Rose bit the inside of her cheek.

"I'll make sure she gets some poppy seeds, but you're not to tell anyone, understand? Don't want us getting into trouble now, do we?"

"No, Granny."

Rose noted the lightness in Lily's voice: relief at being freed of her task. She shook her head. Fancy asking a child to break the law; she'd have strong words with Hyacinth later. Headache or no. The wind picked up, blowing dust across the starlit dunes. They tugged their cloaks tighter.

"Do you know what that flower is called?" Rose asked, pointing towards a star-shaped white blossom.

"Oh, yes. That's a lily."

"And did you know that my name is also a flower?"

"Rose?" Lily shook her head. "What do they look like?"

"Ah, beautiful. They were the flowers of romance. Gifted as a symbol of love, but I don't think they do well in hot weather. I haven't seen one in a long time. Not since before the Great Flood."

Lily's eyes widened. "You saw the Great Flood?"

"Oh yes," Rose said. "I am very, very old."

"How old are you, Granny? A hundred?"

Rose chuckled. "Not quite *that* old," she said. "I was born in 1999. I'm eighty-one."

A gust of sand blasted into Lily's open mouth. She spun round, coughing and spitting. Rose waited in amused silence. When she was younger, she'd never thought that one day she would be proud of her age, especially after having lied about it so much.

Her gaze drifted over the desert, over the dunes which rose and fell like dusky sea waves. If she tried hard enough, she could hear the crash of surf, feel the foamy tide between her toes. She glanced sidelong at Lily, wondering if her granddaughter would ever see the ocean. Lily huffed, shaking the gritty powder out of her cloak.

"What was it like?" she asked.

"The Great Flood?"

"No. What was it like *before*?"

"Oh." Rose cocked her head to one side. "It's hard to explain. It was... different. We tried to stop it from happening, but we were too late."

"What did you do?"

"Me? Not much really. I was part of a movement that campaigned and protested against climate change, the heating of the polar ice caps, deforestation... but even we didn't expect this." Rose swept one hand out in front of them, encompassing all that Lily knew. "No one expected this."

Rose's wrinkled hand gripped her walking stick tighter. Rarely did she speak of the past, but Lily's curiosity spurred her on. When she spoke again, her voice trembled.

"I remember when the sea boiled," she said. "Every single living creature in those waters died. I saw their lifeless bodies bobbing up and down. Millions and millions of them washed up on the shore."

Lily's face blanched or maybe it was the glow of moonlight. She was probably too young to hear these stories, but who else would tell her? Hyacinth never spoke of such things, being only a babe in arms when Rose made the journey.

To their right, a puff of sand particles announced the presence of a mouse. Its whiskers twitched and it scurried off, hopping down the sandy slope.

"I remember a lot that I'd rather forget."

"But you survived," Lily said. "You saved Ma and brought her here. She always talks about how brave and strong you are. That we're survivors."

Rose inclined her head. "Indeed."

Morbid images clouded her vision. Piles of the dead, lines of the wretched. The cold, cramped corner of a lurching cargo hold. Her tiny baby suckling at her breast, blissfully ignorant of the catastrophe surrounding them. Rose clicked her tongue. Snap out of it, she thought. You are here. Now.

"Why don't people talk about it?" Lily asked.

"It was a dark time. Those that lived through it saw things no one should see. Many will have done things they wouldn't normally do. Things they would rather forget. That is what happens." Enough, she thought. You'll give the poor girl nightmares.

They both stared into the middle distance for a moment, lost in their own thoughts. Rose breathed in the cool night air and reached out for Lily's hand; she needed to tell her one more thing.

"I was lucky," she said. "And ruthless. You need that edge. You must be tough like this desert. Don't put yourself in danger for others, consider the consequences of your actions, and follow the rules of the tribe."

With the last statement Rose's eyes flicked towards the poppies and back to Lily. Her granddaughter nodded; she would not break the rules.

"But you said you were going to get the poppy seeds for Ma."

"And I will."

"But—"

"You do as I say and not as I do." Rose smiled. Some things never change.

"Where did you live before you came here?" Lily asked.

"In a city. A place of big, tall buildings, all packed tightly together."

"Sand?"

"No sand."

Lily fell silent, considering this concept. Above them, a nighthawk soared and Rose wondered if the mouse they had seen earlier was aware of the imminent danger. Probably, but it will continue on its way, hoping that death befalls another. Much like humanity.

"There were no stars either," Rose said.

"No stars?"

"Well, they were there, but we couldn't see them. Too much pollution."

"What's pollution?"

Rose sighed. "Never mind."

Behind them, people were starting to wake up, chattering, kindling their fires, preparing for work. It would be a productive night. Rose elbowed her granddaughter.

"Keep a lookout. Tell me if you see someone coming. And remember, you don't know what I'm doing."

"Okay."

Lily faced the darkened kutcha houses. The central fire had been lit and flames danced beyond the thatched roofs. Rose's pulse quickened; anyone who chose to glance in their direction would see them immediately.

"Granny, let me do it. I'll be so much faster."

"Don't you dare! Just keep watch like I asked."

A few minutes later, she reached the poppies which were huddled under the branches of a spindly cactus. She sniffed and looked over her shoulder. Moonlight bathed the whole settlement in an ethereal, creamy glow. Rose grimaced. Brilliant, she thought. I'm lit up like a fucking Christmas tree.

She grinned then, remembering the shiny baubles and rustling tinsel. Presents wrapped in brightly-coloured paper with a festive sheen to it. Cinnamon and nutmeg and mince pies and advent chocolates. Carrot noses and coal buttons. Frosted breath. Her smile faltered. All things Lily will never know…

"Granny!"

Rose cursed, scolding herself. Mooning over the past was a slippery slope: indulge too often and you'd get stuck there, trapped in the ravine, never to return.

Jaw set in grim determination, she plucked four flowers from the base of their stems, not daring to take more, and secluded them within the folds of her undertunic.

She turned, praying no one had seen, and headed back towards Lily. She wasn't even halfway, however, when a gruff voice froze her in place.

"What's going on here?"

Lily flinched. They both knew who it was.

"Oh, is that Akran?" Rose said, feeding serenity and innocence into her words. "How are you, my dear?"

"Concerned." He stepped out of the shadows, revealing sharp features and dark eyes full of suspicion. "What were you doing over there by the wildflowers?"

"Have you never stopped to smell the flowers, Akran?" Rose asked.

"You're up to something," he said, moving closer. "Empty your robes."

Lily gasped, but Rose kept her face impassive and her voice steady. "No."

She tilted her head up and looked straight into Akran's feverish eyes. Her peaceful expression melted into one of hard realisation: he knew what he'd seen. It pained her to resort to foul play before her granddaughter, but some things couldn't be helped.

"I don't think you need to search me," she said, "not when I know so much about you."

He stiffened. "What is that supposed to mean?"

"We all have our secrets. And some" —she dropped her voice to a menacing whisper— "are worse than others."

Rose stared at him and he stared back. Dust swirled.

After a few minutes, Akran broke away. He marched back to the camp, keeping his eyes fixed ahead and gave Lily a wide berth.

Once Rose was sure he had left, she picked her way back to her granddaughter's side, taking care with her stick in the sand. All hostility had evaporated from her features, leaving nothing but a sweet, elderly woman.

"What did you say to him, Granny?"

"Oh, nothing much." She winked. "Just enough to get his imagination going."

Her free hand patted down on Lily's shoulder and squeezed.

"Now then," she said, "let's go tend to your ma."

The Big Bang

The laboratory hummed, a pale-yellow glow emanating from the small centralised time capsule. Thick wires and cables disappeared into the smooth white ceiling, finding their way to the numerous bleeping machines that lined the walls. Backlit by this yellow light, four figures debated in very professional, very controlled voices.

"Obviously, I have to be one of those to make the journey." Debra said, straightening her refined Notplastic overalls. "I invented the Unibend Timeflux Collaborator and I've been working on this project from the very start."

"I agree," her boss, Herbert, said. "A scientist must go and I would rather stay here, monitoring the space gauges and time fluctuations for any irregularities. Also, I must admit that I'm frightened of what might happen." He swept one hand out, gesturing to all three people. "I'll say it one last time. We can still delay and carry out further research."

Miss Humdin shook her head, the all-natural green leaves of her dress rustling with each movement. It must have cost a fortune.

"I funded this project so I'll decide whether or not it's going ahead. And it is indeed going ahead, with me as the first visitor to the beginning of the universe. I want results and *in person*, thank you very much."

Debra groaned inwardly. They had expected this, but it was still frustrating. The amount of power required meant that only one trip would be possible in their lifetimes and the capsule could only take two people. No more. A select committee had agreed that the two travellers should represent science and religion, not wealth.

Unfortunately, Miss Humdin owned the project so they couldn't just disregard her opinion. She needed to be convinced.

"But Miss Humdin," Herbert said, pressing his hands together, "we've never attempted to go back that far. We've gone back years, a century or two, but this is almost fifteen billion years! Those shorter trips didn't cause the travellers any noticeable discomfort, but it's too early to tell of any long-term side effects. A trip of this magnitude could have unprecedented consequences. Dangerous ones."

Miss Humdin listened, her expression unreadable. Debra glanced over at the fourth member of their group — her imminent travel partner — Eldrin Undiere. A solid square of a man with black hair curling past his ears, not quite as tall as Debra, but imposing. Though dressed simply in a marine-blue t-shirt and black trousers, Debra doubted that he could go anywhere unnoticed. There was something magnetic about him, which she hadn't been able to explain despite hours of musing.

As a highly-regarded member of All Faith, Eldrin was an expert in every known religion and spirituality, keeping a neutral, all-inclusive stance.

There were whispers that he would eventually hold the Univean Seat, a position devoted entirely to peace. And as if that weren't enough, he held himself with a grace and humility that Debra had never previously encountered.

It was hard not to stare.

Herbert continued, "You might not return, Miss Humdin, and if you did, you may well be insane. What if the capsule falls off some kind of time cliff? Maybe the machine simply won't work or perhaps the travellers will vanish from existence. Fifteen billion years is a long time. It leaves a lot of room for error." He shook his head. "There are too many unknowns."

Debra knew all the risks — she had calculated most of them — but it was still disconcerting to hear them laid out like this. Miss Humdin, however, did not seem perturbed.

"They didn't know what would happen when they first went to the moon, or Mars, or Saturn's asteroid belt, or Neptune. This is the next big discovery and I want to be a part of it." She lifted her chin. "I could be one of the first people to meet God. I'm going."

Taking great care not to roll her eyes, Debra discreetly signalled over to Eldrin.

"Seems to me," he said, calm, thoughtful, "that you are far too important, Miss Humdin. If you went and were erased from existence, you would not be remembered. Your name wouldn't be entered into history books. You would literally cease to have been. Forever." He paused, letting that sink in. "Are you willing to take that risk?"

Nicely done. Miss Humdin protested a little to save face, but the thought of being forgotten was too much for her and everyone knew it. She stood to one side as Debra and Eldrin stepped into the time capsule and fastened themselves in place.

It was cramped; their knees touched.

"You still haven't told me why you're willing to take this risk," Debra said. "Now would be a good time."

Outside the capsule, Herbert tapped the control screen, waiting for the various energy levels to calibrate. His left hand hovered over the UTC ignition switch.

"I first noticed you when you spoke at the environmental summit of '74," Eldrin said. "Your achievements were more than impressive, but it wasn't until I actually met you that I was sure."

"Sure of what?"

Herbert engaged the UTC and the capsule doors closed, separating Debra and Eldrin from the world as they knew it. She gripped the Kevlar straps, her leg muscles flexing. Eldrin braced himself as if he were preparing to dive into black waters.

He still hadn't answered her question.

"Sure of what, Eldrin?"

He smiled. "That you were going to change the world."

Molten citrine light surrounded them, oozing from the air, pressing against their eardrums. They'd both read the reports of previous missions, but none came close to describing this. It was as if her body had been disconnected from her consciousness, shooting off too quickly for her soul to keep up. Her chest tightened, tingled, her breath coming in shallow rasps. She was going to die, to unexist, to—

Stillness.

Silence.

Her body snapped back into itself.

She looked down at her temporal display: minus fourteen-point-nine billion years. The capsule's air stabiliser had kicked in automatically, meaning that whatever was outside wasn't habitable for humans. Well, she knew that already. At best, they were in space. At worst…

"What do you think is out there?" she asked. "God?"

"Of course," he said. "God is everywhere."

"Even here?"

"Especially here." His hand found hers and their fingers interlocked. This was it. They were going to witness the beginning of the universe. "Ready?"

She nodded and flicked her fingers over the control panel,

engaging discovery mode.

Debra expected black space, an infinite nothingness.

She was wrong.

In all directions, waves of green, red and white swirled, effervescent, like a swarm of fireflies. Millions of molecules extrapolating, surging and pulsing. Each one giving birth to thousands… *billions* more.

The backdrop was dark and in her peripheral vision, there was a point beyond which she couldn't focus. She tried, but her eyes slid away, unwilling. It reminded her of when a piece of paper is set alight, the edges burning and crawling inwards; but in reverse with darkness expanding out into that unseeable space.

"Did we get the time wrong?" Eldrin asked, gasping as a magenta stream of light rocketed upwards.

"We must have," she said. "It looks as though the Big Bang has already happened."

"Uh, Debra" —Eldrin pointed to the left of the purple blaze— "What is that?"

A huge dark-grey form floated. It swayed, the way it moved seeming almost fluid. Abruptly, a voice — no, a knowledge, a communication — entered their minds.

WHAT ARE YOU?

"H-Humans," Debra said out loud. "What are you? Are you… making something?"

YES. THIS IS MY EXPERIMENT. I THINK IT'S WORKED, BUT IT'LL TAKE SOME TIME BEFORE IT YIELDS ANY RESULTS. It paused, rippling in the void. I DIDN'T EXPECT ANY OTHER LIFEFORMS TO BE HERE. WHERE DID YOU COME FROM?

"Planet Earth."

WHERE'S THAT?

"It's, uh, very far away."

MUST BE IF I HAVEN'T HEARD OF IT.

"Are you a god?" Eldrin asked.

WHAT'S A GOD?

"Do you" —Eldrin waved a hand— "create universes?"

SOMETIMES.

Eldrin nodded. "That makes you a god."

DOES IT NOW? THAT'S FUNNY.

"Why is it funny?"

MY FRIENDS WILL LAUGH, THAT'S ALL. It jerked to one side and a new stream of cerulean light emerged from nothing. WHAT ABOUT THE BEING WHO CREATED ME? ARE THEY A GOD?

"I suppose so."

CAN YOU HAVE MULTIPLE GODS?

"Sometimes. It depends." He shifted in his seat. "But you're eternal, right?"

NO. I LIVE AND I WILL DIE, LIKE ALL THINGS. EVEN THIS UNIVERSE.

Debra perked up at that. "Can you tell us the lifespan of this universe?"

THEY USUALLY LAST ABOUT THREE GALACTIC CYCLES.

"What's that in Earth years?"

I TOLD YOU I'VE NEVER HEARD OF YOUR PLANET.

Debra gritted her teeth. She had to go back with some concrete knowledge!

"What usually causes universes to perish?" she asked. "Why do they only last three cycles?"

THAT IS INTERESTING. IT'S OFTEN THE SAME THING. INTELLIGENT LIFE GETS TOO CURIOUS AND DOES SOMETHING INCREDIBLY STUPID.

"Like harming their own planet?"

THAT WOULD BE VERY STUPID INDEED.

Eldrin cringed and muttered something to Debra, but she ignored him: she needed to focus. What could she ask of this creature? The things it could tell her if only she asked the right questions.

"Has time travel ever been discovered?"

YES, BUT NEVER FOR LONG. THAT'S ONE OF THE WAYS UNIVERSES END.

Debra swallowed. "What do you mean?"

WELL, IF SOMEONE AT THE MOST RECENTLY DEVELOPED TIME NODE OF A UNIVERSE JUMPS BACK TO THE BEGINNING, IT WARPS THE TIMELINE INTO A SELF-DESTRUCTIVE LOOP.

Debra broke out in a cold sweat.

"It destroys the universe?"

YES. HAPPENS ALL THE TIME. SUCH A SHAME.

"How long does it take?" Eldrin asked. Then, to Debra: "Hopefully, it's another few of those galactic cycles of theirs."

THAT'S WEIRD.

"Uh, something wrong?" Debra asked.

The grey blob began flitting to and fro amongst the nebulous balls of light, plucking at stars and nudging planets which cracked and crumbled beneath its touch.

MY PLANETARY SYSTEM IS UNRAVELLING, AND I'D ONLY GOT TO THE THIRD ONE! WHAT'S GOING ON? The creature's despair reached out, drowning Debra and Eldrin. I DON'T UNDERSTAND.

"We've angered the gods," Eldrin said, "and now we pay the price."

"Wait!" Debra screamed. "It's us! We did it! We travelled back in time!"

I SHOULD HAVE KNOWN. FOOLS. DO YOU HAVE ANY IDEA HOW LONG IT TOOK ME TO GET THIS FAR?

Debra's heart pounded in her ears. Her mind raced; there must be something they could do… and after a few seconds, it came to her.

"Oh! I have an idea!" she said. "The timeline is looped because we came back to the beginning of our universe, right? So, what if this isn't the beginning? What if you start again, doing it all the same, but just a little bit later. Then, technically, we won't have travelled back to the birth of our universe because the beginning will be in a different place… or, uh, time. Do you see?"

If the blob had shoulders, they would have slumped dramatically.

YOU HAVE NOT UNDERSTOOD. THE TIMELINE HAS BEEN WARPED, REVERSED AND IMPLODED. THERE IS NO UNIVERSE ANYMORE AND THERE NEVER WAS.

Debra looked to Eldrin and screamed. Half of his face was fuzzy as if made of sand, particles of which were drifting out into the ether. She tried to lift her arm, but nothing happened. They were coming undone, dissolving, ceasing to exist.

The grey form of the creator swept through the centre of its collapsing masterpiece. Its contemptuous, desolate voice the last thing any human ever heard.

IDIOTS.

A Tachinomiya Tale

Standing alone at the smooth hinoki bar, Makaira bathes in the pulsating vibrance of Tokyo's Shibuya district. Locals chatter, decompressing, unmistakable in their crisp business attire, whilst warm scents of melon – or is it pineapple? – rise from the rim of her sake. She savours the encompassing aromas of craft beer and cigarette smoke: smells that remind her of her father.

Did he ever stand here? In this exact spot? Her fingers brush against the chain around her neck, the silver fox head medallion cool and comforting against her skin.

Her gaze wanders over the folkloric mural adorning every inch of wall. Images she knows all too well. Bunbuku Chagama, the shape-changing teakettle, is nestled amidst those creatures known to have supernatural powers: the raccoon-dog, the badger, the cat and her father's favourite, the fox. Painted in fantastically intricate detail, they parade and cavort above the heads of the bar's patrons. Some shapeshift into human or semi-human form, whilst others simply pose in enduring elegance.

Oh, how her father regaled her with those tales! Igniting the spark of wonder that would catch and burn in her heart forever. He believed in the magic, and no one told the stories better. Eyes twinkling, he would put on the voices and make shadows dance in the languid glow of autumnal moonlight. She would squeal, hiding beneath her woollen blankets or giggle, nuzzling into his chest.

"The fox is very mischievous," he would say, "loving nothing more than transforming into a beautiful woman and punishing men that mistreat her."

"What else does she do?" Makaira would ask, despite having heard the answers a thousand times over.

"She makes liars tell the truth and cheaters own up to their crimes."

"Have you ever met one?"

"I think so," he said, flashing her a conspiratorial wink, "and Bunbuku Chagama."

"No!"

He nodded solemnly. "There was a time when I was young and working in the city that I saw a badger darting down the street. Men chased after it, shouting and hollering." He leant in close and whispered, "It had a teakettle clasped in its paws."

Makaira gasped. "Did they catch it?"

"The teakettle wobbled and jumped and puffed out a huge cloud of incandescent purple dust. And when the dust settled, the men were nowhere to be seen…"

Such wonderful stories.

Makaira rolls her shoulders, trying to shake off her melancholy, but it's no use. This city is so different to her village: a tempestuous ocean to her secluded lagoon, where all manner of mysterious creatures reside. Perhaps it was silly to leave, to come on this pilgrimage, but she wanted to know more about her father.

Everything, in fact.

In his youth, he walked these streets under the lurid glare of neon lights, but who had he been then, before he met her mother? What kind of man? Would she have liked him?

She frowns, swallowing the hard lump in her throat with another sip of sake. Why is it that all of these questions only occurred to her once he was no longer around to answer them? Her stomach twists. Maybe coming here wasn't such a good idea.

The bar's owner, Kitsu, a woman who holds herself like a queen, notices that Makaira's glass is empty and glides over. Abruptly, a young man slots into place on her right. He fits in with his short black hair and smart grey jacket, the sleeves pushed up over his elbows. There is a slow dissipating intensity in his demeanour that makes her mouth go dry.

"Hello, I'm Nezumi," he says. "Sake?"

She nods and Kitsu serves the drinks. A flick of the wrist sending the glasses directly into their hands. They drink and Makaira forces herself to relax. Maybe she is trying too hard to feel some connection. Her father was never broody, and he certainly wouldn't wish—

Nezumi coughs, wheezes, and slams his palm on the bar. Makaira flinches.

"Uh, Nezumi? Are you—"

He staggers backwards, forcing the men and women behind him out of the way. Somehow, he manages to stay upright and begins spinning, round and round, removing his jacket in the process. Makaira stares, as does everyone else.

The bar is now utterly silent.

And the silence intensifies as a collection of items fall from his jacket pockets and thump to the floor. Brown leather wallets, smooth velveteen purses and jewellery. So much jewellery!

Makaira's hand leaps to her neck, finding nothing but bare skin. She growls, but Nezumi is already being hauled away by three other men. Seconds later, his body makes a satisfying thwack on the pavement outside.

"My necklace is in there," she says to Kitsu, who is

already sequestering the valuables. "Please, my father gave it to me. It's a fox head with nine tails."

Kitsu pauses to search through the pile, fishes out the necklace, and returns it to Makaira with both hands.

"Thank you," Makaira says, pressing the cool metal to her chest before sealing the clasp around her neck.

The hubbub of conversation resumes as if nothing happened, and Makaira reclaims her spot at the bar.

"Good riddance," Kitsu says, sliding a fresh cup of sake across the bar with her slender red-tipped fingers. She winks. "This one's on me, Makaira."

"Thank you," she says, taking the drink.

Kitsu saunters away and Makaira raises the glass. It is halfway to her parted lips when she freezes, her eyes so wide that tears begin to form.

She is staring at the white-tipped, perfectly-pointed fox tail peeking out from the bottom of Kitsu's layered skirts.

The Man Who Lives Beyond the Horizon

Sweet dreams, my love.

I hope you will return to me, and to the world. It misses you.

I miss you.

You came into being some time after me. I know this because I remember the hollow, black-and-white time that preceded your kaleidoscopic influence. When you painted the earth in layers of rich brown, dabbing turquoise here and magenta there, paying no heed to anything else — utterly absorbed by your art.

Besotted in an instant, I wished to attract your attention. And so, I poured over the world, searching for an offering both timeless and pure.

It wasn't long before I noticed the haze of molten planetary magic clinging to the little ones: the babies and children. Around their bodies it swirled, twisting and swooping like a murmuration of starlings. Hypnotic, golden dust in the wind, each particle shining with its own inner light — they were children's wishes.

But they had nowhere to go. As each child grew up, these sparks would inevitably wane and perish. Forgotten.

This, I decided, was unacceptable.

With a cosmic flare, I wove my personal magics so these embers of hope could find passage to my tiny realm beyond the horizon. And so, I returned to prepare for their arrival.

Within hours they came.

From my workbench, I heard them: a light fizzing, like the sound of liquid on hot iron. As they swarmed closer, I gazed out, my palms itching, eager to get started. Endless flurries of amber danced across the ocean, feverishly quick, and I grinned as they skipped over the boundary, their luminous wakes forever blurring the horizon.

I gathered them into a deep, broad well adjacent to my forge and set to work. Handling each cluster of wishes, one at a time, I hammered them into shape, moulding them to my will.

The particles fused and glowed white hot. Reverently, I quenched each one in the silver river, watching as they took on a platinum sheen.

Once I had enough to fill a small basket, I strode into the neighbouring field, placed them by my feet, and one by one, propelled them into the sky.

Thus, I created the stars.

They winked at you, illuminating my love for all the world to see. You said nothing, but distinct shades of pink and scarlet blossomed over the land. Flower petals and gemstones shone, blushing; and I ached to show you more.

Lucky for me, one day a beautifully-rounded asteroid passed close enough for me to lasso and pull into the planet's orbit. Humanity called it the Moon, and it was my gift to you so the night sky wouldn't be so dark.

Your artistry had enhanced the earth, but overhead remained either black or white. Dusk and dawn were shades of these, a sliding scale of monochrome nuance.

Then you made it blue.

Blue, you said, because it's a soothing colour and all earth's creatures — indeed all manner of beings — need peace and comfort from time to time. Why not every day from the sky above?

My infatuation grew.

And my love deepened.

The planet rejoiced from one frozen pole to the other. Over blasted desert sands, verdant grasslands and rushing ocean tides. Dinosaurs, monkeys, mammoths and whales stopped what they were doing and looked to the skies.

I welcomed you to my home of astral forges and silver rivers. You wept at its beauty, and I thought you would stay.

I hoped you would.

Our love collided and melded and burst forth, sending streaks of passion across the heavens, just as the sun sank low enough to sit on the horizon. Wow, it said. Do that again.

And we did.

We transformed the skyline, the dawn and the dusk, into a wondrous blend of our favourite colours: a mirror to our ageless romance. Artists and lovers and poets spoke of our radiance without knowing of us. It is a pity, though I know you like your secrecy.

Alas, these same creatures that adored our splendour broke your heart. Your very spirit. Whatever they did, it brought great woe to all existence. Acid rain ate through your beautiful rainbows, dissolving them till the colours bled into the soil.

It was then, as you watched your creations burning, that you took it away. The gift you had given the world, and me. Perhaps they deserved it, to be refused your magnificence, but there is more to this planet than those who seek to destroy.

Please, my love, bring yourself back to the world.

The Moon weeps, and the stars drip their grief into the night. My rivers are overflowing with tears, their banks wet and glistening.

Children ask, "Daddy, where did the rainbows go?"

No one can answer them. Least of all myself, adrift as I am in an eternity of greys, undertones of asteroid bleakness.

You are the Rainbow God, the King of the Sunset, my Queen of roaring violet and astonishing gold.

You are here, in my domain and you sleep, turned away and folded inwards like a collapsed, dying sun. You have removed your touch from the world, abandoning us in mind and spirit. I understand your anger, I really do, but can you not forgive? It seems a harsh punishment for so many innocents to suffer for the sins of others.

However long it takes, I will wait, pulling the sun up and pushing it down. Comforting the Moon and flinging the stars into place.

I will wait.

***

The Moon and the sun say it hasn't been that long, but time has no meaning to me now. My existence has been split in two: with and without you.

The latter is unbearable. I am dejected and forsaken with no words strong enough for this insidious void. I continue to manoeuvre the sun and console the Moon. I lie, saying I know you will return. She doesn't believe me.

You are fading just as the wishes once did, but I cannot lure you into my forge and rekindle your heart. I beg and plead, receiving nothing but leaden silence. Every night, I hammer away at my anvil, too hard and too fast — the new stars keep breaking. Their snapped off fragments litter the ground, crunching underfoot.

I look down at myself and feel that I should be seeing red,

but my skin has taken on a greyish hue. I've been washed out and hung up to dry. We all have. And it's not fair.

How could you give up? How *dare* you. I see you flinch at my scorn, but it's true. That is what you have done.

I will endure because I don't think you would want me to fail. Not truly. I will suffer in shades of grey, in this halftone misery, until you return.

I will not give up.

***

I'm running out of stars.

Children aren't wishing as much as they used to and hope itself is crumbling. It is my fault as much as yours because I keep forgetting to raise the stars — the few that remain.

The Moon is alone in an inky pool, obliterated by whiteness when the sun is visible. The creatures of this planet fret, asking themselves why the stars are disappearing, but I cannot muster any compassion for them.

Why do I bother? Why continue without you to share the rotations and ellipses, the spins and undulations of this planet's lifecycle?

The Moon curses me as I slink away from my duty and curl up next to you. She says I'm a hypocrite, that I've abandoned a world I promised to cherish. She's not wrong, but I don't have the energy to care.

I no longer tend to the stars. Nor do I pull up the sun. The planet rotates in darkness and the Moon screams, bereft and furious. I ignore her, snuggled as I am against your waning light. Eyes closed, I sigh, resigning myself to the abyss.

It is not long, however, before the Moon's exaltant cheers stir me. Curious, I open my eyes to find the sun grappling with the sky, hauling itself up. Impossibly slow, it crawls to its zenith and holds itself in place. Defiant, it blasts warmth upon the world, shaming me. My mouth hangs open. I did not expect the sun to fight back.

In a daze, I look around. My realm scintillates no more. It is a dull stone-grey. I return to my forge and touch upon my dwindling collection of stars. The sun no longer needs me. What use am I if I cannot bring back my one true love?

Once again, I leave my territory and go out into the world. My heart breaks all over again to see it like this: a uniform, spiritless grey; every bird is either a raven or crow; the people are as ghosts, drifting, their eyes cast downwards.

Children still play and teenagers sit atop high brick walls, their legs dangling; they are happy to a degree, but without colour that happiness is tinged in melancholy, in nostalgia, as if I'm looking at a memory, trying to snatch at past joy and finding nothing but smoke.

I travel to each continent and every home, telling my story. Our story. But it doesn't work. They stare blankly, lacking credence; but in their faces, I see a pallid hunger. They need a sign, something tangible, something visible. On the street, a child crouches, head down, their finger drawing shapes in the dirt. And it gives me an idea.

Back at my forge, I fill my basket with what wishes remain and head into the field. This time, I am more deliberate, judging the precision of my throw, calculating its placement. With my stars, I map out images to which the humans can relate: a plough, a dog, an eagle, a crown. The last five I form into a giant W — I told them I would do this, and it stands for wish.

Their disbelief begins to thaw and when I regale them with our story once again, they listen with ears pricked up and eyes wide. The word spreads, inflaming every heart with wonder.

They strive to heal the planet and my celestial pictures twinkle encouragement, urging them onwards. The smog that billows from exhausts and chimney pots is snuffed out and gradually, the air purifies and water shines.

Wishing comes back to life. Stardust begins to trail me as if I am shooting through deep space until finally, I add my own wish to the iridescent stream.

I can only hope it's enough.

***

You are awake, standing in a sea of glitter. A thousand million wishes reverberate, whispering, all saying the same thing — Forgive us. Come back. Please.

A citrine gloss seeps out of you, tinting the wishes, returning them to their former glory. I rush to my forge, pick up my hammer and set about crystallising the magic. As each star is formed, you reach out and launch them into the sky. Together we work until the heavens gleam with unrivalled brilliance.

It is so bright the Moon requests shade and the sun obliges, gliding into a position that casts her in a crescent of shadow. But not before I catch sight of the smile etched upon her ivory surface.

You say you're sorry, and so do I.

At long last, we gather each other up like ruffled silk and your colours surge, exploding out in a miracle of saffron, heliotrope, and cerulean surf. My rivers sparkle. The planet sings and I tell you, emphatically, urgently, that you will never be alone.

Because I am the man who lives beyond the horizon.

And I am yours.

The Vicar of Coffinswell

In the back annex of the Church of Divine Mercy, as the full moon slunk across a cloudless sky, a priest and a vampire were locked in battle, figuratively speaking.

Drake flexed his long fingers and moved his knight into place. "Check mate, Father."

John sighed. "Just once I'd like to beat you."

"Don't feel bad. I've been playing chess for over a century."

"Still." John began returning the pieces to their respective squares. "Another?"

"Go on."

John poured them both another glass of Pinot Noir and took a sip. He eyed Drake's outfit, which he hadn't commented on yet despite it being rather flamboyant. Their friendship had warped everything he thought he knew about vampires.

"You're looking better," John said tentatively. "I like the shirt."

Drake grinned. "I got a yellow one too, but I think the periwinkle is my favourite."

John nodded. It had been months since he found Drake kneeling in the graveyard pre-dawn, wailing about how his life held no meaning. John had invited the poor soul into his private quarters to talk it over before realising he was a vampire.

Drake continued, "I think dressing in my old clothes

helps. I was always a beach surfer type, never one for wearing black or lurking in shadows."

"Is that the reason for the" —John waved a hand over his face— "spray tan."

"Part of it. Yes. I used to get a brilliant tan in the summer. A real bronzed God." He sighed wistfully.

"I think you're having some sort of... mid-death crisis," John said.

Drake nodded. "Something like that. Pathetic, isn't it?"

"No. I don't think so." John moved a pawn forwards. "It can't have been an easy adjustment."

"Some people are made for it. Pale skin, broody countenance... I never fit in. Even my name was..."

"Your name? Wait, Drake isn't your real name?"

Drake cringed.

"It's alright. You don't have to tell me if you don't want—"

"It's Brian."

"Brian?" John kept his expression neutral through a gargantuan force of will. A muscle in his face twitched. His neck constricted.

"Yes," Drake said, moving a pawn of his own. "Brian the vampire. Doesn't have quite the right ring to it, does it?"

They stared at each other for a few seconds before John exploded, the laughter pouring from him in belly-wobbling waves. Drake took it in silence for a moment before joining in.

"Oh dear," John said, wiping tears from his eyes. "So, let's see. You've redone your wardrobe, but that's not enough. Now you need some purpose. What do other vampires do? Run blood banks?"

Drake rolled his eyes. "No. They do all sorts of things."

"Can you turn into smoke and slip under doors?" He

brought his knight out in front. "Or turn into a bat? You could do magic tricks with that stuff."

Drake groaned and moved another pawn with unnecessary force. "That is such an outdated stereotype."

"No need to be quite so sensitive." John almost touched his bishop, then thought better of it. "I don't suppose you're any good with the ladies?"

Drake leant forwards and waggled his eyebrows. "I might be. Why? Got your eye on someone?"

John blushed. "Miss Berger."

"The baker?"

"Yes."

"Didn't you award her second place in the village cake fête?"

"That's the one."

"And why didn't you award her first place?"

"I couldn't give her first place when I've got… feelings. It wouldn't be right."

"Was her cake better?"

"I think everything she makes is heavenly."

Drake laughed. "Alright, so who did win?"

"Mr Flandin."

"Careful, Father. She might think you're into men, or worse, *boys*."

John narrowed his eyes. "That's *Catholic* priests."

"Now who's being sensitive."

They carried on playing in contemplative silence for a while. More wine was poured.

"Can I stay here tonight, Father? Or… today? You know what I mean."

John almost choked. "Here? Why? What's wrong with your crypt?"

"It's so depressing! All gloomy and dark and well, full of

dead people! It's awful. A constant reminder of what I am, what I can never be again." Drake blinked up at the ceiling, his jaw trembled. "There's this spot on the eastern side that lets in a slab of sunlight. Sometimes I wonder if I could lie there and let the light take me. Who would miss me? Who would mourn me? Who—"

"Alright," John said. "You can stay here."

"Thanks, Father." His relief was palpable. "You're a good friend."

John smiled, said, "Contribute to the needs of God's people, and welcome strangers into your home. Romans 12:13."

Not for the first time, he wondered if he'd taken his scripture readings just a little too far.

The following morning, John woke to find Drake lying on his back on his sofa, blankets strewn over him, naked feet dangling, flip flops on the floor. He seemed so peaceful John left him and went about his morning chores.

It wasn't until the afternoon when Mrs Hovis approached him after Mass that he remembered his dormant friend.

"Did Miss Berger catch you, Father?" she asked. Her grey hair formed an impeccable cone on top of her head.

"No?" He glanced about the pews, the mingling villagers. "She's here?"

Mrs Hovis nodded knowingly. "She said you sent her a beautiful letter. Found it posted through her door this morning, and she wanted to thank you personally."

"A letter? Oh dear, uh…" John cursed Drake. What had he done? Written a poem? He shuddered at the thought. Heat rose up his neck, burning his cheeks. Mrs Hovis grinned. "I thought so! I'm so glad you finally got the courage to tell her how you feel, Father. And a love letter! How romantic!" She winked.

"Where is she?" he asked.

"I encouraged her to go round the back to your private quarters."

"To my... Oh, God in heaven!"

He leapt into a full sprint down the aisle, leaving a stunned Mrs Hovis gawping after his flapping priests robes.

"Miss Berger!"

John blustered into his quarters to find Miss Berger standing in the centre of the room, eyeing the unfinished game of chess. The curtains were open, spilling sunlight into the room. There were few dark corners. Where was Drake?

"Father Matthews," Miss Berger said. "Please, call me Gwen."

"Oh, uh, alright… Gwen." He liked the way her name sounded, and the way her gaze held his. "Mrs Hovis told me that you received my letter?"

The long curtains that separated his bed from the rest of the room were half-closed. John glanced at the shadows. Were they moving? That must be where Drake was hiding.

"I had no idea you felt that way," she said.

He rubbed the back of his neck. "If I've got it all wrong, I'm sorry, but I wanted to let you know, on the off chance…"

Gwen crossed the space between them in two fluid steps and tilted her head back. She was almost as tall as him. "Shh, it's OK. I feel the same," she said quietly.

John's chest fluttered as he leant in for their first kiss, but just before their lips met, a loud bang made them both jump and look towards the curtained-off portion of the room. Oh no! Gwen couldn't find Drake skulking in here. How would that look? How could he explain a fully grown man hiding in his bedroom?

"What was that?" she asked.

"I, uh, I don't know."

Gwen frowned and moved toward the curtains, but John darted in front, blocking her off.

"What's going on?" she asked. "Who's back there?"

"No one! It's uh… it's my bedroom, and um…"

"You're hiding something." She crossed her arms, and her left foot began tapping.

John flapped. "I'm not. It's just that—"

A high-pitched screech cut him off. He whirled round, peeked behind the curtains and threw them back, revealing the entire space to Gwen. No sign of Drake. But what was that noise?

Then, Gwen screamed.

"A bat! A bat!"

"Oh, my word."

John stared as a grey bat fluttered round the ceiling, landing on shelves momentarily, knocking off books and ornaments in the process. Gwen backed away from it, edging closer to the doorway. It flew round and herded her away from her escape route and straight into John's arms.

"It'll be alright, Gwen," he said, ushering her behind his bedroom curtain. "I will deal with this."

He cursed the glorious sunlight streaming in through the windows: no escape there. Where could Drake hide? Bat-Drake alighted on the chess board table, cocked his head and let out another screech. The sound was horrific. It made John's spine quiver.

"Is it still there?" Gwen called out. "Have you tried opening the window?"

"Yes, but it's not gone yet," John said. "Just stay there!"

Where could he hide Bat-Drake? How long would he manage to stay like this? As if in answer to his thoughts, the bat flew over to John, hovered in mid-air and then *expanded*. It sprouted new dimensions of black and then flesh, here, there, until it was a bat no more, and Drake once again.

And he was naked.

"Urgh," Drake said. "That was disorientating."

"Shh!"

"Who's that?" Gwen said.

John launched himself at his wardrobe, unhooked a plain black robe—

"Please, Father. Anything but black."

Holding back a scathing retort, John grabbed a purple robe and shoved that over Drake's head.

"Ooo purple."

Gwen pushed aside the curtain and stepped out. She scanned the room, saw no sign of the bat and exhaled with satisfaction, absently smoothing her skirt.

"Hello," she said. "I do apologise. I was hiding from a bat, would you believe it? Thank goodness it's gone now."

Drake grinned a wolfish smile that made his eyes flash. "Whatever you say, Madame."

Gwen blushed. "Hang on, I wasn't—"

"Whatever you and Father Matthews get up to in his bedroom is none of my business."

"Who are you?" Gwen moved to stand by John, who couldn't believe Drake was ruining this for him.

"Father Drake, at your service, Madame."

"*Father* Drake?"

"Yes. I am visiting Father Matthews from… Coffinswell."

"Coffinswell?" Gwen asked.

John raised an eyebrow, doing his best to control the mirth sneaking up his throat.

"Tiny place. In Cornwall. Lovely views."

"I see." Gwen touched her neck. "No dog collar?"

"Oh, we're very relaxed about that. I wear it when I'm performing services, but go without otherwise. Can't be all work and no play, can we?"

"No. No, of course not." Gwen turned to John. "I need to be going, actually. I've got errands to run. But I'll see you later?"

"I'll call you tonight."

Drake stepped aside for Gwen, pulling a triumphant face at John once her back was turned. John waited until her footsteps had echoed out of the church before rounding on his friend, who had drawn the curtains, turned on a lamp, and was sitting at the chess board, smirking. He moved his rook three places closer to John's bishop. "She likes you."

"Did you have to say you were a priest?" John sat down and moved his bishop out of harms way.

"Don't be such a stiff."

"A stiff? I'm not the one who's dead."

"Touché."

Drake glided his rook along, tucking in suspiciously close to John's king.

"Gwen got the letter," John said.

"I figured as much."

"Well? What did it say?"

"That you fancy the pants off her."

"Drake!"

"Don't worry. It was very poetic."

"It better have been." John thought back on the almost-kiss, the press of Gwen's body against his. "Thanks, Drake."

"No. Thank you, Father."

"What for?"

"I've found my purpose! Match-making."

"Match-making?"

"Who better to teach the art of seduction… than a

vampire?"

"Who indeed."

John examined the chess board and smiled. Drake tilted his head, his expression falling into despair as John picked up his queen. He moved her two places and leaned back, regarding Drake, his eyes twinkling as he said, "Check mate."

The Threads that Hold Us Together

Arthur glared at the flimsy plasterboard wall that separated his student room from Tahlia's — it was *undulating*. He forced his attention back to *Enchanted Flora: A Guide* and tried to shut out the roaring crescendo of thrash metal and the faint tinkling of wind chimes.

It didn't work.

Again, the wall wobbled, sending his already-cracked picture frames tumbling to the floor. He closed the book and pinched the bridge of his nose.

He'd already complained to the housing officer about the noise, but all he got was a sympathetic head tilt and a hearty reassurance that it would be a good learning experience.

Even more preposterous were the two neighbours on the other side of the hall, who claimed not to hear or see anything untoward coming from Tahlia in 4b. Not even when purple smoke curled out from beneath her doorway and ingrained itself in the carpet, giving the hall that swirling pattern which made his eyes groan.

Boom!

His book — and indeed everything not bolted to the floor — suddenly leapt a foot in the air and crashed back down. Arthur, who'd shuffled forward at the wrong moment, was now slotted between his chair and the table, his coccyx throbbing.

"Right!" He shoved the table away. "That's it!"

He staggered into the hallway, knocked twice on Tahlia's

door, and waited.

"Who is it?"

"Arthur."

"Oh!"

The screech of guitars subsided to the sound of bare feet padding towards the door. He squared his shoulders, determined not to be distracted this time.

Two weeks ago, he'd banged on her door, requesting that she keep it down. She'd had a party with students from another dimension, making her apartment a temporary temporal node or lobe or somesuch (which apparently, according to the aforementioned housing officer, was so difficult to prove it wasn't worth trying). Somehow, he'd ended up apologising to her.

The door opened. Tahlia stood there, draped in some light-blue contraption trimmed with beads that drew attention to her every movement and every curve. Not that he looked.

"Everything alright?" she asked.

"Uh no, you see, I was trying to study and my entire room just, well, *jumped*."

"Oh! I'm so sorry. Are you OK? I must have got the parameters wrong again." She ran the palm of her hand over the wall — their wall — and clicked her tongue. "I bet it's because it's so damn thin."

"Yes, maybe, but in the meantime, could you not—"

"It's just so tricky working with exploding fungus."

Arthur cocked his head; he hadn't yet reached the chapter on unstable fungi. "I didn't realise it did that."

"Oh yeah! Why do you think they call it a mushroom cloud?"

He frowned. "Because it looks—"

"Come in," she said, stepping aside. "I'll show you."

"I don't think—"

"Come *on*."

He took one step, and stopped. She's doing it again, he thought.

"Look, I just want to be able to study in peace," he said. "Can't you ask your tutor or someone for a better containment spell?"

She raised an eyebrow. "It's more complicated than that."

"You manage to keep the others out of the loop." He gestured behind him. "They never hear anything."

"They wouldn't," she said. "They don't want to."

"What do you mean?"

"They're studying *politics*, they only hear what they want to hear."

"But I don't want to hear it either!"

"If you say so."

She placed one hand on her hip, numerous bracelets jangled. Was everything about this woman noisy? Even her eyes – big, dark and hooded – were mesmerising in a way that drowned out the rest of the world.

Arthur glanced past her, but the layout didn't allow him to see much from the doorway. Exploding fungus...

"Alright. I'll take a look." She grinned as he slid past her, and told him to have a seat whilst she made some tea.

A forest-green armchair appealed, which would have looked incongruous in any other student room, but not hers. Once settled, Arthur examined the space, enjoying the eclectic style.

A vibrant red dreamcatcher spun by the open window, along with the silver wind chimes. Every surface appeared to be draped in colourful handmade blankets with tassels hanging over the edges. Her room looked more lived-in than his; clearly, she liked to nest.

Or was it that he hadn't made an effort?

"What were you looking at?" she asked. Arthur flinched, picking up on her snappish tone. Did he do something wrong?

"Oh, just, you know." He waved a hand. "The wind chimes and that."

"What else?"

"Uh, the dreamcatcher?"

She froze, and for a second he thought she was going to cry, but then, just as quickly, she wasn't.

"Are you OK?" he asked.

"Of course." She glided over and placed the steaming mug on a midnight-blue, fabric coaster. "Here you go."

"Thank you." He lifted the mug. "Oh, that's… "

"Ginger and orange blossom."

The vapours tickled his nose and tugged at his memory. He'd had this tea before, but where? Tahlia perched on the wooden chair opposite. Hands clasped on her knees.

"So, uh, why are you studying magic?" he asked. And even as he said it, another part of his mind was trying to remember why he was there.

"My grandmother," she said, smiling. "When I was little, she told stories about all the people she helped with her potions and spells. She was one of those types who lived in a cabin in the forest, surrounded by a temporal field so only those seeking aid could find her."

Arthur nodded. "A lot of prejudice in those days. She must have been very brave."

"Yes. I always wanted to be like her and, you know, help people."

"That's good."

In an effort not to stare at her, he focused on the pinewood table. The coasters looked handmade, asymmetrical. He liked that. "Did you make these?"

"Oh no," she said. "My grandmother made those. She loved knitting."

"That's… uh… that's…"

He reached out and touched one, gently, reverently.

And something happened.

Happens.

"Arthur?"

"What's going on?" He moves to put down the tea, only to find it isn't in his hand anymore. "Uh, something's not…"

"Arthur, don't—"

"Why are you saying my name like that?"

Tahlia blinks and the hands clamped together on her knees start to tremble.

"Like what?"

"Like you *know* me."

It strikes Arthur that the room is wrong. There's too much in it, he thinks. The wind chimes clink and he turns to look just as the red dreamcatcher begins spinning. Faster and faster.

Tahlia is not sitting opposite anymore. She is on her knees before him, soft hands cupping his face, drawing his gaze back, her dark eyes search his.

"Because I *do* know you, and you know me." Her voice wavers. "Please, Arthur. Try to remember. This is where it all began. Right here in this room. I just need to find out how… Oh Arthur, please look at me."

He frowns. "But I am looking at you." His breath becomes ragged as panic overpowers everything else. What's going on?

"Who are you?" he asks.

Tahlia tries to say something, her expression pleading, but it's too late.

In his peripheral vision, the room *dissolves*, and then, shatters.

***

In forty-five years, Tahlia only managed to sneak up on Arthur once.

The flowers had budded early with honey bees roaming amidst a cacophony of birdsong. Arthur liked to joke that the woods were almost as noisy as her. He was at the bottom of the garden, tending the wildflowers, confident in his ability to hear her coming from a mile away.

At the patio doors, she removed her sandals first, then her wrap-around lilac dress, bangles and earrings, right down to the multi-coloured beads entwined in her hair. She left everything in a dishevelled pile and stepped proudly into the sunlight.

Grass tickled the soles of her feet as she crept past the daffodils and slipped between the weeping cherry tree garlands. A field mouse ran across her painted toenails, but she didn't scream. She dared not *breathe* for there he was, right on the other side of the misty rose blossoms; the bronzed skin of his forearms working, one hand pushing back the unruly chestnut-brown hair that he kept long specially for her.

Then, she leapt out from her hiding place, not bothering to hold her wobbly bits, and charged.

"What the—"

It was worth the effort to see the surprise on his face, and even more so when, a little while later, she rested her palm against his gorgeous face and whispered, "I'm pregnant."

His eyes widened and dilated, crinkling at the edges. Disbelief and hope surged, fighting, and he didn't try to hide any of it. He never did.

"You were right," she said. "Life did find a way."

He gave her stomach a gentle pat. "No. This is love," he said, leaning in for another kiss. "*Love* found a way."

***

Waiting for her to make the tea, Arthur settles into the armchair and admires the handwoven coasters. He is aware that her grandmother made them, but not how long they took. He leans forward and traces the pattern with one calloused finger. It looks complex, but what does he know? Maybe it doesn't actually take that long. Still—

"What did you do?" Tahlia asks. She sounds angry. No. Urgent.

"Nothing."

"The coaster," she says. "It *flashed*."

"No it didn't." But even as he says it, the strands begin to glow. A slow build of energy.

Tahlia leaves the counter and walks towards him, looking so determined he holds his breath. She reaches out and deftly pulls a thread of that waxing moonlight into her light fingertips and walks to the window, stretching the thread, manipulating it, and links it to the windchimes.

It sticks.

And burns brighter.

Tahlia moves back to stand in front of him. She can tell she doesn't have much time; the light is already waning. It won't last. Arthur is older by ten years or so. He was thirty-two when they got married. His hands grip the armchair, his jaw muscle flexing. She can't let him panic or she'll have to start over.

Again.

"Arthur," she says softly. "I'm playing a game, OK?"

He relaxes back in the chair, though his muscles are still tight. "Alright."

"This is the day—"

"I know what day this is." A smile flickers. "I remember."

"But I think you remember it differently than me. This" — she picks up the coaster— "is significant to you, isn't it?"

He cocks his head and his expression passes from confusion to joy. A dimpled smile warms his face. He nods.

"Why?"

"Your grandmother made it for you. It was precious, but you didn't keep it on display behind protective glass or wrapped in plastic at the back of a cupboard. My mother would have done that, but not you. You used it. You loved it."

"And?"

"I think… yes… this is the moment I knew I loved you. Or at least, when I felt that the possibility existed. It was exciting! I buzzed all over. It was as if a swarm of bees was trying to tell me that the most exquisite honey was within reach and all I had to do was look."

Tahlia's breath catches in her throat. It's been a long time since she heard him say such things. So long since he said *anything*. And he used to be so romantic, so surprising and annoying and frustrating, and *funny*!

She misses his laughter. And her own.

"Tally?" he says. She's given too much away. Concern etches the nascent lines of his face. "This isn't a game, is it?"

***

Tahlia stands, slowly, cursing her arthritic joints. Reaching out, she dabs the corner of Arthur's mouth with a tissue she keeps up her sleeve. His gaze passes over hers, not quite meeting it, and her chest muscles constrict, stifling a sob.

How much heartbreak can one person stand? This must surely be the limit. The patio doors are open, and scents of orange blossom sweep in from the back garden, mingling with Tahlia's freshly made green ginger tea.

This cabin is much larger than they ever needed, especially since Poppy left home, but it's theirs. Tahlia is responsible for the colourful rugs and ornaments and the rock music that she used to play (she doesn't anymore for fear of not hearing him if he needs her). Arthur can be seen in the rich mahogany bookshelves, the smooth rounded edges of their dining table, and above all, the garden. That was his domain.

Is.

It's one o'clock.

Her colleague from the Academy, Jon, is due to video call. She moves into the kitchen, not wanting to do it in front of Arthur in case he can still hear.

"How's the research going?" Jon asks. Straight to business. "Any change in the patient?"

"Not yet," she says, resenting the impersonal though necessary wording. "But I'm close! There's just something I'm missing, something small…"

"Tahlia." The use of her first name puts her on guard. They've been friends and colleagues for over twenty years, but work was work. "It's been *nine years*."

"I know," she says. "Curing diseases takes time, but I'm getting closer."

"That's what you said last year." He pauses. "Listen, I hate to be the one to tell you this, but…" She closes her eyes; she knows where this is going. A cold hard ball forms in her belly. No results mean no funding. It's not personal. It's never personal. Jon is starting to ramble in the face of her uncharacteristic silence.

"It's alright, Jon," she says. "I understand."

He nods. "It's terrible, but there are some things that can't be healed."

"No." She turns away. "No, I won't accept that."

"Tahlia. He's in the final stages. His neural pathways are gone. Who knows what's going on in his mind? His memories are all jumbled up, their links broken. That cannot be fixed. We — I mean us at the Academy — need to focus on preventative measures, ways to slow down the disease's progression, and—"

"Give up?"

She paces, her bare feet smacking on the stone kitchen floor, each turn punctuated with a swish of fabric and a sharp snap of jewellery.

Quietly, tentatively, he asks, "Does he still recognise you?"

Tahlia shoots him a look brimming with hurt. He changes tack.

"Have you spoken to Poppy recently? What does she think about all this?"

"She visits every weekend and tends the garden for him."

Jon lets that one slide: the insinuation that Arthur is merely on holiday and will be right back to it as soon as he returns. That he isn't sitting in his favourite green armchair ten feet away, drifting in and out of consciousness.

"Listen, Tahlia. I'll only say this once and then I won't bother you with it again. But I have to say it. Arthur told me" —he clears his throat— "he told me he didn't want this for you. He said that when it got this bad, he didn't want you to... He didn't want you to suffer. Those were his wishes."

"I know what he said."

"And?"

Tahlia halts and lifts her chin, radiating defiance.

"Tough."

***

"Daddy, I'm scared," Poppy said.

Arthur smiled, his chest swelling; she looked so small and cute with her starry duvet pulled right up to her nose.

"Don't worry. It'll be alright," he said. "Because I got you *this*."

From behind his back and with a flourish, he pulled out a beautiful crimson dreamcatcher. Poppy gasped.

"This," he said, "will catch all the bad dreams and lock them up tight."

"So they can't get me?"

"That's right." He thought about it for a second, and added, "And any that do, won't be able to hurt you."

He tucked her in and kissed her forehead. He worked with flowers and herbs all day long, but his daughter's head, in his opinion, was the best smell going.

"I love you, Daddy."

"I love you too."

***

Love always finds a way. His words, echoing in Tahlia's mind. Nagging her.

She goes back in.

Arthur is in his chair, surveying her room. The room his mind has conjured up. Festooned with snatches of other memories, slipped in when she wasn't paying attention: the wind chimes from their back porch, the dreamcatcher he bought Poppy, the smells of his favourite tea, the thrash metal music that he *loathed*.

She waits, eyeing him sidelong. After what feels like an eternity, he focuses on the coaster, reaches out and brushes it with his thumb.

It glows, and she leaps into action.

"What are you doing?"

She doesn't answer. With a speed that belies her real age, she pinches thread after thread of the silvery starlight and darts about, creating a tapestry of luminescent spider silk. Each connection seems to feed the light, making it expand and grow. She forges links with the wind chimes, the dreamcatcher, the cracked pictures of all three of them together, the tea, the bed, the armchair… her.

"Arthur." The light is now a sphere hovering in the air, blinding in its radiance. "Hold my hands."

He does and for a brief moment, he is him again. The whole him.

"Tahlia, if this doesn't work—"

"It will."

"You don't know that."

"It has to."

A thousand suns explode in glittering majesty, showering them. She holds her breath as the threads surrounding them shimmer, flicker, strengthen, and *hold*.

Not daring to hope too hard, lest it destroy her forever, she leaves his mind.

Outside, she can hear the wind chimes and the soft rush of the afternoon whispering through the patio doors.

She sits on a small footstool in front of Arthur, her hands on top of his.

She looks into his eyes, and he looks right back.

Smiling, he laughs and squeezes her hands. For once, she has no words, so he speaks for both of them.

"I *missed* you."

3022: The Final Launch

Earth's dual suns blazed in the clear morning sky as anticipation rushed up the shore and oozed into the sand. Carried by a warm ocean breeze it swept through the forest, finding those early risers in the camping grounds, stretching their muscles amidst the nascent birdsong.

Bode was one of the first to wake and, stealthy as the ebbing night, she gathered her things and found a spot at the edge of the clearing to do some yoga. She touched her toes, placed her palms flat on the cool earth and walked her hands forward, breathing steadily.

She'd slept well, surprisingly, though a million worries still chittered, clamouring to be heard. Would her sister, Mayra, remember to check on the new nest? What if there was a problem with Sufi, the mother-to-be? What if—

She sensed Raphus, her dodo, approaching. His blue-grey feathers ruffled as he walked, impatient to be on the move. Opening her eyes, she found his yellow feet inches away, black claws scratching at the soil.

"Alright," she said, straightening up. "I'm ready."

Raphus nuzzled her hand.

I don't want to miss it. So many are there already.

"Don't worry. I wouldn't miss the launch for anything!" Bode shouldered her backpack and began walking down the shadowed forest path towards the coast. "We'll be there in plenty of time."

Raphus waddled along, easily keeping up with her,

contentment flowing through their bond. They seemed to be alone; the tents were dark and quiet; hundreds of soft little snores like a chorus of frogs. How anyone could sleep in today bewildered Bode. To think, in a few hours she'd be watching the last—

"Hey!" A man with white-blond shoulder-length hair jogged over from the tents to their right and skidded to a halt. He had a cheerful face and green eyes bristling with enthusiasm.

"You're the dodo breeder, aren't you?"

Bode unconsciously stroked Raphus' smooth brown head. "Yes, that's me. Why?"

"Sorry, I uh, I'm Theodorus Chalut." He grinned. "Call me Theo."

Something about him — that smile? — felt oddly familiar. "Did I sell you a dodo?"

"No, but I live in town. Everyone knows who you are." He glanced at his feet. "I'm on my own as well and I thought we could—"

"I'm not on my own," Bode said, scratching behind Raphus' ear.

"Oh, right. Sorry."

Let him come.

Bode glared at Raphus, but said nothing. It would be incredibly impolite to debate the matter in front of Theo, especially since he would only hear her part of the conversation. She considered him for a moment.

"Fine," she said. "As long as you can keep up."

Despite her best efforts, Theo did manage to keep up, happily trotting along until she relented and slowed to a more comfortable pace. Sunlight dappled their path as the swelling noise of crowds up ahead filled the air.

"Are you excited?" Theo asked. "Can you, you know, feel anything different yet?"

"What do you mean?"

"I just thought with the launch being so close, that people like you would be able to… sense something?"

Bode shot him a look, but didn't slow down. "People like me?"

"Yeah, those more attuned to the Oneness, to the AllMother." His voice took on an air of undeniable devotion, of spiritual awe. "Well," he continued. "If you don't feel anything yet, you're expecting it. That must be why you're here."

Bode frowned as history lessons from school came back to her. Almost a century ago, the world stopped producing plastic and began replacing everything with biologically engineered materials: lab-enhanced spider silk, electro-conductive fungus and aerolium microlattice — things Bode took for granted.

That was when the Great Amassment began on what became known as Plastic Island. Using nanoscale lasers they shrank the plastic piece by piece, fitting one billion tons in a single space shuttle at a time, and set it on a collision course for the nearest black hole. More or less one launch occurred every lifetime and today marked the fulfilment of that entire project, leaving the planet one hundred percent plastic free.

A truly monumental historic event.

"I am here to witness history being made," she said. "My parents talked about it all the time. They would have loved to see the final shuttle blast off." Bode clicked her tongue. They would arrive at the beach in less than an hour and then she could lose him. She didn't want to spend today being lectured by some Earther spiritualist. "That should be reason enough for anybody," she said. "Why are you here?"

"To witness, well, potentially witness the ascendance of our connection to the AllMother."

"Oh really?" Bode rolled her eyes. "Did the AllMother tell you that? Talk to you, does she?"

Raphus winced at her tone, but Theo didn't seem to notice. He just smiled to himself and said, "Not yet."

They didn't speak again for the rest of the walk. It was obvious that Theo wanted to talk more, but he kept quiet. Perhaps he wasn't a complete idiot.

Once they arrived at the edge of the forest, Bode paused and filled her lungs with the salty-fresh sea air. Gulls screeched overhead and vast white sands glistened in the sunlight, stretching north and south, all the way to where the land curved inwards.

The beach was full of people, talking, lounging, and playing games. The hubbub of voices crackled with the promise of great merriment.

Raphus gestured with his head for her to move away from Theo, who was taking in the scene with childlike wonder.

"What is it?" she asked.

Raphus' grey beak poked at her hand.

You were rude.

"Oh Raphus, I wasn't that bad." Bode reached out and smoothed the tuft of white at the nape of his neck, but he jerked away.

Apologise to him. He's nice.

"He didn't seem to think I was being rude."

That's not the point. Raphus turned away from her. *And you know it isn't. What would your father say?*

Bode froze. The words were a harsh slap of honesty that only good friends can successfully deliver. She rolled her shoulders and swallowed the bitter taste in her mouth.

There was just something about Theo that rankled her, though not in an altogether unpleasant way. Was it his incessant positivity? Quite possibly. Even the way he walked was jolly.

She glanced at Raphus who was now behind Theo, idly picking at some buckthorn berries, close enough to hear what she said.

"Listen, Theo," she began, "I didn't mean to mock your belief in the AllMother. I…" He waited. It was impossible to gauge his reaction. He looked like he could stand there all day. "My parents died six years ago in an avalanche. They were on holiday up north, rock climbing and… it shouldn't have happened." She looked to the sky. "But it did."

Theo nodded. "I know."

Bode frowned and he rushed to explain. "My mother told me. I was in the Broken Isles at the time and well, it shocked the whole town. They were good people…" He trailed off, ran one hand up the back of his neck. "I'm sorry for your loss."

A companionable silence settled over them; Bode wondered how long Theo had been in the Broken Isles and what he'd been doing there, but she didn't ask.

The breeze lifted her hair, a few strands fluttering over her face. They both looked out towards Plastic Island and the white rocket – so far away and yet, so tantalisingly close. Walruses and sea cows languished in the gentle lapping current, a few had climbed onto some smooth rocks to their left and flopped down to bask in the sun. To their right, a massive digital countdown was suspended in the air: one hour to lift off.

"Sometimes," Bode said, "I think I'd like to believe in the AllMother, but…"

"Please don't feel like you have to explain yourself to me.

We all have our separate beliefs and hopes, and that's a good thing. I made the assumption that you shared mine and I shouldn't have."

"Even so, isn't having separate beliefs and hopes in opposition to the whole Oneness principle?"

He smiled. "Not at all. You see those sea cows over there on the rocks?"

"Uh, yeah."

"They chose to lie in the sun whereas the others are lolling in the water, but they're all still sea cows."

Bode scratched the back of her neck. "That seems like a very simple explanation."

"Too simple?"

She opened her mouth and closed it again.

Theo continued, "Does an ideology need to be perplexing to be worthy of belief?"

She wanted to say no, but that was clearly what he wanted, so she didn't. Instead, she crossed her arms and surveyed the beach some more, feigning deep thought. Theo grinned. Infuriating man.

A young girl of about Mayra's age was doing backflips whilst juggling to an audience of goggling children and farther down, a volleyball game was being set up.

Mayra.

Bode checked her phone. One message from her little sister:

Morning! Have an amazing day! I'll be watching for it. We should be able to see the smoke trail if we're looking in the right direction. Exciting! And yes, I've checked on the nest and Sufi is totally fine. STOP WORRYING. Love you.

Bode closed her phone and sighed. Mayra was eighteen, the

same age Bode had been when their parents died and she took over the dodo range.

"Hey, uh, Bode?"

She knew Mayra could cope, but letting go wasn't easy. What if she met someone tomorrow or today and fell in love? She might want to move out and—

"Bode?" It was Theo. "Bode!"

"What?"

"It's Raphus. He made this squawk and when I turned around, he was gone. Is that normal?"

She stared, horrified, her stomach suddenly ice-cold; she could barely sense her dodo.

"Raphus!" Bode ran over to where he had been a moment ago. The earth was disturbed, broken twigs from the bush littered the ground and a lonely blue feather was impaled on a thorn right next to the berries he'd been eating.

Had he been snatched? She ran her fingers along the feather and closed her eyes to concentrate. She opened her mind to their bond, straining for some clue as to what had happened. Her heart skipped a beat as the emotions reached her.

He was afraid.

Panicked.

And fighting desperately to stay calm.

***

As a tiny brown dodo chick, Raphus had fit perfectly in Bode's two hands. Her father had brought him to see her because he was refusing to eat.

"Can you ask him what's wrong?" he asked. "Did he eat something he shouldn't have? Does his stomach hurt?"

She was so proud to be able to help, but as it turned out,

Raphus was faking. He just wanted to see Bode and from then on, they were inseparable.

On the range, she helped her father more and more often. She could tell him immediately if one of the birds was pregnant, which birds were fighting, and why.

And it didn't go unnoticed in the town.

Before spending money on a vet, people would stop by to see Bode. One time, a woman came in with her son and their rabbit, which was acting out of character: disappearing for hours on end, biting if anyone tried to pick him up. The mother used gardening gloves to bring it in and did all the talking whilst the boy leant against the doorframe exuding boredom and contempt.

That was until Bode said, "Your rabbit is angry because he" —she pointed at the boy— "keeps trying to flush it down the toilet." The son called her a liar and stormed out, slamming the door behind him.

But that wasn't as bad as when Mr Buster brought in his prize stallion. It was refusing to breed and the vet had been no help. Visiting Bode was a last resort.

"He says…" Bode glanced nervously at the big man. Her father placed a hand on her shoulder.

"It's alright, love," he said. "Just tell us what the horse says."

She cleared her throat. "He doesn't like the fillies, sir."

"Impossible! What doesn't he like about them?"

"Uh, well, that they're fillies, sir. He says he prefers stallions."

"Oh." That was her father, attempting half-heartedly to hide an enormous grin.

Mr Buster erupted in accusations, threats and a string of curses Bode had never heard before as she hid behind her father's legs. Once Mr Buster was gone, her father kissed the top of her head and said, "Don't worry. Your gift is new or perhaps very, very old and not everyone will believe that you can hear what you hear."

"They think I'm making it up?"

"Some will think that. Yes."

"But I'm not."

"I know Bobo." He crushed her in a hug, his black moustache tickling her cheek. "And your mother knows, and your sister… and *you* know, which is all that really matters."

***

Fury smothered Bode's panic as they thrashed their way through the forest, hot on Raphus' trail. He would never run off like this. Someone had taken him. Thankfully, Theo was an excellent tracker — something he'd learnt in the Broken Isles — but the trail zigzagged all over, taking them farther and farther north.

Suddenly, Bode cried out and doubled over as an acute flash of pain stabbed at her from Raphus.

"Can you feel him?" Theo asked. "Are we close?"

"Yes!"

A human voice shouted something up ahead and they sprinted towards it.

Not Raphus. Please, not him.

When she thought of all the times she had visited her parents' graves beneath the flaming-red maple trees with Raphus by her side. Silent and understanding, he would settle next to her as she wept or spoke to them, sending comfort through their bond.

Bode had to be strong for her sister, but with Raphus, if she needed to cry, she could do so without feeling weak or selfish. She didn't think she would have managed without him by her side. The mere thought of losing him made her shake as if she might split open.

"Through here!" Theo shouted. "I can see something!"

They burst out into a clearing and skidded to a halt, exchanging baffled looks. Raphus was surrounded by two women, a man and about seven dodos. This didn't feel dangerous, but everyone looked incredibly tense. For one thing, no one looked up when they arrived.

"Raphus?" Bode called. "Are you alright? What's—"

Quiet. Come see.

They approached and saw that Raphus wasn't actually the one surrounded. In the centre of the group, a female with pale-blue feathers was quivering over a huge yellow egg.

She began laying in the forest, Raphus explained. *It came over her all of a sudden and then, a badger attacked. She was helpless in that state, but I was nearby and sensed her distress.* Raphus' plumage stuck out proudly. *I fought off the badger and guarded her until her family arrived.*

"Are you hurt?"

I'll live. And more importantly, so will they.

Another female dodo stood next to Raphus, her plumage equally puffed up so their feathers were almost touching.

Oh. How had Bode not noticed straight away?

Because she'd never felt these emotions from Raphus before: a fierce yearning to nest, to procreate and protect. All at once, she realised that these feelings of his were warring with his loyalty to her and he was uncertain of how to proceed.

Instinctively, and for the first time, Bode sent her thoughts through the bond to Raphus: *Stay. Be with them. I'll be alright.* She'd always known this day would come, but it was still a shock as she knelt down and Raphus shuffled into her embrace.

You're stronger than you realise, Bode. And this isn't the end for us. You will always be my friend.

Not caring that tears were dripping from her chin, she kissed the top of his head and watched as he made his way back to his new family, his blue-grey feathered form mixing with theirs.

She wept, but not out of loss.

Out of love.

***

Fifteen minutes remained.

The beach was electric with thousands of eyes turned towards Plastic Island.

"Hey," Theo said, pointing at the suns. "Did you know that when the second sun was made, the Earthers believed it would awaken the AllMother?"

"No, but I can see why."

Earth's man-made solar absorption centre or the 'second sun' had eradicated the need for any other source of fuel centuries ago. It was hard for Bode to imagine their world without dual suns in the sky.

"It was massive," Theo said. "They organised huge gatherings when it was sent into orbit and nothing happened. I hope this is the moment, but…" He shrugged.

Bode couldn't help but smile at his stubborn, unshakeable faith.

"How long were you in the Broken Isles?" she asked.

"Three years. Since then, I travelled around a bit, but I'm back home now. Couldn't miss the launch, could I?"

"I suppose not."

"So," Theo said, his foot tracing a semi-circle in the sand.

"You really don't believe, like, at all?"

Bode shook her head. "Sorry."

To her surprise, he chuckled. A light chuckle that quickly transformed into hoots of belly laughter. He bent forwards, hands on his knees, overcome with mirth.

"What is so funny?"

"Oh!" He straightened up and shot her that lopsided grin of his that was – she decided to admit – disarmingly attractive. "Because *you* are the reason that *I* believe."

Confused, she cocked her head to one side and with a gasp, she saw it.

"The rabbit," she said. "The rabbit that was being flushed down the toilet! That was you!"

"Yeah," he said, smiling as she too began laughing. "That was me."

Just in time, they found a good spot in the shade of a fig tree to view the launch. Theo leaned in and whispered, "Take your shoes off."

"What?"

"Trust me. Please?"

She blushed at the thrilling feel of his breath on her neck.

"Fine," she said, slipping off her shoes, wiggling her bare toes. The countdown ticked: ten seconds… nine… eight…

"Here we go," Theo said.

… seven… six… five…

Without thinking, Bode reached out and intertwined her fingers with his.

…four… three… two… one…

A puff of white smoke spewed forth from the base of the rocket and instantly covered the entirety of Plastic Island. Up into the sky it went, history itself piercing the clouds, penetrating the stratosphere and roaring forth into the void.

Every molecule of Bode's body hummed, vibrated, and throbbed. The soles of her feet tingled and then, like a magnificent river held back for eons by a thick concrete dam, pure bliss flooded her being. A happiness as clear-cut as polished diamond leapt from cloud to striated cloud.

"What is that?" Her words came in ragged gasps. Theo's hand in her own felt as if it had always been there, as though it was part of her. "What's happening?"

Stronger than ever before, she sensed Raphus, his joy, his hope and the mirrored sentiments of his newfound mate. Bode was happy for him and ashamed that she had held him back for so long.

And there was Mayra, standing in the centre of their dodo range, eyes following the rocket, wonder pulsating through her body. Her future stretched out: an intoxicating, mysterious tapestry that Bode could not control. That she didn't want to control.

Not anymore.

And herself. Bode. The dodo breeder. Friend. Sister. Daughter. Opening her heart for the first time since her parents died. She hadn't realised that she'd locked it away, shielding herself from future pain and loss. To be strong for her sister she'd stifled her own emotions, not allowing them to interfere.

But that is not living.

How many years had she lost? She squeezed Theo's hand. No matter. This was the beginning of something new. The thrumming joy melded with her deepest heartache, weaving together, making her whole.

Anything was possible.

"It's the AllMother," Theo whispered, the tears on his cheeks shining like frozen jewels. "At long last, we are forgiven."

The End of the Line

I don't know how long we have, so when the train slows I stand ready at the doors with one hand at the centre of your back, guiding you. Passengers rise in the carriages to either side of us. Some shuffle forwards, just as eager, whilst others remain seated, staring out the window.

You are looking too, in complete tranquillity, as a billion comets flash through an eternity of purest black, their wakes smouldering in the void. When you speak, your voice is dreamy and detached.

"Where am I?"

"You'll see."

You don't remember how you got here, but you will. Your brain is beginning to toss up childhood memories: your younger brother, Jake, sitting on your lap, crying because he'd shoved a pink crayon up his nose and couldn't get it out; Mum waving from the school gates, her smile a little too wide; Dad throwing you high in the air under a blazing hot sun. You squealing as the rush of wind tickled your skin…

The train docks, the doors slide open and we step out onto the platform. A few people hurry past, the face of a loved one spurring them on. I exchange nods with the conductor, a petite woman in a hi-vis vest and bright pink hair. Ellie. That's the name she chose anyway. I glance over my shoulder to see her moving effortlessly through the alighting passengers, watching for trouble.

Some – mostly the younger ones who had farther to

travel – have made new friends on the train and excitement zips around them like silent lightning.

Then there's me. And you.

"Something happened," you say. Your eyes take in our surroundings, but your brain struggles to catch up. "I was with Melissa. She was upset…"

I smile to myself; you've got a good one there. It was Melissa who convinced you to get on a plane for the first time and you weren't even afraid, not with her brandishing a passport crammed with stamps, hazel eyes glittering, infecting you with adventure.

"Where is she?" You still can't quite remember. "Is she alright?"

"She's fine."

The station gleams. A lucent snow-white. People of all ages fill the space, lounging on sumptuous cream couches or leaning against the station wall, lost in thought or reading. That singular wall disappears into the distance, separating the station from the Other Side. A few children sit on the pristine white carpet playing a complicated version of rock-paper-scissors and somewhere, a baby is laughing.

"Everyone looks strange," you say, as we exit the platform. "They're too…"

"Perfect?"

The ceiling is impossibly high, fashioned into elaborate glass domes. Looking up, one sees only an infinite night glistening with forlorn stars. On either side, the unnumbered platforms stretch on and on with trains drifting in and out, continuously, forever.

You're starting to freak out.

"What is this?" You jerk back from my hand. "Am I… Am I…"

"You're not dead."

"But—"

"You're. Not. Dead." I smile. "Alright?"

"Then what's going on? Who are you? Why am I in this... this *train station*?"

"This is the end of the line."

A muscle in your cheek twitches. "That sounds an awful lot like—"

"You're not dead! How many times? And you won't be here long. Relax."

This particular part of the station has a piano. An upright studio model with a rosewood body, positioned against the wall. The cover is lifted up, begging to be touched. I draw your attention to an old man in a long brown coat. He approaches the piano and prods the keys, testing them. Then, with a grunt of satisfaction, he settles down and flicks the tail of his coat so it hangs to the floor.

His fingers fly over the keys. He's chosen a soothing melody, full of minor chords and elongated, pensive notes. Within seconds, he is lost in his own creation. He lifts his chin and closes his eyes, a wry smile tugging at his lips.

The chatter in the station halts and heads turn — who is this man? Children see their own grandfather in the delicate pale hair whilst others imagine a father, a favourite teacher, a friend.

You see your brother. Home for Christmas, hunched over your dad's piano, belting out Elton John with one foot stomping on the hardwood floor, his green paper hat falling off as the rest of the family sing along, completely out of tune. Melissa giggling as your golden Labrador, Toby, jumped up to lick her face...

The memory is ferociously vivid and you grab me to steady yourself.

"That'll keep happening," I say. "The memories. They'll

come faster and faster until you remember everything with intense clarity. It should straighten your head out."

"What's wrong with my head?"

"Listen to the music," I say. "It helps."

You do, begrudgingly, but it's impossible not to get swept up in the magic. Moments flash, important and inconsequential, but they are all yours: a high school dance, one hand finding the slope of her lower back; carefree laughter by a fountain in Rome, coins plinking into crystal-clear water; a crisp bedsheet littered with tears, the smell of antiseptic, a farewell.

The tempo changes and the key shifts to the major scale. The pianist presses one foot down on a pedal whilst the other taps out a jaunty rhythm. His face cracks into a wide grin, radiating life and love and joy. A couple in matching purple berets begin to dance. No one sees merely an old man, alone, tinkering at a piano.

What do people see when they look at you? you wonder. I feel this thought and how it makes your stomach grow cold.

"Hey" —I snap my fingers in front of your nose— "come over here."

A café and bookshop are off to the left and I head towards them. You obey, but reluctantly and making a show of it: arms crossed, dragging your feet, eyeing me askance like I'm luring you into a dodgy drug deal.

I pause in front of the station entrance so you can get a good look at that brilliant white light.

"I brought you here," I say, "to show you a glimpse of what happens when you die. And no, I can't tell you when that will be. No one knows and trust me, you don't really want to. It would upset the balance of things, like when people read the last chapter of a novel before the rest."

"No one does that."

"Sure they do." You roll your shoulders, still not getting it. I'm being too vague. "Take a look" —I sweep one arm out— "The peace, the stillness. Quite different to being alive, no?"

"Well, yeah—"

"Nothing exciting goes on here. It's very uneventful, isn't it?" I gesture towards the endless platforms. "The trains stop in all kinds of places and it's up to you whether or not you get off and take a look around. You know, people always reminisce about things they did when they were alive. The sad ones are those that kept to themselves, that never went anywhere or did anything—"

"What are you getting at?" We reach the café and I order myself a double espresso. You shake your head, claiming you're not thirsty. "My life isn't 'uneventful'." Frowning, you add, "I went to South America."

"So you did. First time on a plane, wasn't it?"

"Yes—"

"First time out of the country? At twenty-seven?"

"Not everyone likes to travel."

"No." I blow on my coffee. "But that's not *your* reason."

When your brother, Jake, turned eighteen, he did an online TEFL course and hopped on the first plane to Peru. It hit your mother like a sledgehammer to the heart. Every so often (a year, six months, you never knew) he would return from some exotic corner of the globe bearing gifts and stories, which you always thought were exaggerated.

Your parents framed photos of him with varying backdrops — pyramids, tropical gardens, mountains — and scattered them all over the house. At least they knew you weren't going anywhere.

Melissa was a friend of a friend. She worked in the travel agents on Turner Road and loved Karaoke. Every Friday night she'd be in the Swan Inn, swaying to the house band and playing pool. She always asked after Jake, where he was and when he'd next be back.

You ached to be fascinating enough for her, more well-travelled, higher income, flash car maybe? You didn't think she was like that, but it wouldn't hurt. You couldn't very well impress her with your extensive collection of vintage Pokémon cards and your half-decent golf swing. To be part of her life, however, you were willing to settle for friendship.

It was only when she actually met Jake one blustery Sunday in late autumn that things changed. The three of you were enjoying a drink in the pub's beer garden. Mostly it was the two of them discussing places they'd been and where they'd like to go next. But when Melissa went to the toilet, Jake said, "She's lovely. When are you introducing her to Mum?"

"Oh no." You'd leant back, waving your hands. "We're just friends. She doesn't like—"

Jake smacked you up the side of your head.

"Ow!"

"She likes you."

"How can you… But she's always asking about you."

"Because I'm your *brother*, you moron. It's called showing an interest. Does she ask about Mum and Dad too?"

"Uh, yeah."

"She likes you," he said with finality. "Ask her out."

Exhilarated, you took a tentative sip of your beer and blushed as Melissa returned to the table. Her red hair glowed in the pale sunlight and her feet beneath the table settled right next to yours. Jake shook his head.

"You're such a doughnut."

Over the ensuing three years, Melissa ignited your wanderlust. You booked mini-breaks in Europe, and holidays in Singapore, Cape Town, and Iceland. Her list was huge and yours was only getting longer. Your parents loved her immediately and extra space was made at the Christmas dinner table.

But then one year, Jake didn't come home.

He'd been living in Spain, which was bizarrely close for him. Sure, you hadn't seen or heard from him in about eight months, but he never missed Christmas. On December 27th, whilst you were all watching *Home Alone* in front of the roaring, spitting fire, the phone rang. Your mum disappeared into the kitchen, but you could all hear her voice as it trembled and cracked.

Your Dad turned off the TV and the three of you gathered around her, steeling yourselves for the worst.

"Jake got cancer," she said. The moment froze and for a split-second, you thought: *It's OK. Jake can beat anything. He's young. Strong. There's great treatment nowadays, lots of options—*, but your mum wasn't finished. After a slow steadying breath, she said, "He died this morning."

I grimace as you double over and gag. He'd known for four months and told no one. The doctor had explained, which did little to ease your guilt: *Didn't want to be a burden… remember him the way he was… his wishes.*

In your dreams, you're by his side in the hospital, holding his hand through it all, just like you did when he got that stupid crayon stuck up his nose.

He'll forever be your baby brother, pink and tiny, gripping your little finger and refusing to let go.

"I'm sorry," I say, "losing someone close is never easy."

"Why are you doing this to me?"

At the funeral, the priest read a passage about tragedy and forgiveness which made your blood curdle. And of course it rained. Umbrellas bobbing towards the graveside, shiny shoes covered in mud, Melissa's hand sliding into yours, squeezing.

People asked you with ever-decreasing tact: *Did he smoke? Drugs? Ah come on, it's alright, you can tell me.* They needed a reason why this vibrant young man had been snatched away, as if they didn't know that there were no rules. No pity or justice. You thought you'd done well not to punch any of them until Melissa's gentle smile reminded you that, even at your brother's funeral, you'd never do such a thing.

I soften my voice.

"You love Melissa, don't you?"

"What?" You still don't remember. "Why are you asking me that? She's the best thing that ever happened to me. I'll grow old with her."

"Have you proposed?"

"Got the ring." You pat your jacket pocket, but it's empty as are all the others. Baffled, you look at me. "Where…"

Three weeks ago, in your and Melissa's apartment, you both stood facing each other in the living room. A glass lay shattered on the floor. The TV was muted; the images jumped and flickered. You felt sick.

To do the deed, you'd fixed your gaze on the wall behind her, unable to look at her freckled face which was red and blotchy from crying too hard. Mechanically, you repeated the same empty stock phrases: *I'm sorry. It's for the best. You deserve better.* She told you to leave and you did.

The next day, you returned the engagement ring to the jewellers and deleted your relationship status on Facebook.

Over the next few weeks, you replayed the whole scene in a savage never-ending loop, hating yourself more and more with every repetition. On your walk home from work, your vision blurred and you didn't bother to wipe away the tears as it played again. Melissa grabbing her gorgeous auburn hair, choking back the sobs, stammering… But, but *why*?

And that was when you stepped out into the main road without looking.

"Oh God," you say, placing an open palm against your chest, "what have I done?"

"It's not too late," I say, "Just remember—"

But our time's run out. I barely manage to smile encouragement as your form dissolves and you return back to your body, far away from here. A few people gasp having not realised what you were.

Before I leave, Ellie, the conductor, catches my eye. She wants to know if I've been successful, but all I can do is shrug.

It's up to you now.

You don't open your eyes at first. Instead, you listen. There are voices, the faint bleep of a machine, pained groans, the swish of a curtain. Your memories are dislocated fragments, but after a moment they slot back into place. You flutter your eyes open, slowly for the light is stark and unforgiving.

To your right, Melissa is slumped in a plastic chair, red hair sticking out at odd angles and a light-blue cardigan falling off one shoulder. Numerous Styrofoam coffee cups are on the table next to her.

You raise your left hand and discover a needle, tube and bandage strapped to the back of it. You want to reach out and tell her everything is going to be alright, that you're sorry, that you take it all back. Every word.

The thought of one day losing Melissa still terrifies you, but you're not going to let that get in the way anymore.

You'll marry her, if she'll still have you. Create mini-Melissas and mini-yous. Buy a small house in the country next to a park with swings and slides and an enormous oak.

You'll kiss those tear tracks on her face and breathe in the scent of her herbal shampoo.

You're going to ride the train to the end of the line, getting off at every stop that life has to offer, and you want to do it all with her.

I never told you my name because, technically, I don't have one.

But you can call me Hope.

ACKNOWLEDGMENTS

A big thank you to my writing tribe for providing invaluable feedback and encouragement. You truly are a wonderful group of people! A specific shout-out to those who helped with this project: Robert Burns, J. C. Lovero, Riel Rosehill, Jon Casper, Shea West, Jay McKenzie, Alex Sultan and Claire Lindsey.

Thanks, of course, to my friends and family for their continued support and enthusiasm.

And lastly, a special thanks to my dad, who shared my love of fantasy and science fiction, who never stopped believing in me, and who was taken far, far too soon.

CREDITS

Originally published by the online magazine Secret Attic:
"Global Architects" - Vol. 1 Issue 9
"The Mirror of Youth"- Vol. 1 Issue 13
"The Last Voyage"- Vol. 1 Issue 19
"A Second Chance"- Vol. 1 Issue 20
"Playing with Your Food"- Vol.1 Issue 21

Shortlisted in the Reedsy Prompts short story competition:

"Star Status" - written in response to: *Write about a character named after one of our contest's judges.*

"Emotional Intelligence" - written in response to: *Write about an android just trying to blend in with their human companions.*

"The Threads that Hold Us Together" - written in response to: *Write a story involving a noise complaint.*

"The End of the Line" - written in response to: *Make a train station an important part of your story.*

Longlisted / Honorable Mention in Globe Soup's 7-day story writing challenge:
"The Last Christmas"
"The Vicar of Coffinswell"

Featured on Tall Tale TV podcast:
"Star Status"
Featured on Crossroads Cantina podcast:
"I Don't Believe in Fairies"
Featured on Mark Wilhelm's Frightening Tales podcast:
"Beneath the Sand"

ABOUT THE AUTHOR

Zelda C. Thorne grew up in a pub in Essex and spent over a decade living and travelling abroad in Canada, USA, New Zealand, and France. Amongst other things, she has become fluent in two foreign languages and flown a plane solo.

Now, she lives and writes in Norfolk with her family.

www.zeldacthorne.com

Printed in Great Britain
by Amazon

40389799R00162